He had been desperate

the night he randomly chose her house to break into, seeking food and shelter for a few hours. Desperate men did things they wouldn't ordinarily do. Like take a blameless woman hostage. It was still incomprehensible to him that she hadn't made him pay for that.

But now that he had accomplished his mission and thanked her, he was reluctant to leave. Odd. He had thought that once he said what he had come to say, he would be more than ready to leave Aislinn Andrews for good and close that page of his life's history.

He hated to admit, even to himself, that he had thought about her while in prison. It had been months since that morning on the mountaintop when she had given herself to him. He still found it hard to believe that it had really happened. Before his escape, his desire had been for a woman, period.

But after his escape, his desire had had a face, a name, a tone of voice, a scent. And all of them belonged to Aislinn.

Dear Reader:

We at Silhouette are very excited to bring you a NEW reading **Sensation.** *Look out for the four books which will appear in our new Silhouette* **Sensation** *series every month. These stories will have the high quality you have come to expect from Silhouette, and their varied and provocative plots will encourage you to explore the wonder of falling in love – again and again!*

Emotions run high in these drama-filled novels. Greater sensual detail and an extra edge of realism intensify the hero and heroine's relationship so that you cannot help but be caught up in their every change of mood.

We hope you enjoy this new **Sensation** *– and will go on to enjoy many more.*

We would love to hear your comments about our new line and encourage you to write to us:

Jane Nicholls
Silhouette Books
PO Box 236
Thornton Road
Croydon
Surrey
CR9 3RU

ERIN ST. CLAIRE
Honour Bound

Silhouette Sensation

First published in Great Britain in 1991 by Silhouette Books, Eton House, 18-24 Paradise Road, Richmond, Surrey TW9 1SR

© Sandra Brown 1986

Silhouette, Silhouette Sensation and Colophon are Trade Marks of Harlequin Enterprises B.V.

ISBN 0 373 58092 4

18–9103

Made and printed in Great Britain

Chapter 1

The refrigerator door was open, projecting a pale, blue-white wedge of light into the dark kitchen. A carton of milk was standing on the countertop. Beside it was a loaf of bread, gaping open, two slices lying half in, half out.

But even without those peculiarities, she instinctively knew the moment she came through her back door that something was amiss. She sensed another presence, dangerous and motionless, waiting.

Automatically she reached for the light switch.

Before her hand made contact, it was manacled by iron-hard fingers, twisted behind her and painfully shoved up between her shoulder blades. She opened her mouth to scream, but another hand, callused and tasting slightly of salt, clamped over her mouth, so that her scream came out only as a frantic, guttural sound, that of an animal entrapped.

She had always wondered how she would react in such a situation. If assaulted, would she faint? If her life were imperiled by an attacker, would she plead to be spared?

It came as a mild surprise, now, that besides being frightened she was angry. She began to struggle, trying to twist her head away from the unyielding hand over her mouth. She wanted to see her assailant's face. Get a description. Wasn't that what the rape-prevention centers advised? Look at his face.

Easier said than done, she realized. Struggling proved to be futile because of her attacker's strength. He was tall. That much she knew. She could feel his breath, ragged and hot, against the crown of her head. Occasionally her head bumped into his chin. So he must be well over six feet tall, she reasoned, and filed that bit of information away.

The body she was being held against was hard, but she wouldn't use "bulky" or "muscle-bound" in her description to the police. Indeed, it seemed to her that he was whipcord lean. From the corner of her eye, his biceps looked as firm and round as a green apple.

Her struggles were only succeeding in wearing her out. Rationalizing that she should conserve her energy and strength, she suddenly ceased her efforts to escape his inescapable hold and became still. Her breasts rose and fell with every insufficient breath she tried to draw through her nostrils. Gradually the arms restraining her relaxed, but only a trifle.

"My name is Lucas Greywolf."

A raspy voice, as soft and sandy as the wind that blew across the desert, spoke directly into her ear. It was a gentle sound, but Aislinn wasn't deceived. Like the winds it reminded her of, she thought, it could be whipped into a fury with the slightest provocation.

And considering the source of that whispery voice, such a whimsical shift was probable. Frightfully so.

The name Lucas Greywolf had been repeated over television signals and radio frequencies throughout the day. Last night the Indian activist had escaped from the federal prison camp in Florence, about fifty miles away.

Law-enforcement agencies were combing the state in search of the escaped convict.

And he was in her kitchen!

"I need food. Rest. I won't hurt you if you cooperate," he growled close to her ear. "If you even try to scream I'll be forced to gag you. Do we have a bargain?"

She nodded once in agreement and the hand came away from her mouth cautiously. As soon as it was removed, she gasped for air. "How did you get here?"

"On foot, mostly," he replied, without elaboration or apparent concern. "You know who I am?"

"Yes. They're looking all over for you."

"I know."

Her initial anger had dissipated. She wasn't a coward, but she wasn't a fool either. Heroics had their place, but now wasn't the time to start playing Wonder Woman. This intruder was no petty thief. Lucas Greywolf should be considered dangerous. All the news reports said so.

What was she to do? Overpowering him was unthinkable. He'd have no difficulty subduing her, and in the process she would probably get hurt. No, the only way she could possibly hope to outmaneuver him was by using her wits, while waiting for an opportunity to escape.

"Sit down." He nudged her shoulder roughly.

Without argument, she went to the table in the center of the kitchen, laid her purse on it and pulled out a chair. She lowered herself into the seat carefully.

He moved as silently as smoke and as nimbly as a shadow. She hadn't heard him cross the floor, and only knew that he had when his shadow stretched across the tabletop. Timorously lifting her eyes, she saw his silhouette looming in the eerie light of the open refrigerator door. Like a panther, he looked dark and lean and lethal when he crouched down and took a summer sausage from the meat drawer.

Apparently believing that she had capitulated, he negligently closed the refrigerator door. The kitchen went dark. She lunged from her chair, aiming for the back door. He caught up with her before she had taken two steps, bisecting her middle with a steely arm to anchor her against him.

"Where do you think you're going?"

"To...to turn on the light."

"Sit down."

"The neighbors will know—"

"I told you to sit down. And until I tell you otherwise, that's what you're going to do." He hauled her across the kitchen and pushed her into the chair. It was so dark that she didn't quite make the seat's center and nearly toppled out of it before regaining her balance.

"I'm only trying to help you," she said. "The neighbors will know something is wrong if they saw me come in and I don't turn on any lights."

Her threat was an empty one, and she rather imagined he knew it. She lived in a new condominium complex on the outskirts of Scottsdale. Fewer than half the units had been sold. No doubt he had selected her house for pilfering because of its remote location.

She heard a metallic whispering noise coming out of the darkness. The sinister sound filled her with dread. She knew the terror of a small jungle animal when rustling leaves alert it that an unseen predator is nearby. Lucas Greywolf had spotted the rack of butcher knives on the countertop near the sink and had slipped one from the wooden scabbard.

Expecting any moment to feel its cold metal edge slicing across her throat, she was stunned but at least grateful that she was still alive when the kitchen light came on, momentarily blinding her. She adjusted her eyes to the sudden brightness. He was still holding the long, gleaming silver blade of the knife to the light switch.

From that intimidating sight, her eyes tracked the length of a brown, sinewy arm up to a curved shoulder, over to a determined, square chin, along a straight, narrow nose, and into the most chilling pair of eyes she'd ever seen.

All her life she'd heard the expression "heart-stopping." Countless times she had casually used the adjective herself, describing any number of inconsequential things. But she'd never actually experienced that graphically descriptive sensation. Until now.

Never had a pair of eyes conveyed such unmitigated contempt, such uncompromising hatred and undiluted bitterness.

Unlike the rest of his features, which were clearly American Indian, his eyes belonged to an Anglo. They were gray, so light a gray they were almost transparent, which only made the pupils in their centers look even deeper and blacker. They seemed to have no necessity to blink, because they stared at her without movement. Set in that dark, brooding face, those steadfast, gray eyes were a startling contrast that held her attention far too long.

She lowered her eyes, but when she saw the knife flash, she fearfully jerked them back up to him. He had merely sliced off a disk of summer sausage. As he raised it to his lips, the hard, set line lifted at one corner to form a smirking smile before straight, white teeth bit into the meat. He was enjoying her fear and that made her furious. By an act of will, she rid her face of any telltale expression and surveyed him coolly.

Which might have been a mistake.

Before tonight, if she had been asked to conjure up a picture of an escaped convict, it would never have resembled Lucas Greywolf. She vaguely remembered reading about his trial when it was making the news, but that had been several years ago. She recalled the prosecutors making him out to be a chronic trouble-

maker and rabble-rouser, a dissident who went around
spreading malcontent among the Indians. But had the
reports ever mentioned him being so handsome? If they
had, she hadn't been paying attention.

He was dressed in a blue chambray shirt that was no
doubt prison issue. The sleeves had been ripped out,
leaving ragged, stringy armholes. One of the sleeves had
been fashioned into a headband, tied Apache-style
around his head to hold back hair so unrelievedly black
that it barely reflected the light shining directly on it. But
then the dust clinging to it might have been partly responsible for that dull finish; his jeans and boots were
covered with it.

Around his waist he wore a belt made of intricately
worked silver set with chunks of turquoise. Dangling
from a chain worn around his neck was a silver Chris-
tian cross. The charm nestled in a thatch of dark hair on
his chest. He wasn't pure Indian.

Again she let her eyes fall away. Under the circumstances, it disturbed her deeply that the sweat-stained
shirt was open almost to his narrow waist. It was equally
disturbing that the earring in his right ear didn't repel her.

The tiny silver kachina mask represented a spirit of
another religion and was incongruent with the cross worn
around his neck. Yet if Greywolf had been born with that
earring pierced into his earlobe, it couldn't have looked
more in keeping with the total aspect of the man he was.

"Won't you join me?" he asked in a taunting voice,
holding out a slice of sausage on the blade of the knife.

She lifted her head and thrust her chin out defiantly.
"No thank you. I'll wait to eat dinner with my husband."

"Your husband?"

"Yes."

"Where is he?"

"At work, but he'll be home at any moment."

He tore off a bite of bread from the slice he raised to his mouth and chewed it with an unconcerned leisure that made her want to slap him. "You're a terrible liar."

"I'm not lying."

He swallowed. "I searched the house before you came home, Miss Aislinn Andrews. There's no man living here."

Now it was her turn to swallow, and she did so with great difficulty. She willed her heart to settle down and stop drumming against her ribs with mounting anxiety. Her palms were perspiring. She pressed them together beneath the table. "How did you know my name?"

"Your mail."

"You went through my mail?"

"You sound alarmed. Do you have something to hide, Miss Andrews?" She refused to be baited and kept her lips firmly closed over the vituperative rejoinder that pressed against them from the inside. "You got a telephone bill today."

His sly grin set off her temper again. "They'll catch you and send you back."

"Yes, I know."

His calm response rendered her mute and made the threatening, argumentative speech she was about to voice unnecessary. Instead she watched him raise the carton of milk to his mouth, tilt his head back and drink thirstily. His neck was deeply tanned. The sliding action of his Adam's apple intrigued her as a hypnotist's pendulum would. He drank until there was no more, then set the empty carton down and wiped his mouth with the back of the hand that still held the knife.

"If you know they'll catch you, why make it harder on yourself?" She asked out of a sincere curiosity to know. "Why not just turn yourself in?"

"Because there is something I have to do first," he said grimly. "Before it's too late."

She didn't pursue her question further, because she thought it might jeopardize her well-being to know what criminal acts he was contemplating. However, if she could get him to talk, maybe he would relax his guard and she could make a dash for the back door. Then once in the garage, she would hit the button that raised the automatic door and ...

"How did you get in?" she asked abruptly, realizing for the first time that there had been no visible signs of forced entry.

"Through a bedroom window."

"And how did you escape from the prison camp?"

"I deceived someone who trusted me." His hard mouth curled derisively. "Of course he was a fool to trust an Indian. Everybody knows Indians are untrustworthy. Right, Miss Andrews?"

"I don't know any Indians," she answered softly, not wanting to provoke him. She disliked the way his taut body seemed about to snap with tension.

But by trying not to aggravate him, she only seemed to have aroused his temper. His eyes poured over her slowly, spilling heat on everything they touched. She was made painfully aware of her blondness, her blue eyes and fair skin. His sneer deepened into a scowl. "No, I don't suppose you do." Faster than her eyes could monitor the motion, he crammed the knife into his waistband and reached for her. "Get up."

"Why?" She gasped with fright as he roughly pulled her to her feet. Holding her back against his chest, with his hands on her shoulders, he propelled her out of the kitchen. On their way through the door, he switched off the light. The hallway was dark. She stumbled ahead of him. He was going toward the bedroom and her mouth went dry with fear. "You got what you came for."

"Not all of it."

"You said you wanted food," she countered frantically, digging her heels into the carpet. "If you leave now, I promise not to call the police."

"Now why don't I believe you, Miss Andrews?" he asked in a voice as smooth as melting ice cream.

"I swear it!" she cried, despising her weakness and the panicked sound of her voice.

"Promises have been made to me before by white men . . . and white women. I've learned to be skeptical."

"But *I* had nothing to do with that. I—oh, God, what are you going to do?"

He shoved her into the bedroom. As soon as he had cleared the door, he closed it behind them. "Take a wild guess, Miss Andrews." He spun her around and pinned her between the door and his unyielding body. He closed his hand around her throat just under her chin and bent his head down low over hers. "What do you think I'm going to do?"

"I . . . I . . . don't know."

"You're not one of these sexually repressed ladies who entertain rape fantasies, are you? Hmm?"

"No!" she gasped.

"You've never fantasized about being taken by a savage?"

"Let me go, please."

She turned her head away and he let her, but he didn't release her. If anything, he moved nearer, lewdly pressing himself against her, holding her against the door with his hardness and strength.

Aislinn squeezed her eyes shut and bit her lower lip in fear and humiliation. His long, tapering fingers strummed her throat, moving up and down in an evocative rhythm.

"Well I *have* been in prison for a long, long time." His fingers slid down her chest. He hooked his index finger on the top button of her blouse, then fiddled with it until it popped open. She whimpered. His face was so close to hers that she could feel his breath falling warmly on her skin. It struck her cheeks, her nose, her mouth. She inhaled it by necessity, hating the forced intimacy of breathing the air he expelled.

"So if you're real smart," he warned silkily, "you won't give me any ideas."

When she realized what he was telling her, her eyes sprang up to meet his. They clashed, a meeting of wills and a battle of tempers. For a long moment they seemed suspended, taking each other's measure, analyzing the strengths and weaknesses.

Then gradually he pulled back. When his body was no longer making contact with hers, she almost sank to the floor with relief.

"I told you I needed food and *rest*." There was a strange new quality to his voice now. A gruffness.

"You've rested."

"Sleep, Miss Andrews. I need sleep."

"You mean . . . you intend to stay? Here?" she asked, aghast. "For how long?"

"Until I decide to leave," he answered obliquely. He crossed the room and turned on the lamp beside her bed.

"You can't!"

He returned to where she still stood by the door and took her hand. This time he pulled her along behind him. "You're hardly in a position to argue. Just because I haven't harmed you yet doesn't mean that I won't if I'm desperate enough."

"I'm not afraid of you."

"Yes you are." He dragged her into the adjoining bathroom with him and slammed the door. "Or you should be. Look, get this straight," he said through clenched teeth, "I have something to do, and nothing, especially not an Anglo princess like you, is going to stop me from doing it. I knocked a guard unconscious to escape prison and I made it this far on foot; I have nothing to lose but my life, and it ain't worth a damn where

I've been. So don't press your luck, lady. You've got me as a houseguest for as long as I want to stay." To punctuate his threat, he yanked the knife out of his waistband.

She sucked in a sharp breath as though he had pricked her belly button with the tip of the blade. "That's more like it," he said, gauging her fear. "Now sit down." He hitched his chin toward the commode. Aislinn, keeping her eyes trained on the knife, backed up until she bumped into the bathroom fixture and then collapsed onto its lid.

Greywolf laid the knife on the edge of the bathtub, well out of her reach. He pulled off his boots and socks, then began tugging the tail of his tattered shirt from the waistband of his jeans. Aislinn, sitting as motionless as a statue, said nothing as he peeled it off his shoulders and shrugged out of it.

The center of his chest was smattered with dark hair. The brown skin was stretched tightly over curved muscles that looked incredibly hard. His nipples were small and dark. The skin of his belly was stretched as taut as a trampoline, and the shallow part of it around his navel was dusted with black hair. The crinkly fan narrowed into a sleek stripe that disappeared into his jeans.

He began unbuckling the silver belt at his waist. "What are you doing?" Aislinn asked in alarm.

"I'm going to take a shower." He undid the belt, letting it hang open as he bent toward the taps in the bathtub. He turned them until water was gushing from the faucet full blast. Even over that roaring sound, Aislinn heard the rasp of his jeans' zipper as he lowered it.

"Where I can *see* you?" she cried.

"Where I can see *you*." He calmly pushed the jeans down past his hips and buttocks and stepped out of them.

Aislinn's eyes closed. She was overcome by a wave of vertigo and gripped the lid of the commode beneath her to keep from swaying. Never in her life had she been so outraged, so insulted, so assaulted.

Because to look at his nakedness was to be assaulted by masculinity incarnate. He was perfectly proportioned. His shoulders were broad, his chest deep. His limbs were long and leanly muscled, testimonies to agility and strength. Where his skin was smooth, it looked like polished bronze, yet alive and supple. Where it was hair-dusted, it looked warm and touch-inviting.

He raised the lever of the shower and stepped beneath its powerful spray. He didn't draw the curtain. Keeping her head averted, Aislinn drew in several restorative breaths.

"What's wrong, Miss Andrews? Haven't you ever seen a naked man before? Or is it seeing a naked Indian that has you so visibly upset?"

She whipped her head around, stung by his mocking tone. She wouldn't have him thinking she was either a prudish old maid or a racial bigot. But her verbal barb died unspoken on her tongue. She was unable to utter a sound, paralyzed by the sight of his lathered hands as they slid over his sleek nakedness. The water must have been hot, for the mirrors were fogging up and the atmosphere was as steamy as an Erskine Caldwell novel. The mist settled on her own skin. She could barely draw the heavy, sultry air into her lungs.

"As you can see," he taunted as his soapy hands slid to the lower part of his body, "we're equipped just like any other man."

Well, not quite, Aislinn thought with a secret part of her mind, as her eyes took one forbidden glance down his torso to where that beautiful body hair provided a dense, lush base for his impressive manhood.

"You're crude," she said scathingly, "as well as being criminal."

He smiled cynically and whipped off the makeshift headband, tossing it out of the tub and down on top of his other clothes. He ducked his head under the shower's spray just long enough to moisten it, then picked up a bottle of shampoo. He sniffed the top of it before pouring a dollop of the creamy stuff into his hand, slapping it to the top of his head and lathering it into a white foam that soon coated the ebony strands of his hair. He scrubbed mercilessly.

"This smells better than prison shampoo," he remarked as he ran his fingers through the luxuriant lather.

Aislinn said nothing because a plan was formulating in her mind. If he had put his head under the shower nozzle to wet his hair, he'd have to put it under there longer to rinse all the shampoo off, wouldn't he? She didn't have long to think her plan through. Already he was squeezing the suds out of his hair and slinging them off his fingers into the water that swirled around his feet.

There was a telephone on the nightstand beside her bed. If she could dash through the bathroom door and manage to dial the emergency number before—

He plunged his head beneath the shower's nozzle. There was no more time to ruminate.

Aislinn hurled herself toward the door, pulled it open, almost wrenching her arm from its socket in the process, and flew into the bedroom. She reached the nightstand in less than a second, grabbed up the telephone receiver and began frantically punching out the sequence of numbers she had memorized.

She pressed the receiver against her ear and waited for the ring. Nothing happened. *Damn!*

In her haste, had she punched a wrong number?

She clicked the disconnect button and tried again, her hands shaking so badly she could barely hold the receiver. Risking one frenzied glance over her shoulder, she was dismayed to see Lucas Greywolf framed in the doorway between the bedroom and bathroom, his shoulder propped against it in a stance of lazy indifference.

A towel was draped around his neck. Other than that, he was naked. Water dripped from his wet hair and funnelled down his coppery body. Beads of it clung to places she wished she didn't notice. He held the wicked knife in his right hand, idly tapping the flat side of the blade against his bare thigh.

Aislinn realized that the second telephone call hadn't gone through either and that no other calls were going to go through. "You did something to my phone." It wasn't a question.

"As soon as I entered the house."

Rapidly, her hands moving end over end, she reeled the telephone cord up from behind the nightstand. The connector that normally fit into the wall outlet had been ruined, ground by a boot heel as best as she could tell.

Frustration overcame her then. And fury. It enraged her that he could appear so composed when she felt ineffectual and idiotic. She cursed and threw the telephone toward him, then launched herself toward the door, seeking escape at all costs. It was hopeless, of course, but she had to do *something*.

She managed to reach the door; she even managed to get it open a crack before his wide hand splayed over it directly in front of her face and shoved it closed again. She turned, her fingers curled into claws, bent on attacking him.

"Stop it!" he commanded and grabbed for her flailing arms. The knife nicked her on the forearm. She screamed softly in pain. "You little fool."

He grunted with surprise when she drove her knee up toward his crotch. She missed her mark, but succeeded in unbalancing him as he made a dodging movement. They fell to the floor, struggling. His skin was still wet, slippery, and he easily deflected the blows and slaps she frantically delivered. In seconds, he had her pinned beneath him, her wrists stapled to the floor by his widespread fingers.

"What the hell was that for? You could have gotten hurt," he barked. His face was a scant few inches above hers. His chest was heaving in and out from exertion. The anger in his eyes struck terror in Aislinn, but she didn't let it show. Instead, she glared up at him.

"If you're going to kill me, get it over with," she ground out.

She had no time to prepare herself before he jerked her to her feet. Her teeth clicked together. She was still trying to regain her equilibrium when she saw the knife arcing down toward the side of her face. She felt a rush of wind as it passed. She tried to scream, but the sound became a faint little whimper when she saw the lock of her hair dangling from his hand. The wavy blond strand of hair being squeezed between those hard brown fingers symbolized her frailty and emphasized how easily his strength could overpower it.

"I meant what I said, lady," he said, still breathing heavily. "I have nothing else to lose. You pull one more stunt like that and it'll be more than your hair I'll use this knife on. Understand?"

Eyes round and gaping at the strand of curling blond hair still clasped between his fingers, Aislinn nodded dumbly. He opened his fingers and let the light-catching strands of hair filter to the floor.

Accepting her acquiescence, he stepped away from her and retrieved the towel. He dried the remaining moisture from his skin and made a pass over his chin-length hair. He tossed the towel to her. "Your arm is bleeding."

She hadn't noticed. Looking down, she was surprised to see a thin trickle of blood oozing from the nick just above her wrist. "Are you hurt anywhere else?" She shook her head no. "Get over there by the bed."

Fear tamped her resentment at being ordered around in her own house by a fugitive from justice. Without a murmur of protest, she obeyed him. The bleeding on her arm had stopped. She laid the towel aside and turned to face her captor.

"Take off your clothes."

She had thought he couldn't frighten her any more than he already had. She was gravely mistaken. "What?" she wheezed.

"You heard me."

"No."

"Unless you do as I say, that cut on your arm is only a beginning." The naked steel blade of the knife glinted in the lamplight as he waved it back and forth in front of her face.

"I don't think you'd hurt me."

"Don't bet on it."

Cold, unfeeling eyes glittered back at her defiant stare, and she admitted that the odds for her to remain untouched and unscathed through this night didn't look good.

"Why... why do I have to take off my... my...?"

"Do you really want to know?"

No, she didn't think she wanted it spelled out for her because she had a pretty good idea why, and somehow hearing his intent from his own lips only made the prospect more frightening.

"But if you were going to rape me," she said, speaking aloud the question her musings raised, "why didn't you—"

"Take off your clothes."

He pronounced each word carefully. They fell from his stern lips like chips of ice.

She considered her options and decided that she had none. At least if she went along with him, she was granting herself time. Perhaps someone would try to call and find that her phone was out of order. The telephone company would send someone to check, wouldn't they? Someone might come to her door. The paperboy for instance. Anything was possible if she could just keep stalling him. For all she knew the police could have the house surrounded right now, having tracked Greywolf there.

Slowly she raised her hands to the second button of her blouse, the first already having been opened by him. She cast one last, pleading glance toward him. His face could have been carved from stone, his eyes formed from hardest crystal for all the humanity they conveyed. Pride kept her from begging, though she didn't think any amount of pleading would budge this emotionless man.

She pushed the button through its hole and reluctantly lowered her hand to the next.

"Hurry up."

She looked up at him where he stood naked and sinister only a few feet from her. He remained impassive under her seething gaze. She took her time with every single button, testing the perimeters of his patience, until all were undone.

"Now take it off." He made a brusque gesture with the knife. Lowering her head, Aislinn slipped the blouse from her shoulders, but held it up against her chest. "Drop it." Still not looking at him, she let the garment slide away from her body and onto the floor.

After a long silence, he said, "Now the rest of it."

It was summertime in Arizona. She had closed her studio early that afternoon because she had no appointments scheduled. After a workout at the health club, she had slipped on a skirt, blouse and barefoot sandals, not wanting to put on stockings.

"The skirt, Aislinn," he said with tense emphasis.

His use of her first name was the supreme insult under the circumstances and it fueled her anger. Reaching behind her, she virtually ripped the hook on her skirt open, and let it fall from her hips in a show of defiance.

At his strangled sound, she raised her eyes. The skin over his high cheekbones seemed to be stretched so tight she thought it might split. His eyes were moving over her like flickering torches.

She wished her lingerie was plainer, less alluring. The silk bra and panty set was the color of lemon sherbet and was trimmed in dove-gray lace. While they weren't sheer, they were designed for brevity and prettiness, not functionality. They left nothing to the imagination, and a man who had been in prison would have a well-developed imagination.

"The bra."

Trying to stem hot tears she was too proud to shed, Aislinn slipped down the lacy straps, drawing her arms through them and holding the fragile cups over her breasts before unfastening the front clasp. Greywolf extended his hand. Aislinn jumped reflexively.

"Hand it to me," he said hoarsely.

Her hand was trembling as she passed the flimsy piece of silk and lace to him. The garment seemed even less substantial when his fist closed around it and, held in that patently masculine hand, far more feminine. He fingered the soft fabric. Knowing that it would still hold the heat of her body, Aislinn experienced a funny feeling deep inside her as she watched his fingers rubbing the soft cloth.

"Silk," he murmured in a low, growling sound. He lifted the bra to his face and crushed it against his nose. He groaned, closing his eyes, briefly making a fierce grimace of his face. "That smell. That wonderful, woman smell."

Aislinn realized then that he wasn't talking to her. He was talking to himself. He wasn't even talking about her. Particularly. Any woman would have done. She didn't know whether to be terrified or comforted by that thought.

The poignant moment lasted only a few seconds before he tossed the bra down with an angry flourish of his hand. "Come on. Finish."

"No. You'll have to kill me."

He looked at her for an agonizingly long time. Aislinn couldn't bear to watch his eyes moving over her, so she closed hers.

"You're very beautiful." She braced herself for his touch. It never came. Instead, he spun away from her, apparently vexed, either over her stubborn resistance or the vulnerability he had inadvertently expressed.

Whatever it was had made him exceedingly angry. He pulled several drawers in her dresser from their moorings before he found what he was short-temperedly searching for. He came toward her with two pairs of panty hose.

"Lie down." Reaching around Aislinn, who stood rooted to the spot in terror, he flung back the covers on her bed.

She lay down, her body stiff with fright, her eyes wide as he knelt over her. But he wasn't even looking at her. His face was set in tense, remote lines as he reached for her arm and pulled it back toward the rails of her brass headboard.

"You're tying me up?" she asked tremulously.

"Yes," he answered curtly, pulling the nylon tight around her wrist and securing it to the rail.

"My God." A hundred hideous nightmares flitted through her brain. Every deviate practice she'd ever heard about, she was reminded of now.

His mouth tilted into another of those sardonic smiles, as though he had read her mind and seen her fears. "Relax, Miss Andrews. I told you I wanted food and rest and that's what I intend to get."

Still frozen with shock and fear, Aislinn lay docile as he bound her other wrist to his, using the second pair of panty hose. When they were tied to each other, the backs of their hands pressing together, she stared up at him with incredulity. He merely snapped off the lamp and lay down beside her, his back to her.

"You bastard." She tugged hard on the fetter that tied her to him. "Untie me."

"Go to sleep."

"I said to untie me," she shouted, trying to sit up. He rolled over and yanked her back down. Though she couldn't see him in the darkness, the body lying so close to hers communicated a terrible menace that was more repressive than sheer force.

"I had no choice but to tie you up."

"Why did you have me undress?"

"To make it more difficult for you to escape. I seriously doubt you'd go chasing out into the night as you are. And—"

"And what?" she asked angrily.

After a slight pause his reply came through the darkness like a stealthy, sensuous, black cat—anticipated, but unseen until it's there. "And because I wanted to look at you."

Chapter 2

Get up."

She pried her eyes open reluctantly, unable to remember why she dreaded waking up. Then her shoulder was roughly shaken and she was reminded. Her eyes popped open. Coming to a half-sitting position, holding the blanket over her naked body, she shoved the disheveled hair out of her eyes and looked up into Lucas Greywolf's remote features.

It had taken her hours to fall asleep, hours in which she had lain there beside him listening to his rhythmic breathing, knowing that he was fast asleep. She had struggled to release her arm from the headboard until her entire body ached with the futile effort. Cursing him, she had finally surrendered and relaxed enough to get her eyes to close. After that, her body had taken over and she had fallen asleep.

"Get up," he repeated tersely. "And get dressed. We're leaving."

Both pairs of stockings, the one that had bound her to the headboard and the one that had bound her to the man, were lying across the foot of the bed. Sometime earlier he had freed her. Why hadn't she awakened then? Was his touch that deft and light? And now, too, she vaguely remembered being uncomfortably cold in the early morning hours. Had he covered her? It made her insides tremble to think so.

She was relieved to see that he was already dressed in the dusty clothes he had shed the previous night, before availing himself of her shower. The ripped-out sleeve of his shirt had been replaced by one of her own cotton bandannas to serve as his headband. His earring and neck chain were still there, gleaming against his bronzed skin. She could smell her shampoo in his raven-black hair.

No, she hadn't imagined him. Lucas Greywolf was very real and embodied everything that women had nightmares about . . . or dreamed of.

She snapped her mind back to attention. "Leaving? Where? I'm not going anywhere with you."

His dismissive air indicated just how much credence he placed in her protest. He opened her closet and began riffling through the hangers. Designer dresses and silk blouses were bypassed in favor of a pair of old jeans and a casual shirt. He tossed them across the bed toward her.

Bending at the waist, he examined several pairs of shoes before selecting a pair of low-heeled boots. He carried them toward the bed and dropped them on the floor. "You can either dress yourself or—" he paused while his light gray eyes traveled over her form beneath the covers "—I can dress you. Either way, we leave here in five minutes."

His stance was bold: thighs widespread, chest out, chin high. Arrogance was stamped all over his classic American face. Self-confidence emanated from him like the musky scent of his skin.

Meekly yielding to such raw audacity was untenable to Aislinn Andrews.

"Why can't you just leave me here?"

"Stupid question, Aislinn, and unworthy of you."

She conceded that. As soon as he was out of sight, she'd run screaming down the street until somebody heard her. The authorities would be on his trail before he got to the city limits.

"You're my insurance policy. Every jailbreaker worth his salt takes a hostage." He took a step closer to her. "And my patience with my hostage is wearing thin. Get your butt out of that damn bed!" he thundered.

Though it galled, she prudently obeyed, dragging the covers with her. "At least have the decency to turn your back while I dress."

One of his brows, sleek and black and shaped like an inverted V arched slightly. "You're asking a noble gesture from an Indian?"

"I have no racial prejudices."

He looked at her tumbled blond hair and smirked with derision. "No, I don't suppose you do, because I doubt if you even knew we were out there." Then he turned on his heel and left the room.

She took umbrage at the insult and angrily pulled on the clothes he had selected. She had found a bra and a pair of panties in the piles of clothes he had left on the floor after vandalizing her drawers the night before.

As soon as she had snapped the jeans on, she rushed toward the window and opened the shutters. She reached for the lock and twisted it open, but a hard brown arm came around from behind her. Strong fingers formed a vise around her wrist.

"I'm getting tired of these little games, Aislinn."

"And I'm getting tired of you manhandling me," she cried, trying to wrest her arm free. He let go of her only after he had relocked the window and closed the shutters. Resentfully, she massaged the circulation back into her wrist as she glared up at him. She had always despised bullies.

"Listen, lady, if I didn't need you as protection to get where I'm going, I wouldn't give you the time of day. So don't flatter yourself." He spun her around and, placing his hand in the small of her back, gave her a hefty shove. "Get going."

He led her into the kitchen where he picked up a Thermos and a grocery sack.

"I see you made yourself right at home," she said snidely. Inwardly she was cursing herself for sleeping so soundly. She might have made good her escape through the bedroom window while he was brewing coffee and looting her pantry.

"Where we're going, you'll be glad to have the provisions."

"And where is that?"

"Where the other half lives."

He didn't expand on that, but, with his hand securely around her upper arm, he led Aislinn into the garage. After opening the passenger door of her car, he shoved her inside, then went around and slid behind the steering wheel. He placed the Thermos and grocery sack on the seat between them. Reaching beneath the seat for the lever, he adjusted the seat back as far as it would go to accommodate his long legs. Using the electronic transmitter that always lay on her dashboard, he raised the garage door. Once he had backed the car out, he closed the door the same way. At the end of her street, he skillfully maneuvered her car into the flow of traffic on the boulevard.

"How long will I be gone?" she asked. Her question was casual and out of keeping with her busy eyes.

He didn't stay close to another car long enough for her to make eye contact with either the driver or passengers. There were no police cars in sight. Greywolf was driving carefully and well within the speed limit. He was no fool.

Nor was he talkative. He offered no answer to her question. "I'll be missed, you know. I have a business to run. When I don't show up for work, people will start looking for me."

"Pour me a cup of coffee."

Her mouth fell open at the imperious way he issued orders, as though he were the big bad brave and she his squaw. "Go to hell."

"Pour me a cup of coffee."

Had he shouted at her, flown into a fit of temper, she might have met him nose to nose. But the words left his mouth quietly, like serpents slithering from a cave. They sent chills down her spine. He hadn't hurt her so far, but he was a dangerous man. The kitchen knife was still tucked into his waistband. One look into the hard gray eyes that left the road long enough to nail her to the car seat convinced her that he was an enemy to be reckoned with.

She found two Styrofoam cups in the sack he had brought with them. Carefully she poured him half a cup of steaming, fragrant coffee from the Thermos and passed it to him. He didn't thank her, but sipped from the cup, squinting his eyes against the vapor that rose out of it.

Without asking his permission, she poured another cup for herself before recapping the Thermos. She stared down into the coffee as she rolled the cup between her palms and tried to imagine what his plans for her were. She was concentrating so hard that she jumped when he suddenly spoke.

"What kind of business?"

"What?"

"You said you have a business to run."

"Oh, a photography studio."

"You take pictures?"

"Yes, portraits basically. Brides. Babies. Graduates. That kind of thing."

If he understood, approved, or disapproved, he kept it a secret. His chiseled profile revealed nothing. Granted, her work was nothing to get excited about, she thought with an inward sigh.

When she had graduated from college with a journalism degree, she had had aspirations to set the world on fire with her provocative photojournalism, to travel the globe capturing flame, famine and flood on film. She had wanted to evoke intense emotions such as anger, love and pity with each photograph.

But her parents had had vastly different plans for their only child. Willard Andrews was a prominent businessman in Scottsdale. His wife, Eleanor, was a society queen bee. Their daughter was expected to do the "suitable" thing, that being to amuse herself with suitable projects until she decided to marry a suitable young man. There were any number of clubs she could join, any number of committees she could chair. Charity work was permissible, so long as it didn't entail getting personally involved.

A career, especially one as gritty as traveling to remote parts of the world to take pictures of things too horrid to discuss at dinner parties, certainly didn't fit into her parents' plans for her. After months of endless argument, they finally wore her down and she bowed to their will.

As a concession, her father bankrolled a photography studio where Aislinn could take vapid portraits of her parents' friends and their offspring. It wasn't a bad occupation; it was just a far cry from the meaningful work she had always wanted to do.

She wondered what her parents would say now if they could see her in the company of Lucas Greywolf and she was unable to withhold a laugh that bubbled up from her throat.

"Do you find the situation amusing?" he asked.

"Not at all amusing," she replied, becoming serious again. "Why don't you let me go?"

"I didn't intend to take a hostage. I intended to eat your food, avail myself of your house for a few hours' rest, and then leave. But you came in and caught me plundering your kitchen. Now I have no choice but to take you with me." He glanced at her before adding, "Actually I *do* have a choice, but I'm no murderer. At least not yet."

She suddenly lost her desire for the coffee. Instead the acrid taste of fear filled her mouth. "Do you plan to kill me?"

"Not unless you give me no choice."

"I'll fight you every step of the way."

"In that case we might have difficulties."

"Then I wish you'd go ahead and do it. The anticipation you're putting me through is cruel."

"So is prison."

"What did you expect?"

"I've learned to expect little."

"It's certainly not my fault you went to prison. You commit a crime, you pay for it."

"And just what was my 'crime'?"

"I . . . I don't recall. Something to do with—"

"I organized a demonstration at the courthouse in Phoenix. It resulted in violence, injury to police officers and damages to federal property." He said it in a way that made her think he wasn't confessing, but only quoting verbatim what he'd heard repeated numerous times. "But I think my real crime was being born an Indian."

"That's ridiculous. You have no one to blame for your misfortune but yourself, Mr. Greywolf."

His tight grin was mirthless. "I believe the judge said something to that effect when he sentenced me."

They lapsed into a silence that lasted until she ventured to ask, "How long have you been in prison?"

"Thirty-four months."

"And how long did you have to go?"

"Three months."

"Three months!" She was dismayed. "You escaped when you only had three months left on your sentence?"

His eyes sliced across the front seat of the car toward her. "I told you there is something I have to do and nothing is going to stop me."

"But if they catch you—"

"They'll catch me."

"Then why are you doing this?"

"I told you I had to."

"Nothing could be this important."

"It is."

"They'll tack months, possibly years, onto your sentence."

"Yes."

"Doesn't that mean anything to you?"

"No."

"But you're throwing away years of your life. Think of all the things you're giving up."

"Like a woman."

The three words were spoken shortly and, like tiny bullets, put her sermon to death. She closed her mouth quickly, wise enough to keep silent on this particular subject.

Neither spoke, yet their thoughts were running along the same channels. From different perspectives each was remembering the events of the night before. Aislinn didn't want to acknowledge her disturbing memories— Greywolf standing in the doorway of the bathroom, naked and wet, his very indolence a threat. Or pressing her bra to his face, inhaling her scent with such carnal greed. Or untying her and covering her when she wasn't aware of it. The thoughts were stifling; she felt suffocated by them, by his nearness.

Finally she shut him out in the only way she could. She closed her eyes and rested her head on the back of the seat.

"Dammit!"

She must have been dozing. Aislinn awoke abruptly with Greywolf's curse. He pounded the steering wheel with his right fist.

"What is it?" she asked, sitting up straight and blinking her eyes against the afternoon sunlight.

"Roadblock," Greywolf said, his lips barely moving.

Through the heat waves shimmering above the stretch of highway, Aislinn saw that state patrol cars had blocked off the highway. Officers were stopping each vehicle before letting it pass.

Before she could even register what a welcome sight that was, Greywolf pulled her car onto the shoulder of the highway and shoved the gear shift into Park. In one lithe movement, he straddled the console, crouched over her, and unbuttoned her blouse, working the cups of her bra down over the mounds of her breasts.

"What are you doing?" she gasped, swatting at his hands. At first she'd been groggy from her nap, then too astounded to fight him off. By the time she realized what he was doing, he had her blouse unbuttoned halfway to her waist and her breasts bulging up between the deep V.

"I'm relying on human nature, that's what." Objectively checking his handiwork, and apparently finding it satisfactory, he vaulted over the seat. "Your turn to drive. Get us through that roadblock."

"But . . . No!" she protested vehemently. "I'll be only too glad to have you captured, Mr. Greywolf!"

"Get this damn car moving or they'll notice us pulled over and get suspicious. Put your tush in that driver's seat and pull the car back onto the highway. Now!"

The look she shot him over the back of the seat was fiercely hostile, but she obeyed him when he whipped the butcher knife from the waistband of his jeans and waved it at her menacingly.

"Don't even think of honking the horn," he warned, just as she thought of that very thing.

Butcher knife or not, she had every intention of pulling into that roadblock screaming bloody murder. As soon as she braked, she would burst out of the car door and let the authorities handle the savage.

"If you're entertaining any notions of turning me in, forget them," he said.

"You don't stand a chance."

"Neither do you. I'll say you were in collusion, that you harbored me last night and helped me get this far."

"They'll know you're lying," she scoffed.

"Not when they investigate the sheets on your bed."

Shocked by his words, she quickly glanced back at him. He was lying down on the back seat as though asleep. In his hand he was holding a photography magazine, which she assumed he intended to use as a tent over his face. "What do you mean?" she asked shakily, not liking the self-assurance in his gray eyes. "What do the sheets on my bed have to do with anything?"

"The police will find the evidence of sex on them." Her face went pale and her hands gripped the steering wheel so hard her knuckles turned white. She swallowed dryly from profound embarrassment. "Now, if you want an explicit explanation," he said softly, "I'll be happy to provide it. But you're a grown-up, so I think you can figure it out. I hadn't seen an unclothed woman in a long time, much less lain in bed with one, close enough to smell her, hear her breathing." His voice lowered. "Think about it, Aislinn."

She didn't want to think about it. Not at all. Her palms were already slick with perspiration and her stomach was roiling. When? How? He could be lying, making it up. He could also be telling the truth.

Before they arrested her, would the police give any credence to her side of the story? What proof could she show them to substantiate it? There would be no signs of forced entry at her condo. She wouldn't be implicated for long, of course. Eventually it would be proved that he was lying. But in the meantime he could sure make life difficult. And embarrassing. The incident would be something she would never live down, especially with her parents, who would be mortified.

"And I won't surrender without a fight," he whispered as she applied the brake to slow down, taking her place in line with the other cars.

"They won't take me alive." His voice was muffled by the magazine. There was only one car ahead of her now. The patrolman was bending down to speak with the driver.

"Unless you want my blood on your conscience, not to mention that of any innocents I might take with me, you'd better do your damnedest to get us through this roadblock."

Time for making a decision had run out. The patrolman waved the car ahead of her on and signaled for her to move forward. *Lord, how did I get into this situation and what am I going to do?*

It was strange, but when the time came, she didn't have to think about it. Nor did she weigh her decision in the delicate balance between common sense and conscience. She merely reacted spontaneously.

She rolled down the window and before the state patrolman could utter a word, she blurted out, "Oh, officer, I'm *so* glad you stopped me. I think there's something wrong with my car. This little red light keeps blinking on and off. What do you think that means? Nothing bad I hope."

The ruse worked. Aislinn looked up at the patrolman wide-eyed and short-winded. At least the shallow, anxious breaths she was taking made her appear short-winded.

Her hair, which Greywolf hadn't given her time to comb properly that morning, was even more tousled from her nap in the car. It fell over her shoulders in a disarray that was most appealing, particularly to an underpaid state-highway patrolman who had drawn the thankless task of stopping cars on a lonely stretch of highway in the midday August heat to look for some renegade Indian who, in his opinion, was probably well into Mexico by now.

"Well, now, little lady," he said expansively, pushing his hat back from his sweating forehead, "let's see what the problem is here."

He leaned into the open window, ostensibly to check on which "little red light" was blinking on and off, but Aislinn knew his eyes were trained on her breasts. His expression changed, however, when he glanced into the back seat.

"Who's that?"

"Oh, that's my husband," she said with distaste, giving a negligent shrug. She twirled a lock of hair round and round her finger and suddenly wondered if the strand Greywolf had cut off would be noticed. "He gets as cranky as an old bear if I wake him up while we're traveling. He always makes me drive. Today, I'm glad he did." She batted her eyelashes over her big baby blues, and the officer smiled again.

Greywolf was a fair judge of human nature. Why she was going to such extremes to protect him at that moment, he couldn't say and didn't have time to analyze. The patrolman was speaking to her again.

"I don't see any red light right now." Ridiculously, he was whispering, apparently not wanting to wake up the sleeping husband who might prove to be a little more than cranky toward anyone who ogled his wife.

"Oh, well, thank you." Her bravery was in short supply. Now that she *had* aided and abetted a criminal, she was anxious to get away from the roadblock without being detected. "I guess it was nothing, then."

"It could mean that your motor's overheated." The patrolman said, leering. "I know mine is," he whispered in an even lower voice. Aislinn smiled weakly even as her skin crawled with repulsion.

Greywolf stirred and mumbled something. The officer's smug smile collapsed.

"I'll be seein' you," she said, easing her foot off the brake and gently applying it to the accelerator. She didn't want to appear too eager to be off, though the driver behind her was honking impatiently.

The patrolman shot him an intimidating look. "Better have that light checked if it comes back on. I could radio ahead and—"

"No, no, don't bother about me," she called back through her window. "I'll wake up my husband if it comes on again. Bye."

She cranked up the window and stamped on the accelerator. Looking through the rearview mirror, she saw that the patrolman was now engaged in explaining the situation to the irate motorist who had been detained longer than necessary.

Only when the roadblock was out of sight did she let her muscles relax. She had a death grip on the steering wheel and forcibly unclenched her fingers. Her nails had gouged crescent-shaped wounds into her palms. Letting out a long, shuddering breath, her body sagged within the confines of the driver's seat.

Greywolf climbed over the seat with a lithe agility surprising for a man as tall as he. "You did just fine. No one would ever guess that you're new to a life of crime."

"Shut up!" Aislinn shouted at him. With the same carelessness he had shown earlier, she wheeled the car onto the shoulder of the highway. Gravel sprayed from beneath the tires when she applied the brakes. As soon as the car came to a skidding stop she laid her head on the steering wheel and began to sob.

"I hate you. Please let me go. Why did I do that? *Why?* I should have turned you in. I'm scared and tired and hungry and thirsty. You're a criminal and I've never deceived anyone in my life. A law officer! I could go to jail now, too, couldn't I? Why am I helping you when you'll probably kill me anyway?"

Greywolf sat unmoving at her side. When she had at last cried herself out, she dried her wet cheeks on the backs of her hands and looked up at him with tear-swollen eyes.

"I'd like to tell you to cheer up, that the worst is behind us, but it seems our troubles have only started, Aislinn."

He was gazing down at her breasts, which she immediately remembered were indecently displayed. Her hands trembled as she pulled the cloth of her blouse over them. "What do you mean?"

"I mean the damn roadblocks. I hadn't counted on them. We need to find a television set."

"A television set?" she parroted in a thin voice.

His eyes scanned the stretch of highway behind and ahead of them. "Yes. I'm sure there will be a news story about the dragnet. Hopefully it will give us a thoroughly detailed account of how the authorities plan to apprehend me. Let's get going."

He hitched his chin forward. Wearily she steered the car back onto the highway. "What about the car radio? We can hear the news on that."

"Not as detailed," he said, shaking his head. "And haven't you ever heard that a picture is worth a thousand words?"

"I suppose you'll tell me where to go and when to stop."

"That's right. You just drive."

For almost an hour they rode in silence, though he passed her cheese and crackers he took from the sack. He peeled an orange and divided the sections between them. She didn't like eating from his hand, but opened her lips obediently each time he pressed a section of the orange against them.

As they approached the outskirts of a dreary-looking town, Greywolf instructed her to slow down. They were driving past the beer taverns that lined the highway like sad old whores in desperate need of customers.

"There," he said shortly, pointing with his finger. "Pull into the Tumbleweed."

Disgust registered on Aislinn's face. The Tumbleweed was the sleaziest-looking of all the honky-tonks. "I hope we're in time for happy hour," she remarked sarcastically.

"They have a television," Greywolf said, having spotted the antenna sticking out of the tin roof. "Get out."

"Yes, sir," she mumbled, tiredly shoving open her door. It felt good to stand. She placed her hands at the small of her back and stretched, then stamped circulation back into her feet.

There were only a few other vehicles parked in the dusty gravel parking lot in front of the tavern. Greywolf took her arm and dragged her along with him to the door. A good portion of the rusty screen had been ripped from its frame. The jagged edge, which curled outward, looked as intimidating as the rest of the place. Aislinn's plan was to appear resigned, but the moment they cleared the doorway, to scream for help.

"Forget what you're thinking."

"What am I thinking?"

"That you're going to escape me and run into the safe arms of a rescuer. Believe me, I'm the safest companion you could have in a joint like this." That wasn't saying much, considering that she had seen him slide the knife down into his boot before he left the car. "No," he said, slinging his arm across her shoulders, "look like you're having a good, sexy time."

"What!"

"That's right. We're having an illicit afternoon affair."

"You're insane if you think— And stop that!" she exclaimed when he slipped his arm around her waist and his hand came up her side alarmingly close to her breast. His hard fingers pressed into the tender flesh, securing her in a hold there would be no escaping from.

"Why, honey, is that any way to talk to your lover?" he whined.

Assuming an ambling, none-too-steady swagger, he pulled open the screen door, pushed open the rickety door and stumbled into the murky, smoky interior. To maintain her balance, Aislinn gripped the front of his shirt, pressing her hand against his stomach. He glanced down at her and winked, as though she had won his approval. She wanted to shout at him that she wouldn't have touched him had it not been a choice between that or falling down.

However, she said nothing. She was disheartened into speechlessness by her seedy surroundings. Such places as the Tumbleweed were portrayed in movies, but she had certainly never been inside one. The low ceiling was all but obscured by a pall of tobacco smoke. It took her eyes a moment to adjust to the darkness, but seeing the place clearly only distressed her more.

In front of the bar was a row of stationary stools with red vinyl seat pads. At least they had been red once. Now they were all aged to a greasy, dirty maroon. Only three of them were occupied. As the door slapped shut behind Greywolf and her, three pairs of mean eyes turned toward them and gave them a suspicious once-over.

One pair, laden with crusty make-up, belonged to a blowsy blonde who had her bare foot propped up on the stool next to her. She was painting her toenails. "Hey, Ray, we got customers," she hollered.

Ray, Aislinn assumed, was the obese man behind the bar. He was leaning forward with his massive forearms braced on a refrigerator, his eyes glued to the television set that was mounted high in the corner. He was engrossed in a soap opera. "So wait on 'em," he bellowed back. He hadn't taken his eyes off the screen.

"My nails ain't dry."

Ray let go a string of obscenities that Aislinn thought were reserved only for public rest room walls in seaports. He pushed his fat bulk off the refrigerator and shot Greywolf and her a sour look. She was the only one who saw it. Her escort had his face buried in her hair and his tongue in her ear.

But apparently he hadn't missed anything. "Two cold beers," he said loud enough for Ray to hear. Then he gave Aislinn a slight push and maneuvered her toward one of the ratty-looking booths along the wall. It would provide them with a clear view of both the TV set and the door. "Sit down and scoot over," he whispered for her benefit.

Since he all but shoved her down, she had no choice. She didn't have a chance to inspect the cleanliness of the seat, but it was probably just as well. Greywolf slid into the booth after her and crammed her against the wall. "You're squashing me," she complained beneath her breath.

"That's the general idea."

He was gnawing on her neck when Ray waddled over carrying two beers in his hands, which looked like hams with dirty fingernails. The bottles of beer made solid thumps on the chipped Formica table when he set them down. "Three bucks. You pay as you go here."

"Pay the man, will ya, hon?" Lucas wheedled, sliding his hand over her shoulder in a circular, caressing motion. "I'm busy."

She ground her teeth together in an effort not to scream at him to take his hands off her, or to take her out of there, or to go to hell. But right then, she was glad he was there. He had known what he was talking about. Even if she could coax some sympathy out of Ray and the others, she doubted she would want to entrust herself into their care. At least Greywolf was a familiar villain.

She dug into her purse for three one-dollar bills and laid them on the table. Ray, still looking over his shoulder so he wouldn't miss a second of his soap opera, scooped them up and shuffled away.

"Good girl," Lucas spoke softly into her ear.

She wished Greywolf wouldn't be so earnest in his playacting now that Ray no longer posed a threat to him. He could at least remove his hand from inside her blouse, where his fingers were fiddling with her bra strap. "Now what?" she asked.

"Now we neck."

"You go—"

"Shh!" he hissed angrily. "You don't want to attract Ray's attention, do you? Or maybe those two cowboys are more to your liking. They'd just love rescuing a damsel in distress."

"Oh, stop," she said, when his lips slid down her neck. "I thought you came here to watch television."

"I did. But I don't want them to know that."

"So I'm supposed to sit here and let you paw me?" He made a humming sound of affirmation. "For how long?"

"For as long as it takes. Every half hour or so we'll order fresh beers so Ray won't get mad at us for taking up his valuable space."

How a man could talk so rationally while nibbling so dedicatedly, she didn't know. She squirmed away from his seeking lips. "I can't drink that much."

"When no one is looking, pour the beer on the floor. I doubt it will ever be noticed."

"So do I," she said with a shiver, lifting her foot off the floor. It was sticky with substances she thought it best not to identify. "Are you sure this is going to be worth it?"

"What's the matter, sweetheart? Ain't you having a good time?" His hand found the placket of her blouse and plucked at the buttons.

"No."

"Do you want to go through another roadblock? Or did you enjoy driving that poor cop a little crazy?"

"You're despicable." She leaned back against the hard, lumpy upholstery of the booth and tried to be passive under the gropings of his hands and mouth.

"I'm not convinced you're hot for it, sugar, and neither will they be. Put a little more into it," he growled, his lips very near her mouth.

"No. This is disgusting."

His head snapped up and he stared down at her coldly. "Why?"

He had taken offense. Why? Because he thought her comment was a racial slur, or because he thought she was maligning his lovemaking expertise? And either way, what the hell did she care if he was offended or not? "I'm not accustomed to making out in public places, Mr.—"

She never said his name. She never had a chance. He mashed his lips over hers and sealed his name inside. It was a functional kiss, impersonal, delivered only to keep her quiet. He kept his lips closed. Still, Aislinn's insides somersaulted and she couldn't utter a sound.

Which was the point, after all. When he finally lifted his mouth off hers he whispered, "Careful."

She merely nodded her head, wishing that her heart would cool. One thing she knew, she wouldn't provoke him with any more questions or conversation. She didn't want him to kiss her again.

She was ambivalent as to why, but she did *not* want him to kiss her again.

Thankfully no one took much notice of them. It seemed to be an unwritten rule that the patrons of the Tumbleweed minded their own business unless invited to do otherwise.

Though he gave every semblance of being absorbed in his lovemaking, Greywolf was fully aware of what went on. His eyes were never still, though he made them appear slumberous with arousal by keeping his eyelids at half-mast. From beneath the hood of his brows, he watched each face for signs of recognition, but no one paid them any attention. Ray—or his waitress when her nails had dried—carried beer to the booth when Greywolf drunkenly called out an order for it. Beyond that, no one paid them the slightest heed.

Customers drifted in and out. Most stayed only for a couple of drinks before leaving. Some drank alone. Others entered in groups of two or three. One played on the pinball machine until the pinging bells and flashing lights nearly drove Aislinn crazy. When he finally left, the television provided the only distraction. Situation comedy reruns now held Ray enthralled.

For Aislinn the time dragged by. Not because she was bored. Her nerve endings were sizzling. She kept telling herself it was because she was waiting for a potential savior to walk through the door. But honestly she thought her skittishness had more to do with Greywolf's foreplay.

And what else could it be called? What other term applied to the way he slid his fingers up through her hair, holding her head still while his lips nibbled their way down her throat. Or the way he squeezed her upper thigh when the waitress delivered their beer. Or the way his lips were wont to play around her ears.

"Don't," she moaned once, when that particular caress caused goose bumps to break out over her arms.

"The moaning is good. Keep it up," he whispered as a pair of truckers moseyed past the booth on their way to the pinball machine.

He took her hand and slipped it inside his shirt, holding it palm down, against his skin. Aislinn made a feeble attempt to withdraw her hand, but Greywolf wouldn't let her. As long as she was forced to touch him, she submitted to her own curiosity. As unobtrusively as possible, she curled her fingertips into the hard flesh. Her thumb moved a fraction. It encountered his nipple. It was erect.

He sucked in his breath sharply. "Godamighty," he cursed. "Don't do that." His body had been tense all afternoon, but nothing compared to the rigid, still way it pressed against her now.

She snatched her hand back. "I'm just doing what you—"

"Shh!"

"Don't say—"

"*Shh!* Look. On the screen."

She glanced toward the TV. A Phoenix newscaster was reading a story about the search for the elusive prison escapee, Indian activist Lucas Greywolf. A picture of Lucas was flashed onto the screen. Aislinn stared at it, barely recognizing him. His hair was cropped short, almost shaved.

"Not a very flattering picture," she said dryly.

The corner of his mouth twitched with the hint of a smile, but his attention was riveted to the map of Arizona that was now being shown. As he had guessed, the media weren't doing the law-enforcement agencies any favors; they were pinpointing where roadblocks had been set up. Even though leaked news stories like this sabotaged police work, each television station's main goal was to scoop its competitors.

As soon as the announcer switched to other newsworthy events of the day, Lucas scooted to the edge of the booth. "Okay, let's go. And remember to weave. You've supposedly drunk several beers."

He offered her his hand, but his attention was diverted to the door as it was opened to admit another customer. Greywolf's curse was soft, but no less scorching, as a uniformed man came strolling in.

Chapter 3

Casually taking off his hat, the uniformed man ran his sleeve over his sweating brow. Aislinn sat up and took notice. His uniform was that of a sheriff, at the very least a deputy.

"Stella, get me a beer," he called out as soon as the door slammed closed behind him.

The blond waitress turned and gave him a wide, welcoming smile that indicated their level of familiarity. "Well, look what the cat just drug in." Leaning back against the bar, she propped her elbows on it. The posture displayed her huge bosom to its full potential. The sheriff showed his appreciation by giving her a lecherous smile.

"Missed me, didja?"

"Hell no," she drawled, curling her arm around his sunburned neck as he squatted on the stool next to where she was standing. "You know how it is with me. Outa sight, outa mind."

"For two days I've been chasing some damn Indian nobody's seen hide nor hair of. What I need is a coupla cold ones and some tender loving care."

"In that order?" The blonde leaned down and purred the question near his mouth. He kissed her, but then swatted her ample hip.

"Get me that beer."

Stella went to do the hunter's bidding while the hunted sat seething next to Aislinn in the booth. "Damn," Greywolf said beneath his breath, pounding his fist against his thigh under the table. "Just a few more minutes and we would have been gone. Damn."

He kept up the frustrated litany, all the while leaning over Aislinn in the corner of the booth as though they were petting. "Don't you dare do anything to attract his attention. Because to rescue you, sweetheart, he'll have to go through me."

"What do you plan to do?"

"For the time being, more of the same," he said, kissing her neck. "Maybe he'll leave."

But apparently the officer intended to make a night of it. His "coupla cold ones" turned into three, then four. Stella didn't move far from his side, unless forced to wait on other customers. They flirted outrageously, exchanging sexual innuendos, until their provocative banterings mellowed to soft, private whispers punctuated occasionally by Stella's low, sexy laugh. The sheriff's hands were never idle, but caressed her unceasingly. Stella never demurred.

Aislinn's hopes had flared with the unexpected appearance of the sheriff, but now she doubted that the law officer even cared whether the escaped convict was captured or not. There were a lot of people, Indian and Anglo alike, who had felt that Lucas Greywolf got a bum rap and had been in sympathy with his cause. This overworked sheriff might be one of them. He might look the other way if Greywolf crossed his path.

Still, the sheriff represented Aislinn's only hope of getting away from her kidnapper. She planned to use him, though she was sure he wouldn't thank her for ruining the evening he planned to spend in Stella's company.

"When the time is right, we're going to get up and walk out, got it?"

"Yes," she agreed. Perhaps a little too quickly.

Greywolf raised his head slightly and, staring down into her eyes, reached beneath the table. Even before she saw the blade of the knife reflecting the dim lights, she realized he had drawn it from his boot. "Don't make me use this, Aislinn. Particularly on you."

"Why not on me?"

His eyes slid down her body suggestively. "Because after spending such a pleasurable afternoon feeling you up, I'd hate to hurt you."

"I hope you burn in hell," she said, pushing each word of the harsh condemnation through her teeth.

"And I'm sure your wish will be granted." He said no more, but turned his attention back to the couple at the bar. He watched them like a hawk, his gray eyes unwavering. When the sheriff's hand made an exploratory pass across Stella's breast, then paused to investigate, Greywolf said, "Now."

Aislinn had expected him to slink out of the booth and through the door. Instead, he jerked her to her feet suddenly, giving him the element of surprise. It worked to his benefit beautifully. She slumped against him to regain her balance. His arm wrapped around her waist, securing her to his side. She pressed her fists against his chest, angling her body away from his, and opened her mouth. All that came out, however, was a short gasp. He slipped the knife up between their bodies.

"Don't." His raspy voice was dangerously calm, cool, and collected. It effectively changed her mind about trying to escape him now.

They made their staggering progress toward the door, his head bent low over hers as though he was drunk.

"Hey, mister."

Aislinn's footsteps faltered, but Greywolf's didn't. He kept going.

"Hey, mister! I'm talking to you, Chief."

Against her cheek, she felt Greywolf's aggravated expulsion of breath before he halted and lifted his head. "Yeah?" he asked of Ray, who had addressed him.

"We got rooms in the back," he said, hitching his thumb over his shoulder. "You and your lady want one for the evenin'?"

"No thanks," Lucas said. "Gotta get her home before her ol' man gets back."

Ray chuckled lewdly and went back to watching the detective series that was now blaring forth from the television. The sheriff, pouring all his romantic passions into the kiss he was grinding onto Stella's receptive mouth, never even looked up. Once she was outside, Aislinn's lungs drank in the pure air. She didn't think she'd ever filter the dank smell of beer and stale tobacco smoke out of her nasal passages. Greywolf wasted no time on luxuries like deep, cleansing breathing, but hustled her into the car.

Within minutes they had put several miles between them and the Tumbleweed. Only then did he breathe deeply. He rolled down the window and seemed to relish the wind beating against his face. "You're becoming very good at eluding the law," he remarked.

"I didn't like having that knife against my ribs," she shot back.

"You weren't supposed to."

He seemed to know where he was going, though Aislinn knew this wasn't a well-traveled highway they were on now. The lanes were narrow. There were few signs. No lights. Shoulders were nonexistent. Other cars were few and far between. When they met them, she held her breath out of fear of crashing head-on.

Greywolf drove fast, but safely. Before long, staring at the white stripes chasing each other down the center of the highway became hypnotic and she nodded off. But only moments later, Greywolf's blistering curse rent the silence.

"Dammit all to hell!"

"Is somebody following us?" she asked hopefully, sitting up and glancing behind them.

"The heat light just came on."

Her spirits sank as low as her weary shoulders. For a moment she had entertained the hope that the sheriff or somebody in the Tumbleweed had recognized Greywolf, but had played it safe and not tried to apprehend him until reinforcements could be called in. "It was doing that this afternoon," she said, slumping back against the seat.

He swiveled his head around and glared at her. His face was illuminated only by the lights on the dashboard. They lent it a greenish cast, making it look even more fearsome. His eyes were pale, silver, furious. "You mean the engine was actually overheating this afternoon?"

"Didn't you hear me tell that to the highway patrolman at the roadblock?"

"I thought that was just part of your act," he shouted.

"Well it wasn't."

"So why didn't you say something before I pulled onto this abandoned highway?"

"You didn't ask!"

He ended the shouting match with a curse she couldn't possibly champion for fear of being struck by lightning. Her lower teeth almost went through the roof of her mouth when he suddenly steered the car off the highway. "Where are you going?" she asked fearfully.

"I have to let the car cool off or the engine will burn up completely. I can't do anything to repair it in the dark anyway." He drove the car several hundred yards off the highway. The terrain was so rough that Aislinn had to brace her hands against the dash to keep from getting jostled onto the floorboard. When they finally came to a standstill the motor was hissing like a boiling teakettle. Greywolf pushed his door open and got out. He leaned his back against the car and bowed his head.

"Damn! I've wasted so much time today. First in that godforsaken tavern. Now this." He appeared to be extremely upset over the forced delay. He walked toward the hood of the car and viciously kicked one of the tires, cursing expansively.

Aislinn got out on her side and stretched her cramped muscles. "Are we under some kind of deadline?"

"Yes. We're under a deadline." His grim tone advised her to hold her peace and not pursue the subject. After a while, he shook his head and heaved a sigh of resignation. "As long as we're stuck here, we might just as well make use of the time and get some sleep. Get in the back seat."

"I'm not sleepy," she said sullenly.

"Get in the back seat anyway."

His voice rolled over the desert like ominous, distant thunder. Aislinn gave him a murderous look, but she obeyed him. Leaving all the car doors open save one in the back seat, he got in behind her. Settling himself into the corner against the door, he spread his thighs wide and, before she knew what he was going to do, pulled her between them.

"Let me go," she demanded, outraged. She squirmed against him, but since that only served to better acquaint her bottom with the fly of his jeans, she stopped.

"I'm going to sleep. And so are you." He situated her back against his chest and wrapped his arms around her. They felt like bands of steel crisscrossing just beneath her breasts. It was an extremely unnerving position, though not painful. Not even uncomfortable, if she would let herself relax against him. Which she wouldn't.

"I can't go roaming off in the desert, Greywolf. Let me go."

"Not a chance. Unless you'd rather be tied to the steering wheel."

"Where would I go if I escaped?"

"If I've learned one thing about you, it is that you are a resourceful lady."

"We're in the middle of nowhere. It's dark."

"There's a moon."

Yes, she had noticed. And there were stars, the likes of which she'd never seen. They were huge and bright and close, not city stars at all. At any other time, she could have admired this night, savored it, let its magnificence embrace her, and enjoyed her smallness when compared to it.

But she wanted nothing about this night to be beautiful. She wanted to remember only the horror of it later. "I'd be a fool to strike out on my own, even if I knew where I was and could get away from you."

"Which I'm making certain you won't do. Now, for your own good, be still."

The tenseness underlying his warning alerted her to other things as well. Like the tremors vibrating through the arms that supported her breasts. Like the pressure at the small of her back. She swallowed, denying to herself what that could mean.

"Please don't do this." She was willing to swallow her pride and plead with him, because she didn't think she could stand to be this close to him all through the night. Not because she disliked it so much, but because she didn't dislike it nearly enough. "Let me go."

"No."

Knowing that it was useless, she stopped trying to change his mind. But she refused to relax. Her back was as stiff as a board against his chest. Before long her neck began to ache from the tension of maintaining the small distance between them. Not until she thought he was asleep, did she let her head fall back onto his shoulder.

"You're very stubborn, Aislinn Andrews."

Aislinn closed her eyes and gnashed her teeth, knowing that he'd been privy to her stubbornness and her final surrender. He'd probably waited her out deliberately.

"If you'd loosen your arms I could breathe easier."

"Or reach for the knife." They lay in silence, then he said, "You are one of few."

"Few what?"

"Women that I've spent more than one night with."

"Don't expect me to be flattered."

"I don't. I'm sure an Anglo virgin like you can't imagine anything worse than having an Indian between her lily white thighs."

"You're unspeakably vulgar. And I'm not a virgin."

"Have you been married?"

"No."

"Then you lived with a man?"

"No."

"Affairs?"

"None of your business."

She would rather die than have him know that there had been only one. Hardly worth mentioning. It had been a terribly disappointing experience that she had engaged in mainly to satisfy her curiosity.

Between her and the man, there had been only mild affection, little communication, no warmth or closeness, nor even much passion. Afterward, she had been disillusioned and disappointed and imagined that her partner had been as well.

She had never risked that kind of awkward encounter again and recently had begun to think that she simply wasn't sexually inclined. The men she went out with tried, but none stirred even enough interest for her to pursue the relationship beyond dinner dates and an occasional good-night kiss.

Rather than talk about her love life, or lack thereof, she asked him, "What about you? How many affairs of the heart have you had?"

But either he had dropped off to sleep or he ignored her. In any event, no answer was forthcoming.

She snuggled closer to the warmth.

A soft growl, like the purr of a great cat, echoed through the waking chambers of her mind. She stirred and when her brain began to piece together the information her senses were sending she came suddenly awake and her eyes popped open.

"Oh my God," she cried.

"No, that's my line," he groaned.

She was sprawled atop Lucas Greywolf.

Sometime during the night she had turned over, so that now her cheek was resting on his bare chest where his shirt had fallen open. Her breasts were flattened against his stomach and her hips... "Oh, Lord." She repeated her plea to heaven because the cleft of her thighs was cuddling his manhood.

And it was very hard.

Cheeks flaming, she pushed herself up and scrambled to the other side of the back seat. "I'm sorry," she stammered, keeping her face averted.

"So am I," he grated, as he opened the door on his side and practically fell out. For a long while, he just stood there by the side of the car. Aislinn didn't dare ask what the matter was. She knew.

After several minutes, he walked to the front of the car and raised the hood. He fiddled with something beneath it, then came back to crouch down inside the open car door. "Take off your bra."

If he had said, "Sprout wings and fly," she couldn't have been more astounded. "I beg your pardon?"

"You heard me. Either that or your blouse. But hurry up. We've lost enough time."

It was well past dawn, and her blush deepened when she realized how soundly they had both slept. Of course yesterday had been an exhausting day and—

"Either you take it off or I do," he interrupted her thoughts brusquely.

"Turn around."

"Oh for..." He turned around. Hastily she peeled off her shirt, took off her bra, then pulled the shirt back on, buttoning it quickly.

"Here." She thrust the garment at him. He took it without a word and carried it back with him to the front of the car. After several minutes of sweat-breaking work and elaborate cursing, he slammed the hood and got into the driver's seat, wiping his hands on the legs of his jeans.

All he said by way of explanation was, "That might hold it for a while."

But not nearly long enough. They had driven only twenty miles or so when threads of white smoke began ghosting from beneath the hood. Then it began to billow.

"You'd better stop before the car blows up," Aislinn suggested tentatively. They hadn't spoken a word since starting out. If he was as shaken as she by the position in which they had found themselves upon waking, then she could understand his reticence.

She kept remembering things she wished she could physically blot from her mind, like how his chest hair had felt warm and fuzzy and fine against her lips. And how his hands had been cupping and caressing her derriere before she was fully awake. And how good she had felt moments before realization stunned her into consciousness.

His remote features gave away none of what he was thinking as he pulled the car off the road again. It wheezed to a stop. "Well, that bra did no more good there than it did keeping your nipples from showing."

She gaped at him in shock, but he merely opened his door and stepped out. "Come on."

"Come on where?"

"To the nearest town."

"You mean we're going to *walk*?" she asked incredulously. They were in the middle of nowhere, surrounded by rugged terrain on all sides. In the distance was the purple silhouette of mountains. Between here and there was nothing but rock-strewn ground, the callused palm of Mother Nature, unrelieved except for the gray swath of the highway.

"Until someone stops to pick us up," he said in answer to her question. He struck off. Aislinn had no choice but to leave the car and trot along behind him until she caught up.

She wasn't about to stay there alone. He might not come back for her, and it looked as though it could be days before another car came along. She was already thirsty and hadn't helped that by eating a few cookies out of the provisions Greywolf had taken from her kitchen.

They walked for what seemed like hours. She had to virtually jog to keep pace with him. The sun beat down unmercifully on her uncovered head. The terrain was fit only for Gila monsters and other reptilian creatures that occasionally slithered across their path.

Finally they heard the chugging sound of an approaching vehicle and turned to see a pickup truck coming from behind them. It looked like a faded red specter materializing out of the shimmering heat waves. Before Greywolf even raised his arms and waved, the driver was downshifting. Three stoic Navaho men sat shoulder to shoulder in the cab of the ancient pickup. After conversing with them briefly, Greywolf hauled Aislinn into the back of it with him.

"Did they recognize you?"

"Probably."

"Aren't you afraid they'll turn you in?"

His head swung around and, despite the heat, she shivered against the cold glance he sent her. "No."

"Oh, I see. They're honor bound to keep their silence."

He didn't even bother to reply, but turned his eyes toward the northeastern horizon, where she had already deduced they were headed.

They maintained a hostile silence for the length of the ride into a small, dusty town. Conversation would have been difficult anyway. The hot wind pounded her and sucked the breath out of her lungs.

While they were still on the outskirts of the town, Greywolf knocked on the rear windshield of the pickup and the driver downshifted to a halt in front of a service station. Greywolf jumped to the ground and assisted Aislinn down. "Much obliged," he called to the driver, who doffed his straw cowboy hat to them before reengaging the gears of the truck and driving off.

"Now what?" Aislinn asked, tiredly. She had known instinctively that the Navaho men would be in sympathy with Greywolf, but hope had briefly glimmered at the prospect of stopping in a town.

Hope died the moment she saw the community. The streets were deserted. Except for chickens pecking on the barren ground in a yard across the highway, there were no signs of life anywhere. The town looked as unwelcoming and inhospitable as the desert that surrounded it.

Greywolf walked toward the tin building which housed the service station. Aislinn forced herself to follow him, dragging her feet. She had never been so uncomfortable in her life. The perspiration that had soaked her clothes and body while they were walking on the highway had dried now and left a gritty, salty residue on her skin that itched like mad. She was hot, sticky and sunburned. Her lips were parched, her hair a tangled mess.

She groaned when she read the sign posted on the grimy window of the service station. "Siesta!" she exclaimed mournfully.

"They're closed until four o'clock," Greywolf said, turning his head to consult the sun.

Aislinn discovered a meager sliver of shade near the wall of the building and pressed herself against it. Leaning her head back, she closed her eyes. They came open instantly when she heard the crash of breaking glass.

Greywolf had smashed out a window in the door with a rock. Without so much as a blink of his eyes, he reached inside and unlocked the door. It swung open with a protesting squeak and he went inside. Aislinn, who would never have considered deliberately breaking a window, much less trespassing onto anyone else's property, followed him into the marginally cooler interior.

Once her eyes had adjusted to the dimness, she saw that the place was not just a gas station, but a small grocery store as well. Wooden shelves were stocked with potato chips and canned goods, paper products and household cleansers.

There was one dusty glass counter filled with even dustier Arizona souvenirs. On top there were boxes of candy bars, cigarettes and chewing gum. Behind it, the pegboard wall was covered with an inventory of small automotive parts.

Greywolf crossed the aged wooden floor, which protested each of his footsteps with a groan, to an old-fashioned cold-drink vending chest. Lifting the lid, he jimmied the lock that was supposed to prevent thefts, took out two bottled Cokes, opened them and passed one to Aislinn even as he raised the other to his mouth and drank thirstily.

"I intend to pay for mine, " she said sanctimoniously.

He lowered the bottle from his mouth. "I intend for you to pay for mine, too. Also for the broken pane of glass. And for the water hose."

She drank the cold cola, thinking that it was the best-tasting thing she'd ever had. "What water hose?"

He was scanning the various implements behind the counter. "To replace the one that busted. Like this," he said, lifting one off its peg and holding it up to her.

With his other hand, he was opening drawers behind the counter and examining the contents. Metal tools clanked and rattled as he moved them about in the drawers. The sound emphasized to Aislinn how deserted the place was.

She felt alien, consumed by the feeling of desolation that lurked around the place. Greywolf suffered from no such unease. When he found the tools he was looking for, he took them out. Just when she was about to succumb to abject despair, she spotted the pay telephone.

She was sure Greywolf hadn't noticed it. He was still pilfering the tool drawers and hadn't looked in the direction of the corner where the phone was attached to the wall. It was partially hidden by a rack of outdated magazines.

If she could keep him talking, maybe she could get to that phone and place a call without his knowing. But where was she? What was the name of this godforsaken town? What highway had they been on? She didn't recall seeing any signs. Had it even been a highway? For all she knew they could have crossed a state line and were no longer in Arizona.

"Finished?"

She jumped guiltily at the sound of Greywolf's voice. "Yes," she said and passed him her empty bottle. Where only moments before she had felt laggardly, her mind was now alert, whirring with plans for ways to distract him.

"Give me some money," he said, holding out his hand, palm up.

Eager to please him for the moment, she fished in her purse and came up with a twenty-dollar bill. "That should cover it."

He folded the money and tucked it under an ashtray on the counter. "There are facilities in the back," he said. "Do you need them?"

Yes, she did, but she deliberated on her next course of action. She could lie and say she didn't need the rest room, encouraging him to go ahead while she waited for him. But that would seem unlikely and would arouse his suspicions. Better to go along, get him to think that she no longer sought to escape.

"Yes, please," she said meekly. Without a word, he led her out the door and around the corner of the building to the two doors appropriately marked. She dreaded what awaited her inside as Greywolf pushed open the door of the women's rest room. The odor was overpowering, but she stepped inside and switched on the feeble light.

It was better than she had expected, though still bad. Now that she was reminded of how long it had been, she needed very badly to use the facility no matter how offensive it was. When she was finished, she rinsed her face and hands in the rusty sink. Even the tepid water felt cool against her sun- and wind-chafed skin.

Opting to let it air-dry, she went to the door, unlatched it, and tried to push it open. It wouldn't budge.

At first she thought she was pushing the wrong way and tried drawing it toward her, but to no avail. She pushed on it with all her might. It didn't move. Panic welling inside her, she threw herself against it.

"Greywolf!" she cried frantically. "Greywolf!"

"What is it, Aislinn?"

"I can't get the door open."

"That's right."

Her mouth dropped open in dismay. He had locked her in!

"Open this door," she screamed, banging on it with her fists.

"I will as soon as I return."

"Return? *Return?* Where are you going? Don't you dare leave me locked up in here."

"I have to. I don't want you using that telephone you made such a point of not noticing. I'll let you out as soon as I get back."

"Where are you going?" she repeated, desperate over the thought of being cooped up in the rest room for an unspecified period of time.

"Back to the car. As soon as I get that busted water hose replaced, I'll be back to pick you up."

"The *car?* You're going back to the car? How will you get there?"

"I'll run."

"Run." She mouthed the word, but little sound came out. Then a thought occurred to her and she wanted to flaunt her cleverness in his face. "As soon as the owners of this dump reopen at four, they'll find me. I'll scream the place down."

"I'll be back well before four."

"You bastard. Let me out of here." She pushed against the door with her full weight behind her, and still it wouldn't give. "It's stifling. I'll die cooped up in here."

"You'll sweat, but you won't die. I suggest you rest."

"Go to hell!"

He made no reply. Her words echoed off the walls of the public rest room. Pressing her ear to the door, she listened but could hear nothing. "Greywolf?" she called tentatively. Then loudly, "Greywolf!"

Nothing. She was alone.

Slumping against the door, she covered her face with her hands and submitted to the luxury of tears again. A woman like herself wasn't prepared to cope with adversity of this sort. Life-and-death situations were beyond the realm of her sheltered environment. She had grown up in a gilded ghetto guarded by parents who wanted "the best" for their child.

She had never even attended a public school because of the "undesirable elements of society" she would encounter there. She hadn't been trained in survival tactics at the exclusive women's college she had attended. Situations like this made great movie scripts, but no one really believed that they actually *happened*. But this was happening—to her.

For the first time in her twenty-six years, Aislinn Andrews was confronted with real fear. It was tangible. She could breathe it. She could taste it.

What if Greywolf never came back for her? What guarantee did she have that the service station would reopen at four o'clock? That sign could have been posted on the door months ago and forgotten when the owners decided that keeping the business open wasn't worth their effort.

She could die of thirst.

No, the rest room had water. Not the purest, she was certain, but it was wet.

She could die of starvation.

Actually that would take a long time, and surely someone would drive into the place before then. She'd have to keep alert for the sound of a motor and start pounding on the door and shouting when she heard one.

She could die of suffocation.

But there was a window, a small one, located high on the wall just under the ceiling. It was open several inches. The air might be arid and hot, but there was plenty of it.

She could die of rage.

Now that was a very real possibility, Aislinn thought. How dare Greywolf desert her in this disgusting place? Calling him every vile name she could think of, she paced the small rest room.

Finally it was that very anger which fueled her mind and sparked her imagination. Even he had said she was resourceful. She could get out of this rest room if only she would put her mind to it. She knew it! But how?

Again and again, she threw herself against the door, but it wouldn't budge. Whatever he had used to brace it shut wasn't going to give, and she was only wasting her strength trying to move it. Sweat ran down her body in steady streams. She could feel it trickling along her scalp beneath her hair, which was heavy and hot.

Despairing over her futility and weakness, she raised her eyes imploringly toward heaven. And therein lay the answer to her dilemma. *The window!* If she had some way to—

There was a metal barrel standing in one corner of the rest room. Apparently it had served as a trash can for as long as the rest room had been in use. Steeling herself against thinking of its stinking contents, she struggled to upend it. The thing was monstrously heavy and bulky, but she finally succeeded in turning it bottom side up and scooted it beneath the window.

By standing on the barrel, she was able to grasp the bottom of the windowsill. For several minutes she labored, pulling herself up with the strength of her arms alone, searching for nonexistent footholds in the concrete block walls, until finally she levered herself up over the sill. Poking her head through the open window, she hauled in great gulps of air and welcomed the wind against her face. She hung there for several minutes, giving her arms, which trembled with fatigue, a much-needed rest.

Then she used her shoulders to raise the window as high as it would go. The opening was narrow, but she thought that with some effort and good luck, she could get through it. Pulling one knee up and bracing it against the sill, she tried turning herself so she could go feet first out the window.

It was when she raised her other knee to the sill that she lost her balance. Deliberately, she propelled herself toward the outside. With that much momentum behind it, her body slipped through the open window. As she fell, her arm caught on a nail on the sill. It ripped a seam in her flesh from wrist to armpit.

Miraculously, she landed on her feet below, but the ground was uneven. Grasping her arm in pain, she reeled backward and went toppling down a slope, rolling, somersaulting, only to bump her head on a rock at the bottom.

For a few blinding seconds, she stared up at the fiery orb of the sun, which seemed to be mocking her. Then all went black.

Chapter 4

He was anxious to get back. His eyes, missing nothing, had memorized the landmarks. He knew he had only a few miles left to go. Three at most. He pushed the accelerator to the floorboard.

Thankfully, the car responded. It was back in prime working condition. Switching out the hoses hadn't been a problem. The difficulty had been running all the way back to the car with heavy tools in his pockets and carrying a gallon jug of water to replace what had leaked out. He was accustomed to running distance. Even in midsummer heat that wasn't a challenge. But carrying the unevenly distributed extra poundage had been.

Greywolf was grateful for the opportunity to think as the car ate up the remaining miles. The hot wind whipped against his cheeks and through his hair. He preferred driving with the windows down; disdaining artificial air conditioning when he could glory in the elements of the desert. Only because of the woman had he left the car windows rolled up in the first place.

The woman.

His conscience pricked him to think of her locked up in that hot, filthy rest room. But what else could he have done? Left her to phone the nearest sheriff's office? Taken her with him? She would never have been able to walk back to the car, and even if she had, she would have added hours to the time it had taken him. Hours he couldn't afford.

How soon before they caught up with him? How soon? Would he make it there in time? He had to.

He had known what the prison escape would cost him, but he was willing to pay any price. He only regretted that it had cost others as well. He hadn't enjoyed knocking unconscious the trustee who had considered him a friend. He hadn't enjoyed frightening the woman either. She represented everything he despised: Anglos in general and affluent Anglos in particular. Still, he wished he hadn't been forced to involve her.

Forced to?

With an aggravated motion, he switched on the radio and turned it up full volume, telling himself he wanted to catch any forthcoming news bulletins. Actually, he hoped the blaring music would block out thoughts of *her*.

Why had he saddled himself with this responsibility? Why hadn't he just clipped her on the chin and left her house as quickly and quietly as he had come? By the time she regained consciousness and alerted the police, he would have had time to elude them again.

Instead, *stupidly*, he had stayed and heckled the Anglo woman. He had needed a shower, yes, but that was a luxury he could have done without. He had needed sleep, yes, but he could have found a place less comfortable than her bed with its scented sheets and fluffy pillows.

Even granting himself that much luxury, why hadn't he left before dawn the moment he had awakened? Sure, she would have notified the authorities when she woke up, but that could have been hours later. By then his trail would have been cold.

Instead of doing what he knew he should, he had lain there gazing at her blond beauty. She was too easy to look at, and he had never entertained the thought of resisting the temptation. Eyes starved for the sight of a woman had feasted on her. He had breathed deeply of her scent, treating his nostrils, too long deprived, to the perfume of a woman's body.

Rather than sneaking out as he knew he should, he had foolishly decided that he would take her with him. It was never his intention to harm her.

All right, so why did you threaten her with a knife?

Safety precaution.

Did you have to make her strip?

That was unnecessary, I admit. But I just wanted to look at her.

Like hell.

It's true. I wouldn't have forced her. Besides she's an Anglo. I don't even like Anglo women. I sure don't desire them.

You desire this one.

I've been in prison for God's sake! Any woman would be desirable!

You wouldn't like to make love to her?

No.

You're a damn liar.

Well I didn't and I won't.

He would maintain rigid control over his lust if it killed him. He just wanted the woman near him. That's all. To keep that taunting voice of his conscience at bay, he thought of all the reasons he didn't like his blond hostage.

She was rich and spoiled, no doubt. She had about her that Do-Not-Touch look that Indian boys like him had come to recognize on Anglo coeds. That was one of the first things he had learned when he left the reservation to attend college. Girls like Aislinn Andrews might flirt with you, but they sure as hell didn't want to make it with you. Or if they did let it go that far, it was for kicks, for the novelty of it, to brag to their sorority sisters that they'd had an Indian. "No!" "Yes!" "Just how savage was it?" The next day they acted like they didn't know you and the social barriers were up again.

This Anglo woman had spunk, though; he'd give her that. She could have been a real pain in the ass, whining and crying all the time, but she hadn't been. She'd kept a stiff upper lip no matter what he put her through.

His grim face relaxed into a facsimile of a smile when he recalled the way she had handled the highway patrolman. Why had she done it?

He owed her for that, he supposed.

And after last night, he was no longer sure he could keep to his resolve not to touch her. The hours spent in the Tumbleweed had been pure heaven and pure hell. There had been times, far too many for his peace of mind, when he had wanted the kisses to be real, when he had wanted to part her lips with his tongue and taste her, when he had wanted to open her clothes and touch her.

God, she had felt good lying against him this morning, her breath lightly fanning his chest, her breasts so soft and sweet, her thighs . . .

Damn! he thought, *I've got to let her go.*

When he got to the gas station, he would fill up the car, check with her to see that she was all right, then leave a note telling the owners where she could be found. When the police were notified, she would be able to tell them where he had been, but not where he was going. Or rather, not specifically where. They already knew his approximate destination and would be searching anyway. It was only a matter of time.

He only hoped he would accomplish what he had to do before that time ran out.

Sighting the town, he sped forward. Now that the decision to leave the woman behind had been made, Greywolf was eager to see it done and be on his way. He would have to take her car, of course, but for a woman like her, cars were probably easy to come by.

He pulled up to the gas pump and got out to put the nozzle into the tank. While it was filling, he added more water to the radiator. Keeping a careful eye on the time, he even washed the windshield and checked the tires. To avoid another sticky situation like the roadblock, he wanted to be well away when the owners of the service station returned.

Finally he went around the corner of the building to the rest room. Reaching over the salvaged steel girder he had pulled in front of the door, he knocked loudly. When there was no response, he called her name.

"Answer me. I know you're in there, Aislinn. This is childish."

He waited, pressing his ear to the door. After several seconds of intent listening, he knew that the room beyond the door was empty.

Apprehension squeezed his vitals like a cold fist. Before he could account for his actions, he shoved the girder out of the way and pulled the door open. He rushed inside, almost hoping that this was a ruse and that she was planning to launch some sort of amateur attack on him.

But he was met with nothing but an empty heat and a revolting stench. He rapidly deduced the meaning of the overturned barrel beneath the open window. When he did, his apprehension turned to black rage.

The little hellcat had gotten out!

Spinning on his heel, he went tearing out the rest room door and around the corner of the building. He dashed into the main room where they had been before, but there was no trace of Aislinn and no evidence that either she or anyone else had been there.

The broken glass of the window still lay undisturbed on the floor. The twenty-dollar bill was still tucked beneath the ashtray. He checked, but the dust on the telephone's receiver hadn't been smudged.

Puzzled, Greywolf crammed his hands into the back pockets of his jeans. Where could she have gone? And how? Had someone picked her up? He gnawed the inside of his cheek as he paced. Wouldn't she have telephoned someone right away? Wouldn't the authorities have made this their temporary command post while they questioned her and searched for him? It didn't make any sense.

He retraced his steps back to the rest room.

"Easy, easy, drink slowly or you'll choke."

Aislinn's parched throat thirstily welcomed the trickle of cola being poured into her mouth. She angled herself up, but moaned when a pain went rocketing through her head.

"Lie back," the gentle voice said. "That's enough for now anyway."

Her eyes flickered open. Greywolf was bending over her. His face was dark and inscrutable. Then she realized that the sun must have gone down because everything was dark. Moving her eyes caused her head to throb, but she let them wander far enough afield to determine that she was lying in the back seat of her car. The windows were all opened to let in the desert breeze. Greywolf was hunkered down beside her, wedged between the seats, his hip propped on the seat beside hers.

"Where—"

"About thirty miles from the service station. I've got bandages."

"Bandages?"

"You were moaning in your sleep," he said tersely, as though that explained everything.

Garnering all her strength, she reached up and gripped a handful of his shirt. "Talk to me, damn you. I'm sick of your Indian stoicism. Where am I and why do I need bandages? Did you finally use that knife on me?"

The rebellion had cost her every ounce of reserve energy, and she collapsed back onto the seat. But she didn't release Greywolf from her hostile stare. It was like looking into mirrors, but she kept staring into his eyes until he answered.

"Don't you remember climbing out the window and falling?" he asked.

Her eyes slid closed then. Now she remembered. The fear, the despair, and the hatred for the man who had caused it. Everything came rushing back to her in a tide of bad memories.

"I brought some aspirin for your headache."

She opened her eyes. He was shaking the tablets out of the bottle into the palm of his hand. "Where did you get them?"

"From the store. Can you take them with Coke?" She nodded. He passed her the aspirins and when she had laid them on her tongue, he slid his arm beneath her shoulders and supported her while she drank from the bottle he pressed to her lips.

When she was finished, he eased her back down. "The sun blistered your lips." As he informed her of that, he opened a tiny jar of lip salve and gouged into it with the tip of his index finger. He touched it to her lip, smoothing the cool salve over the dried, sunburned skin.

The touch of his finger on her mouth elicited sensations in her middle, sensations she was ashamed of since they strongly resembled curls of arousal. His finger slid from one corner of her lower lip to the other, quickly and businesslike at first, then more slowly. When he traced the shape of her upper lip with his fingertip, she could barely hold still. Her body was restless with an ache that had nothing to do with the injuries she had sustained.

When he withdrew his finger, she tentatively touched
her lips with her tongue. The ointment tasted slightly of
banana and coconut. "Don't lick it off," Greywolf instructed brusquely, staring down at her mouth. "Let the
salve work."

"Thank you."

"Don't thank me. You almost got me caught."

His cruel tone was so vastly different from his tender
ministrations that she flinched. She should have known
better than to expect tenderness from a man of stone like
him. Her eyes flashed up at him angrily. "Well you
should be caught, Mr. Greywolf. If there was no reason
before, then because of the way you've mistreated me."

"You've never been mistreated in your life, Miss Andrews," he said scornfully. "You can't even begin to
grasp the meaning of the word."

"How would you know? You know nothing about
me."

"I know enough. You were reared with all the privileges that go with being rich and white."

"I'm not at fault for the way the Indians have been
mistreated." She knew that all his anger and bitterness
stemmed from that. "Do you indict every Anglo?"

"Yes," he hissed, his teeth bared.

"And what about yourself?" she shot back. "You're
not a full-blood Indian. What about the part of you
that's Anglo? Is it rotten to the core?"

He retaliated, grabbing her shoulders in his hard hands
and pressing her back into the seat. His razor-sharp eyes
were as cold as naked steel. "I am Indian," he whispered, emphasizing his words by shaking her slightly.
"Don't ever forget that."

Aislinn knew she never would. Not now. The fierceness of his gaze dispelled any hopes that he was soften-
ing toward her. He was dangerous. Fully aware of his
brute strength as he leaned over her, she shuddered with
trepidation.

In the sleeveless shirt, the muscles of his arms looked as hard as granite. Most of the buttons on the soiled shirt were undone and his exposed chest sawed in and out with each angry breath he took. His corded throat was a perfect pedestal for a face that could have been hewn out of native rock.

The silver earring fastened in his lobe winked at her like a menacing eye in the darkness. The silver cross hanging from his neck mocked her because of the benevolence it symbolized. He exuded a scent that was part sun, part sweat, and all male.

Any woman with an ounce of common sense wouldn't dare to provoke such a potentially dangerous animal. Aislinn was smarter than average. She didn't even blink.

During that tense silence, he kept his muscles coiled as though ready to spring. Now, he visibly relaxed them and loosened his hold on her. "I should bandage your arm before it gets infected." He spoke with a notable lack of emotion, as though their heated argument had never taken place.

"My arm?" Only when she tried to move it did she realize that her left arm was hurting almost as badly as her head. She remembered tearing open the skin as she fell out the window.

"Here," he said, noticing her grimace when she tried to raise it, "let me." He levered her up and settled her into a half-reclining position in the corner of the back seat. His hands moved to the front of her blouse. Reflexively her right hand flew up and clutched the material to her body. He didn't move, but continued to stare back at her levelly, then said, "It has to come off, Aislinn."

She looked down and was shocked to see that her sleeve was soaked with blood. "I . . . I didn't know," she stammered, suppressing a wave of nausea and dizziness.

"I needed to get away from there in a hurry, so I bundled you into the back seat. I put some distance between us and that place, but now your arm has to be seen to."

Seconds ticked by. Minutes? They stared deeply into each other's eyes. His took a detour down to her mouth, glossy now with the emollient. Hers looked at the grim line of his lips and wondered how they could be both stern and sensual. Then Greywolf shook his head impatiently and muttered, "As I said before, you are my insurance policy."

Once again his hands reached toward the front of her blouse, and this time she didn't forestall him. He unbuttoned it quickly, emotionlessly. Embarrassment rose inside Aislinn like a warm, red tide as her bare breasts were revealed to him button by button. But if he noticed them, his face gave nothing away.

Only when he settled his hands on her shoulders and began to peel the cloth back, did his movements become slow and tender, almost caring. He eased the sleeve off her uninjured arm first, then gradually began lowering the other one. She winced when the cloth tugged on places where the blood had dried.

"I'm sorry." Before she could prepare herself, he ripped the remaining sleeve away. "That's the best way. I'm sorry," he repeated.

"It's all right. I know you had to." Her eyes filled with tears, but she didn't let them fall. He seemed momentarily entranced by her eyes, or was he merely watching to see if an Anglo woman would surrender to pain and cry?

Then, abruptly, and with the same kind of detachment he had shown as he unbuttoned her blouse, he angled her forward in order to remove it. For an infinitesimal second, Aislinn leaned against him, her breasts grazing his chest.

Myriad sensations flocked to her mind like fluttering birds. How fragile her nipples felt against the solid wall of muscle. How his chest hair felt both crisp and soft as it tickled her skin. How warm he was.

They pretended not to notice the brief contact, though his jaw was clenched tighter than ever when he eased her back into the corner of the seat.

The reopened scratch, which ran the entire length of her arm, oozed blood. Greywolf tossed her blouse aside and reached into a paper sack. He took a box of sterilized cotton and a bottle of antiseptic from it. "This is going to burn like hell," he said, uncapping the bottle and pouring some of the liquid onto a wad of cotton. "Ready?" he asked.

She nodded. He lifted her arm and applied the cotton to the wounded skin on the underside. Her knees jackknifed; she gasped; tears spurted out of her eyes. Quickly he dabbed the entire scratch from wrist to armpit, then went back to press the soaked cotton to the places where the nail had plowed deeper.

"Oh, please," Aislinn moaned, squeezing her eyes shut against the fiery pain.

He hurriedly recapped the antiseptic and set it aside. Lifting her arm again, he began to blow gently on the scratch.

Aislinn opened her eyes and was dismayed to find his dark head bending so low over her. One brown hand was wrapped loosely around her wrist, holding her arm up. The other was splayed open just behind her head bracing him above her.

She watched his cheeks beneath the blade-sharp ridge of his cheekbones. They ballooned in and out as he cooled her skin with his gentle breath. His lips hovered scant inches above her arm. His head moved higher as he worked his way up her arm until his mouth was even with her breast.

His breath touched her there. Warm and balmy and soft. Responsively, her nipples reacted. They beaded to the size of small, perfect, pink pearls.

When he saw what had happened, his head made a jerking motion, as though he was going to raise it. But he paused. Lowered his head. Blew on her again. More gently this time, but directly over the tip of her breasts.

Then he became perfectly still. Raw hunger made his eyes look bleak as his gaze became fixed on her. He swallowed. He strained toward her, but, as though an invisible leash were around his neck, he refrained from touching her.

Aislinn was afraid to move, though she was tempted to. She fell victim to an almost irresistible urge to thread her fingers up through his hair and draw his head down to her. A forbidden and unaccountable tenderness for him overwhelmed her. It was unlike any emotion she had ever experienced before. She longed to grant him the use of her body. She wanted to use his. She should hate him and yet . . .

Why hadn't he deserted her at the service station? Why had he wasted his precious time getting aspirin and medicine for her scratch? Was there more to this man than met the eye? Did he have a capacity for human kindness after all? Was his austerity only a reaction to the injustices he had suffered?

Her expression conveyed her bafflement and made her appear extremely receptive and vulnerable. When Greywolf looked up into her face, the fire in his eyes went out instantly and he growled a warning. "Don't look at me like that."

She shook her head uncomprehendingly. "Like what?"

"Like you've forgotten that I've been in prison. Do you want to know if I desire you?" he asked harshly. "Well I do." The fingers encircling her arm became a manacle. "Yes, I want you. I want to touch you all over. I want to feel your breasts. I want to take one in my mouth and hold it there for a long, long time. I want to be so deep inside you I can feel your heartbeat. So un-

less you're ready to take an Indian between your thighs,
I suggest you don't give me that come-on look again,
Miss Andrews.''

Outraged that he could so grossly misinterpret her
expression, and furious with herself for giving him the
benefit of the doubt only seconds before, she shielded her
breasts with her free arm. "Don't flatter yourself," she
hissed. "I'd die first."

He laughed shortly. "I'm sure you would. At least
you'd *want* to die before having your pure Anglo body
tainted by an Indian. But at least you won't bleed to
death. Not if I have anything to do with it," he said bitterly.

She averted her head and didn't deign to look at him
while he bound her arm with gauze he had taken from the
sack. Once that was done, he gathered together the first-
aid supplies and stuffed them back into the paper bag.

Her eyes widened with alarm when he picked up the
knife, but he used it only to cut the sleeves from her shirt,
much as he must have his own. He wielded the sharp
blade viciously, making jagged cuts in the material until
the job was done, then tossed the ravaged garment to her.

"Put this back on. We've wasted enough time here."

He got out and went around to the driver's seat. In
broody silence, Aislinn stared at the back of his head.
While the car made the best of the pockmarked highway, she devised a dozen ways to overpower him. Each
one was eliminated before she could even think it
through. She thought of making a garrote out of one of
her sleeves and strangling him from behind. But then
where would she be? Out in the middle of nowhere without a map or water. The gasoline in the car wouldn't last
forever. Should she succeed in physically besting Greywolf, her chances of surviving in the wilderness were remote.

So she rode in stony silence until exhaustion overcame
her and once again she fell asleep.

She woke up when the car was brought to a slow, gradual halt. Struggling to pull her aching, tired, sore and bruised body into a sitting position, she blinked the sleep out of her eyes and adjusted them to the dark.

Greywolf gave her no more than a cursory glance over his shoulder before opening the car door and getting out. He strode up an incline that led to a structure. She could barely distinguish its outline against the darkness, but she recognized it as a Navaho hogan. Aislinn doubted that the six-sided log dwelling would have been visible at all had it not been for the faint light coming through the rectangular doorway.

The hogan was nestled against the side of the mountain and was cloaked by its dark shadow. The slightly rounded, conical roof was left untouched by the silvery moonlight, which spilled down the mountain like mercury.

Curiosity, as much as the profound desire not to be left alone in such primitive, almost mystical, surroundings, motivated her to leave the car and follow him. She scrambled up the rocky path, trying to keep her eyes both on where she was going and on Greywolf's lean silhouette.

Before he reached the hogan, another silhouette, much smaller than his, was outlined in the patch of light in the doorway. It was that of a woman.

"Lucas!"

His name was uttered in a soft, glad cry before the petite figure left the doorway, ran down the path and launched herself against him. His arms locked around her, hugging her tight. His head and shoulders bent low, protectively, over her diminutive frame.

"Lucas, Lucas, why did you do it? We heard about your escape on the radio and saw your picture on TV."

"You know why I did it. How is he?"

He held the small woman away from him and peered down into her upturned face. She shook her head sadly.

Without another word Greywolf took her arm and
guided her back up the path and through the doorway.

Intrigued, Aislinn followed them. Never having been
in a hogan before, she tentatively stepped inside. The
single-room house was stifling hot. A low fire burned in
the center. Smoke, seeming to lack the energy to make the
climb, was emitted through a hole in the roof. Kerosene
lamps provided the only other lighting. In the fore-
ground was a rough square table with four crude chairs.
A dented enamel coffeepot and several battered tin cups
were on the table. There was a dry sink in the corner with
a hand-crank water pump.

The floor was hard-packed dirt. On the floor, not far
from where Aislinn was standing, someone had done a
beautiful sand painting. The design was intricate and
meticulously executed. She had no idea what it symbolized, but she knew that such sand paintings were used in
ancient curing ceremonies.

Against the wall opposite the door was a low cot
draped with Navaho blankets. Greywolf was kneeling
beside it. Lying on the cot, beneath a blanket, was an elderly Indian man. Long, gray braids framed gaunt,
jaundiced cheeks. Gnarled, callused hands fitfully
plucked at the blanket. His eyes shone feverishly as they
gazed up at the much younger man bending over him,
speaking softly in a language Aislinn couldn't understand but knew was of the Na-dene group.

There were two other people in the room—the woman
who had greeted Greywolf so intimately, and another
man, surprisingly, an Anglo. He stood at the foot of the
cot on which the old Indian lay. He was of average height
and had thinning brown hair streaked attractively at the
temples with gray. Aislinn placed his age at around fifty.
He stared meditatively down at Greywolf and the old
man.

For a multitude of unnamed and unacknowledged
reasons, Aislinn had avoided looking at the woman. She

did so now. She was very pretty. Indian. She had high cheekbones, raven-black hair styled in a soft, straight pageboy to just above her shoulders, and liquid dark eyes. Dressed like an Anglo, she wore a simple cotton dress, low-heeled shoes and inexpensive jewelry. The way she held her small head lent her an air of elegance. She was slender, but her figure was feminine and perfectly proportioned.

Greywolf pressed his forehead against the work-worn hands of the old man, then turned to speak to the man standing at the foot of the cot. "Hi, Doc."

"Lucas, you crazy fool."

A ghost of a smile flickered across Greywolf's austere features. "Some greeting."

"Some damned stunt. Escaping prison."

Greywolf shrugged and glanced back down at the old man. "He says he isn't in any pain."

"I've made him as comfortable as I can here," the man addressed as "Doc" said. "I urged him to go to the hospital—"

Greywolf was already shaking his head and interrupted the other man. "He wants to die here. It's important to him. How long?" he asked hoarsely.

"Morning. Maybe."

The woman shuddered, but didn't make a sound. Greywolf took the steps necessary to enfold her in an embrace. "Mother."

His mother! Aislinn thought, aghast. The woman looked so young, far too young to have a son as old as Lucas Greywolf.

He put his lips close to her ear and murmured words that Aislinn imagined to be consoling. She was awed that the cold, remote man she had been with for almost two days could show such compassion. His eyes were pinched shut. The stark contrast of light and shadow playing over his face made his anguished expression even more pronounced and testified to the depth of his emotion. When he finally opened the light-gray eyes, they happened to fall on her where she still hovered in the doorway.

He eased away from his mother, and bobbed his chin toward Aislinn. "I brought a hostage with me."

The blunt statement brought his mother around and she saw Aislinn for the first time. She raised a dainty hand to her chest. "A *hostage?* Lucas!"

"Have you lost your mind?" Doc asked angrily. "Hell, man, they're looking all over the state for you."

"So I've noticed," Greywolf said with casual disregard.

"They'll slam you back in prison so fast it'll make your head spin. And this time they might throw away the key."

"That's a risk I was willing to take," Lucas said, matching the other man's anger. "I asked permission to leave the prison in order to see my grandfather before he died. The formal request was denied. I played by their rules, but it did me no good. It never has. This time I've learned my lesson. Don't ask, just do."

"Oh, Lucas," his mother sighed, slumping down into a chair. "Father understood why you couldn't be here."

"But *I* didn't," Greywolf said fiercely, baring his teeth and spitting the words out. "What difference would it have made to let me out for a few days?"

The three fell silent because there seemed to be no answer to that question. Finally Doc stepped forward and kindly said to Aislinn, "I'm Dr. Gene Dexter."

She liked him immediately. His looks were unremarkable, but his demeanor was soothing and reassuring...or did it just seem so because she had spent the past forty-eight hours in the volatile company of Lucas Greywolf? "Aislinn Andrews."

"You're from ... ?"

"Scottsdale."

"You look tired. Won't you sit down?"

Gene Dexter offered her a chair and she accepted it gladly. "Thank you."

"This is Alice Greywolf," Dexter said, laying a hand on the woman's shoulder.

"I'm Lucas's mother," she said, leaning forward in her chair. Her dark eyes were filled with sincerity. "Will you ever forgive us for what's happened?"

"He's your father?" Aislinn asked softly, pointing to the still figure on the cot.

"Yes, Joseph Greywolf," Alice answered.

"I'm sorry."

"Thank you."

"Can I get you something?" the Anglo doctor asked Aislinn.

She sighed tiredly and gave him a wry smile. "You can get me home."

Greywolf made a scoffing sound. "I was an unpleasant surprise to Miss Andrews when she came home the night before last and found me scavenging food out of her refrigerator."

"You broke into her house!" Alice exclaimed in disbelief.

"I'm a criminal, Mother. Remember? An escaped convict." He poured himself a cup of coffee from the enamel pot on the table. "Excuse me." He gave Aislinn a smirking smile before he returned to the bedside of the dying man.

"He escaped prison, broke into my house, and took me hostage just so he could come here to see his grandfather before he died?" All the perplexity Aislinn felt went into the question she hardly realized she had spoken aloud.

When she recalled how Greywolf had frightened her, how he had threatened her with the knife, how he had taunted and tormented her, she wanted to get up, walk across the dirt floor, jerk him up by his long hair and slap him as hard as she could.

She had submitted to his threats because she had thought him capable of violence. Looking at him now as he leaned over the old man, whispering tender words, stroking the creased forehead with a loving hand, she doubted Lucas Greywolf would harm a fly.

Aislinn drew her eyes back to the two people who were quietly watching her as though she were an object of curiosity. "I don't understand."

Alice Greywolf smiled gently. "My son isn't easy to understand. He's impulsive. He has a short temper. But his bark is worse than his bite."

"Personally I'd like to whip his butt for involving this young woman," Dr. Dexter said. "Why would he make things more difficult for himself by kidnapping Miss Andrews?"

"You know how determined he is, Gene," Alice said with resignation. "If he made up his mind to get here before Father died, nothing could have stopped him." She looked at Aislinn with concern. "He didn't hurt you, did he?"

Aislinn hesitated before answering. She could tell them he had humiliated her by forcing her to watch him strip off his clothes and take a shower. Then he had made her strip and had tied her to him while they slept. He had mauled and pawed her, but never for recreation. He had verbally abused her, subjected her to embarrassment many times, but she couldn't honestly say that he had *hurt* her.

"No," she answered quietly. Confused, she shook her head as she glanced down at her clenched hands. She was protecting him again. Why?

"Your arm is bandaged," Gene observed.

"I hurt it trying to get out of a rest room."

"A rest room?"

"Yes. He, uh, locked me in."

"What?"

Aislinn backtracked and told them everything that had happened, leaving out the more personal aspects of her encounter with Greywolf and glossing over the incident at the roadblock. "Lucas bandaged my arm just an hour or so ago."

"Well, I'd better check it," Gene said, going to the basin in the dry sink and pumping water into it. He began to wash his hands with a cake of yellow soap. "Alice, get my bag, please. She probably ought to have a tetanus shot."

A half hour later, Aislinn felt better. Her arm had been examined and diagnosed as having nothing more than a painful scratch. She had washed at the sink and had used a borrowed hairbrush to untangle her hair. To replace her tattered blouse and dirty jeans, Alice lent her a traditional tunic blouse and long skirt of a Navaho woman, having taken them from a storage trunk against the wall. "It's very kind of you to agree to wait here until . . . until Father dies."

Aislinn buttoned the blouse. "I expected to be taken to an outlaws's hideout." She glanced toward the bed where both Gene and Greywolf were attending the elderly Indian. "I don't understand why he didn't just tell me why he had escaped."

"My son is often defensive."

"And mistrustful."

Alice briefly laid her hand on Aislinn's arm. "We have some soup that's still hot. Would you like some?"

"Please." Only then did she realize that she was starving. Alice sat at the table with her while she ate. Aislinn used that opportunity to ask questions about Greywolf, questions that had previously piqued her curiosity.

"Am I to understand that he was serving a three-year sentence for a crime he didn't actually commit?"

"Yes," Alice replied. "Lucas was guilty of only one thing—of organizing that demonstration on the steps of the courthouse in Phoenix. He had gone through all the legal channels. He had secured a permit to march. It wasn't supposed to get violent."

"What happened?"

"Some of the marchers, much more militant-minded than Lucas, got rowdy. Before Lucas could regain control, public property was being vandalized and fights had broken out. It resulted in a brawl. Several people, including policemen, were injured."

"Seriously?"

"Yes. Because he had already won a reputation as a dissident, Lucas was the first one arrested."

"Why didn't he tell them he was trying to put a stop to the violence?"

"He refused to name the men who were actually responsible. He represented himself at his trial and wouldn't allow anyone else to speak in his defense. But I think that the judge and jury had already made up their minds before the case ever came to trial. There was a lot of media publicity about it. He was found guilty. The sentence was disproportionately severe."

"Wouldn't he have been better off to hire a lawyer to defend him?" Aislinn asked.

Alice smiled. "My son didn't tell you much about himself, did he?" Aislinn shook her head. "He *is* a lawyer."

Speechlessly Aislinn stared at the other woman. "A lawyer?"

"A disbarred one now," she said sadly. "That's one reason he's so bitter. He wanted to help our people through the legal system. Now he won't be able to."

Aislinn could hardly assimilate everything Alice had told her. It seemed that Mr. Greywolf was more complex than even she had imagined. She glanced at the cot just as he stood and turned toward the table where she was sitting with Alice. Gene Dexter laid a comforting hand on his shoulder.

"You said 'our people,'" Aislinn remarked to Alice. "Your Indian heritage is extremely important to you. Is that why you and Lucas use the name Greywolf?"

"What name *should* we use?" Alice asked, apparently bewildered by the question.

"Why, Dexter," Aislinn said, equally bewildered. "Isn't Gene Lucas's father?"

Aislinn was met with three stunned stares. Alice's velvety brown eyes were the first to look away. A becoming blush stained her dusky cheeks. Gene Dexter cleared his throat uncomfortably. Greywolf's response was somewhat more abrupt and to the point.

"No, he isn't."

Chapter 5

Alice, Joseph is asking for you," Gene said diplomatically. They withdrew, Gene with his arm around Alice's shoulders.

Aislinn wished the proverbial hole would open up and swallow her. "I th-thought since you're only half Indian . . . I mean . . ."

"Well you thought wrong." Greywolf dropped into one of the chairs at the table. "What are you still doing here anyway? I thought that by now you would have wheedled Gene into taking you back to civilization."

"He's got better things to do, like taking care of your grandfather."

Balancing his chair on its two back legs, he looked up at her tauntingly. "Or maybe this life of crime has proven to be exciting. Maybe you don't want to go home."

She gave him a fulminating look. "Of course I do. It's just that I'm not as shallow and unfeeling as you seem to think."

"Meaning?"

"Meaning that I sympathize with you and your mother. Instead of terrorizing me, holding a knife on me and tying me up, you could have told me why you escaped prison. I would have helped you."

He uttered a sound that could have passed for a laugh. It wasn't a jovial sound, but one laden with skepticism and rebuke.

"A nice, respectable, law-abiding WASP like you, giving aid to an escaped convict, an escaped *Indian* convict?" His tone was derisive. "I seriously doubt that. Anyway, I couldn't gamble on your kindheartedness. I've learned to be distrustful." The front legs of the chair hit the floor hard, as though punctuating his statement. "Is there any more of that soup?"

As she dished up a bowl of soup from the pan that simmered over the smoky fire, she realized that the identity of his father was still a mystery. Apparently his Anglo blood wasn't a topic open to discussion, which only made her more curious about it.

He wolfed down the steaming soup. Without his asking, she poured him a fresh cup of coffee. While hours ago her sole desire had been to put distance between herself and this dangerous man, she now sat down in a chair across the table from him. He looked up at her with an inquiring tilt to his eyebrows, but went back to eating without offering a comment.

He no longer seemed so ferocious. Was it the hushed atmosphere or the limited confines of the hogan that had mellowed him? It was difficult to feel terror for a man who would kneel at the bedside of his ancient, dying grandfather and speak with such gentleness.

Greywolf hadn't changed physically. His hair was just as jet black, just as rebelliously long. His eyes were still as cold as a pond glazed with morning frost. The muscles in his arms still rippled with latent violence beneath the sinuous, coppery skin. His expression remained just as aloof.

And yet he was different.

He wasn't so much frightening now as he was intriguing, and so very different from the men her parents often paired her with. They were cookie-cutter replicas of each other. They wore conservatively tailored suits that only varied in their shades of gray. All were upwardly mobile executive types who conversed at length on subjects like market analyses and growth indexes. Their idea of spicing up a conversation was to talk about their tennis game and the expense of maintaining a foreign sports car. So-and-so's recent divorce and so-and-so's hassles with the IRS could always be counted on as good cocktail-party topics.

How boring they all seemed compared to this man, who wore one silver earring and gulped down canned soup as if it might be his last decent meal for a long time, who wasn't embarrassed by sweat and dirt and the fundamentals of life, like dying.

Quite frankly, she was fascinated by Lucas Greywolf.

"You didn't tell me you were a lawyer." He wasn't given to chitchat. Aislinn knew no other way of commencing a conversation with him than to jump in feet-first.

"It wasn't relevant."

"You might have mentioned it."

"Why? Would you have felt better knowing that the man holding a knife on you was a lawyer?"

"I suppose not," she said wearily. He went back to eating his soup. Conversation closed. Information would have to be pulled out of him like a deeply rooted bicuspid. She tried again. "Your mother told me you went to college on a track scholarship."

"That must have been some conversation you two had." He finished the soup and pushed the empty bowl away.

"Well, did you?" she demanded impatiently.

"Why the sudden interest?"

She shrugged. "I just... I don't know. I'm interested."

"You want to know how a poor Indian boy bettered himself in the Anglo world, is that it?"

"I should have known you'd take umbrage. Forget it." Angrily she scraped her chair back and stood up, but when she reached for his soup bowl to carry it to the sink, his hand shot out and captured hers.

"Sit down and I'll tell you all about it, since you're so curious to know."

She couldn't possibly win an arm-wrestling match with him, not the way his fingers were biting into her flesh, so she sat back down. He stared across the table at her for several moments before he finally released her hand. His eyes smoldered with contempt. The degree of it made her squirm uneasily.

"I graduated from a school here on the reservation," he began. His lips were held in a firm, grim line which barely moved as he formed words with them. "I got the scholarship because an alumnus who scouted for the coach had seen me run in a track meet. So I went to Tucson and enrolled in the university. The athletics was easy. But I was woefully ignorant compared to the other freshmen. Dedicated as the teachers on the reservation had been, I wasn't prepared for college by any stretch of the imagination."

"Don't look at me like that."

"How's that?"

"Like I should feel guilty over having blond hair and blue eyes."

"I know someone like you will find this hard to understand, but when you're the outcast to begin with, you'd better be damned good at *something*. That's the only way you even come close to being accepted. While you and your crowd were enjoying the fraternity and sorority parties, I was studying."

"You wanted to excel."

He scoffed. "I wanted to stay even. When I wasn't in class or in the library or on the track, I was working. I held two jobs on campus because I didn't want it said that I had gotten a free ride just because I was an Indian and could run fast."

He folded his hands on the table and stared down at them. "Do you know what a half-breed is?"

"I've heard the word, yes. It's an ugly word."

"Do you know what it's like to straddle a line like that? That's a rhetorical question. Of course you don't. Oh, I earned a certain celebrity from track. I could run," he said reflectively, as though he could still hear the cheering from the stadium fans. "By the time I graduated with honors—"

"So you *did* excel."

He ignored her. "My name was so well-known that they even wrote an article in the newspaper about me. The slant of it was how commendable my accomplishments were...for an Indian." His eyes speared into hers. "You see, there's always that qualification: 'For an Indian.'"

Aislinn knew that he was right, so she said nothing.

"I went straight into law school. I was eager to set up practice, to help keep the Indians from being exploited by mining companies and such. And I did win a few cases, but not nearly enough. I became disillusioned with the legal system, which I found out is as political as anything else in the world. Justice is *not* blind.

"So I began playing dirty ball, too. I became much more outspoken and critical. I organized the Indian protesters so they would have a louder voice. I staged peaceful demonstrations. My activities only served to win me a reputation as a troublemaker who bore watching. When they had the opportunity to arrest me and lock me up for a long time, they did."

He sat back in his chair and eyed Aislinn stonily. "So there. Are you satisfied now? Did you learn what you wanted to know?"

It was a lengthier speech than she could ever have imagined him making. The missing pieces were easy to fit in. He belonged in neither society, being neither wholly Indian nor wholly Anglo. She knew the slurs he must have been subjected to. Words like "breed" would have been intolerable for a headstrong, proud young man.

He was smart and physically superior. No doubt other Indian discontents looked up to him as their leader and rallied to his side. He became someone the Anglo community feared. Still, she thought, most of Lucas Greywolf's hardships stemmed from his own deep-seated bitterness and stubbornness.

He could have saved himself years in prison by naming the guilty parties. Aislinn could just imagine the granite hardness of his jaw when he refused to answer the authorities' questions.

"You've got a chip on your shoulder," she said candidly.

Surprisingly he smiled, though it was a chilling grin. "You're damned right I do. Now. Not always. When I left the reservation to go to college, I was full of naiveté and high ideals."

"But society did a number on you."

"Go ahead, mock me. I'm used to it."

"Did you ever stop to think that the reason you weren't included wasn't because you are Indian, but because of your less-than-charming personality?"

Again his hand lashed out and caught her wrist. "What do you know about it? *Nothing*," he growled. "Even your name reeks of your pure Anglo-Saxon blood. Have you ever been invited to a party and plied with liquor just so the others can see how much alcohol an Indian can really tolerate? 'How drunk will he get?' 'Maybe

he'll put on a war bonnet and do a dance for us.'
'Where's your bow and arrow, Chief?''

"Stop it!" She tried to pull her arm free but she couldn't.

Both had stood, though neither noticed. He had her bent at an awkward angle over the table. His teeth were clenched, and though his voice was as smooth as honey, it carried with it a terrible malice. "After you're subjected to that kind of ridicule, you come back and tell me all about that chip on my shoulder, Miss Andrews. You—"

"Lucas!"

His mother's sharp reprimand ended Greywolf's tirade abruptly. He stared deep into Aislinn's eyes for another heartbeat before he dropped her hand and spun around. "He's calling for you," Alice said. Her beautiful eyes sawed back and forth between her son and his captive, as though wary of the sparks she sensed crackling between them. She took Lucas's arm and led him back to the cot.

Aislinn watched them. The top of Alice's head barely reached his shoulder. The arm he settled across her narrow shoulders as they approached the sickbed conveyed affection and tenderness. She couldn't imagine him experiencing those natural human emotions.

"You have to forgive Lucas." Gene Dexter's quiet voice coaxed Aislinn out of her musings.

"Why should I? He's a grown man, accountable for his actions. Bad behavior is inexcusable, no matter the cause of it."

The doctor sighed and poured himself a cup of coffee. "You're right, of course." As he sipped his coffee, he, too, watched the mother and son kneeling at the bedside of the dying man. "I've known Lucas since he was a boy. He's always been angry. Bitter. Alice's mother was Navaho, but Joseph is Apache. Lucas inherited that warrior spirit."

"You've known them that long?"

He nodded. "I came to the reservation fresh out of my year of residency."

"Why?" She blushed when the doctor looked down at her, a smile curving his lips. Good Lord! Was Greywolf's rudeness rubbing off on her? "I'm sorry. It's none of my business."

"That's all right. I'm happy to answer." He drew his brows together, collecting his thoughts, carefully choosing his words. "I felt a 'calling,' I guess you might say. I was young and idealistic. I wanted to make a *difference*, not a lot of money."

"I'm sure you have." She paused before adding, "At least in the lives of Alice and Lucas Greywolf." When she dared to glance at him from the corner of her eye, she saw that he wasn't fooled by her subtle probing.

"I met Alice when she brought Lucas to the clinic with a broken arm. Over the next several weeks we became friends, and I asked if she would be willing to lend me a hand at the clinic. I trained her in nursing skills. We've been working together ever since."

His feelings for Alice Greywolf ran much deeper than those of a doctor for his dedicated nurse, but Aislinn didn't have the opportunity to press him on the issue. Just then Alice turned toward Gene, her lovely face stricken with alarm.

"Gene, come quickly! He's—"

The doctor rushed toward the cot and shouldered Lucas and Alice aside. He placed his stethoscope against Joseph Greywolf's bony chest. Even from where she stood near the table, Aislinn could hear his rattling, struggling respiration. It sounded like two pieces of sandpaper rubbing together. The abrasive sound didn't cease until daybreak.

When it did, the sudden silence was louder than the racket had been. Aislinn covered her trembling lips with her hand and turned her back to the three keeping vigil at the cot, affording them a modicum of privacy. She, being the outsider, didn't want to intrude on their grief. She sat down in one of the chairs and bowed her head.

She heard the shuffle of feet on the packed-dirt floor, the quiet sound of Alice's weeping, whispered murmurs of consolation. Then her ears were met with the heavy thud of boot heels. The front door squeaked as it was shoved open. Aislinn raised her head and, through the door, saw Lucas stalk off down the rocky path.

His powerful body was as fluid and graceful as ever, but the sinewy muscles were stretching his skin, straining it. He seemed able to hold himself together only by sheer willpower. Since his back was to her, she couldn't see his face, but she could imagine it—tense, hard, unrelentingly stern.

Aislinn watched him stamp past her car and the four-wheel-drive truck she assumed belonged to Dr. Dexter. With that same determined stride, he crossed the floor of the canyon, then took a rocky, uneven path up the side of the hill.

She never remembered moving. She didn't consciously make up her mind. She simply stood up and rushed toward the door, some subconscious area of her brain directing her. She quickly glanced at Alice. Gene Dexter was holding her in his arms, crooning words of comfort into her midnight-black hair.

Aislinn ran through the door and out into the still morning. Dawn light was just peeping over the ridge of the mountains that ringed the hogan. The air was considerably cooler up there in the mountains, particularly at that time of day, when the sun hadn't had time to bake the rocks to a grilling heat.

Aislinn noticed nothing, not even the gorgeous, ever-changing violet hues of the eastern sky as the sun rose higher. Her eyes were trained on the man who was no more than a rapidly shrinking speck against the rocky terrain as he climbed, seemingly without effort, higher.

Her progress wasn't as rapid. The boots he had chosen for her came in handy now, but the borrowed skirt kept getting snagged on brush and wrapped around her legs, impeding her efforts. Innumerable times she skinned her knees; her palms bled from stinging scrapes.

Before she even reached the halfway point to the summit, she was winded and laboring for every breath. But she kept climbing, driven by an emotion she didn't stop to contemplate. It was something she simply had to do. She had to get to Greywolf.

At last the plateau, which formed a tabletop crest to the rocky incline, no longer seemed unreachable. She took heart and began climbing faster. Looking up, she could see Lucas standing at the summit, his body a dark, lean silhouette against the cloudless lavender sky.

When she finally reached the top, she virtually crawled the remaining distance. Once there, she slumped down on the level rock and hung her head in exhaustion. Her breath soughed in and out of her body. Her heart was beating so fast that it actually hurt. She stared down at her hands in disbelief. Rocks had been cruel to her palms. Her nails were broken.

Ordinarily, she would have been horrified by such injuries. Now, the pain meant nothing. She didn't even feel it. Its significance was reduced to nothingness when measured against that of the man.

Greywolf remained motionless, his back to her, staring out over the opposite cliff. His feet were braced a shoulders' width apart. His hands, balled into fists, were held rigidly at his sides.

As she watched, he threw his head back, squeezed his eyes shut, and released a howl that echoed eerily off the walls of the surrounding mountains. The animal wail came straight from his soul. It was an outpouring of grief, despair and frustration, so profound that Aislinn felt his pain as her own. Tears coursed down her cheeks.

Leaning forward, she stretched out a hand as though to touch him, but he was standing several yards away. Her offer of solace went unseen.

She didn't know why she wasn't repulsed by his soul-rending display of emotion. In her family such exhibitions were forbidden. If one felt sadness, rage, even joy, demonstrations of the emotion were kept restrained and refined. Self-expression, just as everything else, was governed by rules. One kept one's feelings bridled. To do otherwise was considered bad taste and vulgar in the extreme.

Never in her life had Aislinn witnessed such an honest, boundless expression of emotion. Greywolf's raw cry opened up a secret pocket of her heart and left a wide and gaping wound. A spear couldn't have pierced her more thoroughly. The impact was that jarring, that sharp, that deep.

He sank to his knees, bowed his back and hung his head low, covering it with his arms. He rocked back and forth, keening and chanting words she didn't comprehend. She understood only that he was a man totally disconsolate, made alien and alone by the measure of his grief.

Still sitting, she inched her way over to him and touched his shoulder. He reacted like an injured animal. His head snapped around and he made a snarling sound. His eyes were tearless and icy on the surface, but the black centers burned from within like the fathomless pits of hell.

"What are you doing here?" he asked disdainfully. "You have no place here."

Not only was he implying that she didn't belong on this wild plateau with him, but also that she couldn't begin to understand the depth of his grief and that he resented her thinking she could.

"I'm sorry about your grandfather."

His eyes narrowed dangerously. "What could you possibly care about the death of an old, useless Indian?"

Tears smarted in her eyes at his harsh words. "Why do you do that?"

"Do what?"

"Cruelly shut other people out, people who are trying to help you."

"I don't need anybody's help." He looked at her with open scorn. "Especially yours."

"Do you think you're the only person on earth who has ever been disillusioned, or hurt, or betrayed?"

"*You* have? In your ivory palace?"

The contemptuous question didn't merit an answer. She could have told him there were endless varieties of abuse but swapping tales of woe would have been ridiculous. Besides, she was too angry at him for spurning her sympathy. "You carry your bitterness like a shield to protect yourself. You hide behind your anger like a coward who is afraid to get caught experiencing some human warmth. Someone offers you tenderness, and you misread it as pity. Anyway, we all need to be pitied at times."

"Well then," he said silkily, "pity me."

He moved with the speed of summer lightning and his touch was just as electrifying. His hand shot out and sank into her hair, winding the long strands around his fist and yanking her head forward. He tilted it back so far she feared her neck would snap.

"You're feeling benevolent toward the Indians, hmm? Well let's see just how much."

His mouth came crashing down on hers. The contact was brutal and punishing. She made an outraged sound deep in her throat, but it had no effect on him. If anything, his fist wound tighter in her hair and his lips pressed harder upon hers.

Moving her head was out of the question, so she gripped his biceps and tried to push him away. The skin beneath her grasp was warm and smooth. The muscles felt like braided cables of steel. Her efforts were to no avail.

Raising his lips only inches above hers, he smiled sardonically. "Ever been kissed by an Indian, Miss Andrews? It'll be something you can tell your friends about the next time you have a tea party."

He ground his lips against hers again. This time, she experienced a sense of falling and realized only when she felt rocks digging into her back that he had lowered her to the ground. He stretched above her, covering one side of her body with his.

"No!" she gasped when he released her mouth to press hot kisses into her neck just below her jaw. She tried to kick, but he threw his long leg over hers, imprisoning them beneath his thigh.

"What's the matter? Lost your taste for pity so soon?" he mocked. "Taste this."

He kissed her again. She felt the probing of his tongue against her lips and stubbornly kept them sealed together. His hand released her hair and caught her just under the jaw. Hard fingers squeezed until she had no choice but to open her mouth or risk her jawbone being shattered.

His tongue thrust its way into her mouth. It was an angry, plundering, ravishing, hurtful intruder. Silently she screamed in mortification and fury, struggling against him, arching her back above the hard ground in an effort to throw him off.

All she accomplished was to get his knee wedged between her thighs and his hips intimately pressing upon hers. Desperate to end the savage embrace, she curled both hands into claws and reached for his face.

But the moment her fingertips came into contact with his face, she felt the wet patches on his cheekbones. Immediately, her wrath was banished and replaced by wonder. Her fingers relaxed their curled tension, and she used them to blindly explore the chiseled ridges of his cheek-bones and the almost gaunt planes beneath them.

Her lack of resistance squelched his brutal intent as well, and he lifted his mouth from hers. Silently they stared into each other's eyes—his so beautifully incongruous with the rest of his face; hers blue, awash with her own tears.

She saw her hand move of its own accord and touch the damp streaks on his face. She traced the salty track of one of his tears all the way down to his chin. To think of the absolute grief it had taken to make a man of stone like him cry caused Aislinn's heart to pound.

Lucas stared down into her face and instantly regretted what he saw. Her lips were discolored and swollen from the anger behind his kiss. Never in his life had he physically mistreated a woman. The thought of it made him ill.

He moved slightly, intending to lift himself off her. But Aislinn's hands were still resting on his cheeks. She was studying his mouth. He paused.

"I warned you not to look at me like that again," he said roughly.

She didn't move.

"I told you what would happen if you did."

She didn't alter her expression either.

It lasted for only a heartbeat, but his hesitation seemed to stretch out for an eternity before he made a hungry, mating sound and lowered his lips once again to hers.

This kiss was vastly different. His mouth was changed. It settled over hers gently, despite the yearning sounds that it emitted. He rubbed his lips over hers, a comfort-giving, forgiveness-asking gesture.

She responded by letting her lips part. But slightly. Slightly. So that when his tongue touched the seam of her lips, it had to probe them gently to gain the sweet inside.

He groaned low and long as his tongue delved into the warm interior of her mouth, reaching far, swirling deep.

He angled his head; she tilted hers in a corresponding movement. Their mouths were sealed.

Aislinn had never received such a blatantly sexual kiss. He brazenly imitated lovemaking, stroking the inside of her mouth with his tongue until she gasped breathlessly. She wanted more.

Her hands moved up from his face. She touched the silver earring in his right ear. He made a catchy, breathy little sound as she fondled it. Her other hand sank into the long, straight strands of his hair. She slipped the headband from around his head and let his hair fall over her fingers. Black silk.

His hand moved between their bodies and fiddled with the buttons on her unattractive, borrowed blouse. She felt them falling open and did nothing to stop it.

Don't think about this. Don't think, she commanded herself. For to think would be to end it. And at all costs she didn't want it to end.

Since she had walked in on him in her kitchen, she had been assaulted by emotions and sensations. Almost without stop, they had come hurling toward her like bullets from an automatic weapon. Sometimes she hadn't dodged them quickly enough and had known their full impact, in her head, her heart, her body. Until three nights ago, her life had seemed as wasteful and barren as the desert compared to the abundance of emotions she had experienced since meeting Greywolf. Now she longed to experience the ultimate emotion. With him.

His breath fell hotly on her neck as his mouth moved over it greedily. He spread kisses across her chest. His hand, without permission or apology, fondled her breast. Just thinking of his strong, brown fingers moving against her pale flesh sent tongues of desire licking through her belly.

She bit her lower lip to stifle a moan when his fingertip located her taut nipple. He dallied with it, circling and fanning it with gentle strokes. When she felt his open mouth closing around it, she released a shuddering cry and clasped his head with both hands, holding it against her.

He exercised no discipline. He used his tongue, his teeth, the suckling ability of his mouth. She couldn't give enough and he couldn't get enough. Each caress brought her higher, further, than she'd ever gone before.

She peeled his shirt open, shoved the cloth aside and spread her hands over his chest. Her fingers engaged in an orgy of discovery. They pressed shallow dents in the curves of his muscles, combed through the pelt of hair, made brief, shy contact with his hard nipples.

Lucas buried his face between her breasts and groaned his pleasure. He gathered a handful of her skirt and lifted it, then laid his hand against the inside of her thigh.

Drums pounded in his head. Heat collected in his sex and spread through his thighs. He had needed a woman, but his desires had focused on this one. This woman. This blond, blue-eyed symbol of everything he hated had become what he wanted most.

Ever since he had seen her standing before him, her body golden in the lamplight of her bedroom, his senses had been humming with desire. He had wanted to seek out every tantalizing inch of her flesh and, once discovered, to know it thoroughly by sight, feel, smell and taste.

Her small, beautifully rounded breasts with their dainty pink crests appealed to him mightily. She was slim, but delectably shaped. He had dreamed of running his hands up and down her slender form, molding it to fit the palms of his hands.

Vividly he could recall how she had looked unclothed. Tremulous, but proud. Vulnerable, but brave. To him her skin had looked as smooth and rich as cream. What he hadn't seen but what his imagination had visualized until he ached.

And now he was touching. That sweet delta was as warm and as soft as he had dreamed it would be. Working his hand deeper inside her panties, he sifted through that silky nest until he found the heart of her womanhood. Impatience overcame him then and he pushed her panties down until she was free of them.

Spontaneously they both fell still, save for their rapid breathing. He braced himself above her and stared down into her face. It was calm. He could appreciate her expression. It held a challenge.

Her breasts were exposed to the new sun and the limitless sky. She didn't flinch as he raked them with his eyes. Her skirt was bunched up around her waist. He lowered his gaze to her womanhood. She was beautiful. He closed his eyes against the immense pleasure that surged through him.

He opened his jeans and positioned himself between her raised thighs. Then, bending his head down to cover her mouth with his, he penetrated her. He entered by slow degrees, savoring every creamy inch of femininity that sheathed him. Only when there was no more of himself to give, did he let his weight settle over her. His face burrowed in the fragrant hollow between her shoulder and throat.

He prayed for death.

Because nothing would ever be this good.

Aislinn, her eyes closed, reached beneath his shirt and ran her hands up and down the supple expanse of his back. His waist was neat and narrow. She loved scooping out the small of his back with her palm. She barely investigated the flare of his hips before she lost her nerve and pulled her hands back. She wanted to slip them into his jeans and cup the hard curves of his buttocks. She wanted to draw him deeper inside her. Not that that was possible. He more than filled her, and yet her body had delighted in accommodating him.

Turning her head, she kissed his ear where the silver earring was secured. He moaned deeply, more vibration than sound. He lowered his head to the tender tip of her breast. He rubbed his open mouth over it until it was quite wet. His tongue was capricious.

Their middles convulsed, reflexively, and then he began to move. Pumping slowly, he entered and withdrew repeatedly. He was smooth and hard and warm. He was animal. He was man. He was wonderful. Aislinn wondered how she had survived all these years without knowing this, without having him.

He whispered something in his native language, then suddenly braced himself above her with stiff arms. "My name is Lucas," he rasped.

"Lucas," she repeated on a breath. Then more loudly, "Lucas."

"I want to... oh, God... I want to see this... us..." He looked down at the place where their bodies were joined, where dark met fair, where male met female. He made a circular, grinding motion with his hips. It robbed Aislinn of breath. Her throat arched. But she couldn't close her eyes, even though the sublime ecstasy of it commanded her to.

She stared into his face and recorded it for memory. It was dark, beautiful, savage. Sweat beaded on his forehead as his movements gained momentum.

"I want to remember I want to remember I want to remember," he chanted as he thrust into her. "When they take me back... oh, God..."

He reared his head back. His gray eyes bore down into hers for only a second before they closed. He grimaced, locked in the throes of exquisite sexual climax. He slid his hands beneath her hips, palmed her derriere and held her tightly as the tremors claimed him.

Aislinn wrapped her arms around his neck, pressed her face into the mat of hair on his chest, and trembled with her own fulfillment.

Endless moments later, he collapsed on top of her. His lips moved against her ear, but if he was actually speaking words, they were indistinguishable. She stroked the back of his head, loving the feel of his hair against her cheek.

How long they lay there, their bodies damp with perspiration, she never remembered. Nor could she ever recall exactly what it was that roused them from that blissful lassitude.

All she could ever remember was the expression on his face when he lifted his head and gazed down at her. For an instant, he looked infinitely sad, resigned, somewhat grateful, before his face closed again and became remote.

He left her. Standing, he zipped his jeans, but made no effort to rebutton his shirt. He walked to the edge of the cliff and looked down toward Joseph Greywolf's hogan.

"You'd better get dressed. They've come for me."

The words struck her chest like heavy stones. She wanted to cry out in protest, but to what avail? Where could she hide him? How could she protect him? Besides, Lucas looked as though he was supremely indifferent to either his immediate or long-range future, much less to hers.

Feeling chilled to the bone despite the rising temperature, Aislinn hurriedly adjusted her clothing. Shakily she stood and dusted off her back as best she could. She reeled with the enormity of what they had done. Her cheeks were hot with shame even as her body continued to pulse with aftershocks.

She wasn't finished yet. It was over too soon. Incomplete. She wanted a tender aftermath. She wanted the closeness that was supposed to follow what they had just shared.

What had she expected, a profession of love, a hearty thank-you, a tension-easing joke? Lucas gave her nothing more than a casual glance with empty, emotionless eyes before he started down the rocky path toward the floor of the canyon.

She covered her face with her hands in a vain attempt to get a grip on herself. Her knees could barely support her as she walked to the edge of the plateau. The sight that greeted her did nothing to restore her composure.

Official cars, each with its red and blue lights flashing, clustered around the hogan. The small dwelling was swarming with men in uniforms, like bees around a honeycomb. One officer was poking around in her car.

"Put your hands over your head, Greywolf," a voice barked at him through a bullhorn.

Lucas complied, though it made his descent down the mountainside hazardous.

Feeling helpless, Aislinn watched from above. An ambulance roared up to the front door of the hogan. Moments later Joseph Greywolf's draped body was carried out on a collapsible gurney. Alice, supported by Gene Dexter's arm, followed close behind.

Two officers came scrambling up the slope toward Lucas. When they reached him, each grabbed an arm and roughly drew it behind him. One clamped on a pair of handcuffs before they started down again.

Lucas walked tall. His bearing was haughty, almost condescending. He seemed impervious to what was going on around him. Only when he saw the ambulance doors closing on his grandfather's body did Aislinn notice a tension in his shoulders. Alice ran toward her son and threw her arms around his waist. Lucas bent his head and kissed her cheek before a deputy sheriff rudely jerked him toward a waiting car.

Seconds before they pushed him inside, he raised his head and looked directly at Aislinn where she still stood on the precipice. Except for that, she might not have existed for Lucas Greywolf.

Chapter 6

When are you going to marry me?"

"When are you going to give up and stop asking?"

"When you say yes."

Alice Greywolf folded the dishtowel she'd been using and carefully laid it on the drainboard. Sighing, she turned and faced Gene Dexter. "You're either steadfast or stubborn. I can't decide which. Why haven't you given up on me?"

He slid his arms around her slender waist and drew her close, laying his cheek against the sleek crown of her head. "Because I love you. Always have. Ever since the first time I saw you in the clinic."

And that was true. The doctor had fallen in love with her that very day. She had been awfully young, incredibly beautiful, and frantic over her rowdy little boy with the broken arm. Within an hour, Gene had set the arm . . . and set his heart on Alice Greywolf. In the years since then, his love hadn't diminished.

It hadn't always been easy to love her. There had been times when, out of sheer frustration, he would issue ultimatums that either she marry him or he'd never see her again. No amount of ranting and raving ever did any good. She still refused his marriage proposals.

Several times he had stayed away from her and deliberately cultivated other romances. They never lasted for long. He hadn't bothered to use that jealousy tactic in years, partially because it wasn't fair to the other women. Alice was the single love of his life, whether she ever married him or not. He had resigned himself to that fact.

Alice rested her cheek against his chest and smiled sadly at the bittersweet memory of the day they had met. Gene Dexter had been a friend to her in every sense of the word for so long she couldn't imagine a life without his solid presence in it. She treasured the first time she had seen him and heard his gentle voice. But at the same time, she had been anxious over her son.

"Lucas had been in a fight," she said reminiscently. "Some of the older boys at school had been aggravating him. One called him an ugly name." Even now it was painful for her to think of the double stigma her son had had to grow up with.

"Knowing Lucas, I guess he threw himself right into the thick of it."

"Yes," she said with a laugh. "I was worried about his arm, of course, but I remember being angry with him as well for not ignoring their name-calling."

Gene thought Lucas probably would have if they had slurred only him. His guess was that Alice had been maligned, too. Defending his mother had kept Lucas in fights during his childhood and adolescence. Gene refrained from mentioning that.

"I never liked for him to cause trouble at school because that only drew attention to him," Alice continued. "Then, too, I was worried about how I was going to pay the new Anglo doctor for his services."

She tilted her head back to look up into Gene's face. He was no longer as young as when she had first met him, but he was just as handsome in his kind, quiet way. "You knew I didn't have the money to pay you. Why did you extend me credit?"

"Because I wanted your body," he said, nudging his nose beneath her chin and making playfully ferocious growling sounds. "I thought that treating your kid on credit might give me some bargaining room."

Laughing, she pushed him away. "I don't believe that for a minute. You're far too nice. On the other hand, you insured payment. Right after you set Lucas's arm, you offered me a job."

He framed her face between his hands and stared down into it lovingly. "All I knew then and know now is that I couldn't let you walk out that day if there was the slightest chance I'd never see you again. All I ensured myself was that you had to come back." He kissed her, his mouth both tender and passionate as it moved over hers. "Marry me, Alice." There was a desperate edge to his voice and she knew that his yearning was sincere.

"My father—"

"Is dead now." Gene dropped his arms to his sides and agitatedly raked back his hair. "I know it's only been several weeks since he died. I know you're still feeling the pain of losing him. But you used him as an excuse not to marry me for years. I understood. You had to take care of him. But now that he's gone, are you going to use his death in the same way you used his life?"

She walked around him, leaving the kitchen and moving into the living room of her small but tidy house. "Please don't badger me about marriage now, Gene. I have Lucas to consider, too."

"Lucas is a grown man."

"He still needs the support of his family, and I'm all he's got left."

"He has me, too, dammit!"

She looked up at him then, apologetically, and reached for his hand. Angry as he was, he let her pull him down onto the sofa beside her. "I know that. I didn't mean to exclude you."

Gene's tone softened considerably. "Alice, Lucas isn't a child any longer, but he's still getting into fights. He's hellbent on making life as tough on himself as he possibly can. With only a few months to go, he escaped prison. He took a young woman hostage."

"She's still a mystery to me," Alice interjected at the mention of Aislinn Andrews. "It was unlike Lucas to involve anyone else."

"Exactly my point. He didn't consult you, or ask my counsel on whether he should escape prison and become a fugitive. Why should you feel it's necessary to involve him in your decision to marry me? He knows how I feel about you. Maybe if you had married me when I first asked you, he wouldn't be as wild as he is." She looked hurt. Gene sighed. "That was a low blow. Sorry."

"Lucas had enough to live down when he was growing up. Having an Anglo stepfather, who was rich by reservation standards, would have been another."

"I know," he conceded. "But you used Lucas as an excuse for years. Then once he was grown and away at school, you said your father was the reason you couldn't marry me." He pressed her hands between his. "Neither of them was a viable reason. They were flimsy excuses, and they just ran out."

"Can't we just go on as we have been?"

He shook his head. "No, Alice. I'll love you till the moment I draw my last breath, but I'm a man. I want and need a total loving relationship." He leaned forward. His voice was low and earnest. "I know why you're afraid to marry me."

Her head dropped forward and she drew a deep breath as though preparing herself to face a firing squad. Gene brushed the raven-black hair away from her face, his eyes compassionate. "You associate sex with being victimized. I swear to you, I won't hurt you as you were hurt before."

Her eyes were glossy with tears when she raised them to look at him. "What do you mean?"

"We've been needing to have this conversation for years, Alice, but I didn't want to antagonize you by bringing it up." He paused momentarily before plunging ahead. "You're afraid to love a man again, especially an Anglo." She clamped her teeth over her lower lip, and he knew he had hit the target squarely. "You think that as long as you maintain your distance you can't get hurt again."

He carried her hands up to his mouth. His lips moved against her knuckles as he said, "I swear I'd never, never, hurt you. Don't you know me well enough by now to know that you are the center of my life? I love you. Let me and I'll cherish your body. Why would I hurt someone who is a vital part of myself?"

"Gene." She whispered his name through her tears and leaned against him. His arms went around her and held her with the fervent passion reserved for something most dear. He kissed her long and thoroughly.

When at last the kiss ended, he asked, "When are you going to marry me?"

"As soon as Lucas gets out of prison."

He frowned. "God knows when that will be."

"Please, Gene, give me until then. He'd never forgive us if we married without him. And we don't want him to break out again," she added on a soft laugh.

He smiled, allowing her that rationalization. Actually, Gene thought that Lucas would feel better knowing his mother was happily married. Now, however, after getting that much of a commitment from her, was not the time to argue. "All right. But I'm going to hold you to that. As soon as Lucas gets out. And in the meantime…" he murmured as his eyes gazed deeply into hers.

"In the meantime...?"

"In the meantime, I'll keep doing what I've always done. I'll impatiently wait for you, Alice Greywolf."

"Come in, Mr. Greywolf." Lucas stepped through the door of the office. "Please close the door and sit down." Warden Dixon didn't extend the prisoner the courtesy of rising from his chair behind the wide desk, but he exhibited no condescension toward him either. He studied the man with interest.

Lucas walked across the office and dropped into the chair the warden of the prison camp had indicated. Dixon was surprised that there was no meekness in the man's attitude. Far from being cowed, the prisoner had the bearing of a proud, undaunted man. His cool, gray eyes made no furtive movements, dead giveaways of guilt. They met those of the warden without a trace of repentance or remorse. Humility and deference were noticeably absent.

"Apparently the ordeal of the past several weeks hasn't cost you physically," the warden observed out loud. Since his return to the prison, the prisoner had been kept in a cell away from the others and disallowed any privileges.

"I'm fine," Lucas said laconically.

"A bit thinner, I think. A few days of cafeteria food should remedy that."

Lucas crossed one ankle over the opposite knee. "If you're going to spank my hands, get it over with, please. I'd like to return to my cell."

Warden Dixon curbed his temper. Years of dealing with recalcitrant prisoners had taught him to withstand the strongest provocation. He got out of his chair behind the desk and went to stand at the window, deliberately putting his back to Greywolf. He hoped the man would interpret that as a sign of trust. "The disciplinary action we've decided to take isn't nearly as severe as your escape warranted."

"Thanks," Lucas said sarcastically.

"Up to the time of your breakout, you were a model prisoner."

"I always try to do my best."

Again the warden exercised extreme self-restraint. "The board and I, after carefully reviewing your records, have voted to extend your sentence by six months in addition to the weeks you've already cost yourself. Our decision met with the approval of the penal-system officials."

Dixon turned quickly, in time to see Greywolf's astonishment before he abruptly masked it. Turning back to face the window, the warden hid his smile. Mr. Greywolf might try to remain indifferent, but he was as human as the next. Perhaps even more so. Dixon hadn't run across too many men who would risk spending more time behind bars to attend the death of their grandfather.

Lucas Greywolf sparked an admiration in the warden that was rare and unsettling. Given the same set of circumstances, would he have done what Greywolf had? It was a question that bothered him.

"Was it worth six more months in prison to see your grandfather before he died?"

"Yes."

The warden returned to his desk. "Why?"

Lucas lowered his leg back to the floor and assumed a more respectful posture. "Joseph Greywolf was a proud man. He clung stubbornly to tradition, often to his detriment. My being in prison bothered him more than it did me. He couldn't stand the thought that the grandson of a chief had to live behind bars."

"He was a chief?"

Greywolf nodded. "Little good that it did him. He died poor, disillusioned, defeated, as many men of my race do."

The warden studied the dossier in front of him. "It says here he was a landowner."

"But he had been swindled out of three-fourths of his land. He gave up. Stopped fighting. Before he got too sick, he was reduced to performing Indian ceremonial dances for tourists. Religious ceremonies that had at one time been solemn rites to him had become spectator sports to others."

Suddenly he lunged out of his chair. The warden jumped and reached beneath his desk for the panic button that would set off an alarm. But when he saw that the prisoner posed no physical threat to him, he placed his hand back on the desktop. He gave his full attention to Greywolf, who was pacing angrily, his body taut.

"Grandfather's only hope lay in me. He forgave me my white blood and loved me in spite of it. He raised me more as his son than grandson. The idea of my being in prison was intolerable to him. He had to see me out of it, he had to know that I had conquered it, before he could die peacefully. That's why I had to do it."

He faced the warden and Dixon thought that if this man couldn't sway jurors, no one could. His physical presence was dynamic. He was eloquent. He was a man of conviction and passion. What a waste that he wouldn't be allowed to practise law.

"I didn't want to escape, Warden Dixon. I'm not a fool. I asked for permission to leave for two days to see my grandfather. *Two goddamn days.* Permission was denied."

"It was against the rules," the warden countered calmly.

"To hell with the rules," he spat. "That is a stupid rule. Don't you people running this place realize how rehabilitative it would be to grant a prisoner some favors, give him back some dignity?" He was leaning over the desk now, full of threat.

"Sit down, Mr. Greywolf." Dixon spoke with just enough firmness to let the prisoner know he was getting out of line. After a considerable time had passed while they stared each other down, Lucas threw himself back into the chair. His handsome face was sullen.

"You're a lawyer," the warden said. "I think you realize how light you're getting off this time." Putting on a pair of silver-rimmed reading glasses, he scanned the report lying on his desk. "There was a young woman, a Miss Aislinn Andrews." He peered at Lucas over the rims of his glasses. The inflection at the end of the statement indicated that it was actually an inquiry.

Lucas said nothing, merely stared back at the warden with implacable eyes that revealed nothing of what he was thinking. The warden returned to the report. "Curious that she didn't press any charges against you." Still Lucas held his silence, though a muscle in his cheek jumped. Finally the warden closed the folder and took off his glasses. "You may return to your regular cell, Mr. Greywolf. That's all for now."

Lucas stood and headed for the door. He had already turned the knob before the warden halted him. "Mr. Greywolf, were you personally responsible for the assault on those policemen during that riot? Did you order the destruction of those government offices?"

"I organized the protest. The judge and jury found me guilty," he said succinctly before opening the door and making his exit.

Warden Dixon stared at the door for a long time after Lucas had closed it. He knew when a guilty man was lying. He also sensed when a man was innocent. Consulting the file on Lucas Greywolf again, he made a decision and reached for the telephone.

As Lucas was being escorted back to his cell, his heart was thudding, though on the outside he gave no indication of his inner turmoil.

He had expected to be told that he was being charged with breaking and entering, assault, kidnapping, and God knows how many other state and federal crimes. He had dreaded the ordeal of another trial, a trial that would further embarrass his mother and add to her heartache.

To learn that his escape had cost him only six more months in prison was a tremendous surprise. He would be busy during that time. By now the small table in his cell would be stacked with letters from people seeking legal advice. He couldn't charge them for it. He could never officially practise law again. But he could offer free legal advice. Among the Indians the name Lucas Greywolf represented a ray of hope. He wouldn't turn down anyone asking his help.

But why hadn't Aislinn Andrews pressed charges? Surely the state and federal authorities had tried to build a case against him. But without her testimony they couldn't prove he'd done anything but break out of prison. Why hadn't she cooperated with them?

Lucas Greywolf hated being indebted to anyone, but he owed Aislinn Andrews his gratitude.

Aislinn slipped through the bedroom door and closed it quietly behind her. The doorbell rang for the second time. She rushed down the hallway to answer it, hurriedly tucking loose strands of hair up into her casual ponytail. She checked her appearance in the hall mirror and saw that she was at least decent. Her face was expectant and wearing a half-smile when she pulled the door open.

The smile never made it to a full-fledged one. Indeed, it froze in place when she saw who her caller was. Her eyes glazed; she slumped against the door for support. For a moment she thought she would very likely faint.

"What are you doing here?"

"Did I frighten you again?"

"Are you . . . out?"

"Yes."

"When?"

"Today. Released this time. I walked out a free man."

"Congratulations."

"Thank you."

The conversation was ridiculous, of course, but for someone having just received the shock of her life, Aislinn thought she was doing fairly well. She hadn't fainted at the sight of Lucas Greywolf. She was maintaining her equilibrium with the help of the door, though her palms had become so slick with perspiration that she might slide down its smooth surface at any moment. Her mouth was dry, but she hadn't completely lost her capacity for speech. If the world had suddenly turned upside down, she couldn't have been more astounded. Taking all that into consideration, her behavior was remarkable.

"May I come in?"

One hand fluttered up to her throat. "I…I don't think that's a very good idea." *My God! Lucas Greywolf in her house? No!*

He stared down at the toes of his boots for a moment, then raised those unforgettable gray eyes up to hers. "It's important or I wouldn't trouble you."

"I—"

"I won't stay but for a minute. Please."

She looked everywhere but directly into his face, knowing that it would exude the determination of the Rock of Gibraltar to remain standing where it was. There was a hint of humility in his tone, but it was backed by generations of Indian resolve.

Finally she nodded briefly and moved aside. He came in and she shut the door behind him. The entrance hall seemed to shrink around them. She had been under the same roof with him for fewer than ten seconds, but already she was having difficulty breathing.

"Would you like something to drink?" she asked hoarsely. *Say no, say no.*

"Yes, please. This is my first stop."

She almost tripped on her way into the kitchen. Why here? Why had he made her house his first stop? Her hands were shaking as she reached into the cabinet for a glass. "A soft drink?" She asked.

"Fine."

She took a can of soda out of the refrigerator and opened it. It spewed over her hand. She yanked up a towel and clumsily blotted the sticky mess off her hand and the countertop. She was all thumbs as she opened the freezer and took out ice cubes, thunking them into the glass. Only when she had poured the soda over the ice did she turn around. Disconcertingly, her eyes were on a level with his chest. She was surprised to find him still standing.

"I'm sorry. Please sit down." She nodded toward the table.

He pulled out a chair and sat down, accepting the cold drink with a terse thank-you. His eyes roamed around the kitchen. They stopped on the rack of knives, then slowly moved to her. "I wouldn't have used the knife on you."

"I know." Before her knees gave way, she sank into the chair across the table from his. "I mean I know that now. Then, I was scared to death."

"You demonstrated remarkable courage."

"I did?"

"I thought so. But then you were my first hostage."

"You were my first abductor."

They should have smiled then. Neither of them did.

"Has your hair grown back out?"

"What?"

"Your hair. Remember that hank of it I chopped off?"

"Oh, yes," she said distractedly. Unconsciously she reached for that shorter strand. "It's tucked in there somewhere. Barely noticeable now."

"Good."

He sipped his drink. She pressed her hands together and slid them between her thighs, keeping her arms stiff. The tension squeezing her chest felt very much as she imagined a heart attack would. She feared suffocation.

From moment to moment she didn't know if she could stand the anxiety any longer without losing control. However, the silence was more unbearable than the stilted conversation, so she asked, "Have you been home yet, seen your mother?"

He shook his head. "I meant it when I said this is my first stop."

He hadn't even seen his mother before coming here? *Don't panic yet, Aislinn.* "How did you get here?"

"Mother and Gene came to the prison last week. Gene left my truck there."

"Oh." She rubbed her palms up and down her thighs, wiping the sweat on her jeans. But her hands were cold and her bare toes felt bloodless. "Why did you come here?"

"To thank you."

Startled, she looked straight at him. His steady stare caused her tummy to do a flip-flop. "Thank me?"

"Why didn't you press charges against me?"

She let go of her pent-up breath on a rushing gust. If that's all he wanted to know, she could live with that. "The sheriff and all those policemen who came to pick you up didn't even know about me." She recounted for him the events that followed his capture. "They had taken you away before anyone even noticed me coming down off that mountain."

Their eyes met fleetingly, each remembering what had taken place on that mountaintop.

Quickly she started speaking again. "They, uh, they questioned me about who I was and what I was doing there with you." She blushed, recalling how awkward she had felt, wondering if the men who interrogated her could tell that she had recently been made love to. Her hair had been a mess. Her lips had still felt swollen from ardent kisses. Her breasts still tingled. Her thighs—

"What did you say?"

"I lied to them. I told them I had met you on the road and given you a ride. I denied knowing that you were an escaped convict. I said that I had agreed to drive you to your grandfather's house because he was gravely ill and I felt sorry for you."

"They believed you?"

"I suppose so."

"You could have been implicated."

"But I wasn't."

"You could have had me charged with any number of crimes, Aislinn." The sound of her name startled both of them. They glanced at each other. Their eyes locked and held for a moment before falling away. "Why didn't you tell them the truth?"

"What would have been the point?" she asked, coming out of her chair and moving restlessly around the kitchen. "I was safe. You were going back to prison anyway."

"But you had been . . . hurt."

The euphemism fooled neither of them. They both realized that had she wanted to accuse him of rape she could have, and probably got him convicted of it. It would have been his word against hers, and who would have believed him?

"The scratch on my arm was superficial. Besides that wasn't your fault." Both knew that he hadn't been referring to the scratch, but it seemed prudent to pretend that he had been. "I think it was wrong of the prison officials not to let you go see your grandfather. In my eyes your escape was justified. No harm had been done. Not really."

"No one missed you?"

It cost her a great deal of pride to answer, but she told him the truth. "No." She had returned home as soon as the officials had released her. There hadn't been any media present in the canyon when Greywolf was arrested, so no one knew she had been involved.

"What about the people at your business?" he asked.

"What people?"

"You told me you would be missed."

"Of course I told you that."

"Oh," he said, shaking his head with chagrin, "there weren't any people."

"Not then. But I have two employees now."

He actually grinned. "Don't worry. I don't intend to pull a knife on you this time."

Aislinn smiled back, struck by how handsome he was. Now that the shock of seeing him had subsided, she was able to truly look at him for the first time. His hair was a trifle shorter in front, though it was still collar-length at the back. No prison pallor lightened his bronzed skin. Had she asked why, he could have told her that he ran every day around the prison yard, encircling it numerous times until he got in his quota of miles, which also accounted for his superb physical condition.

The silver earring still pierced his right lobe. The cross still rested in the soft black hair on his chest which she could see through the open collar of his shirt. His mother and Gene must have brought him new clothes for his release. His shirt and jeans looked new. Only the cowboy boots and the turquoise-studded belt around his trim waist were familiar to her.

"Well," he said, coming to his feet, "I promised you I wouldn't stay long. I just wanted to thank you for not making things rougher on me."

"You didn't have to bother."

"I started to write, but I wanted to thank you in person."

Lord, it would have been much easier on her nerves if he had mailed her a thank-you note! "I'm just glad you're out."

"I don't like being in anyone's debt, but—"

"You're not in my debt. I did what I thought was right, just as you did."

"Thanks all the same."

"You're welcome," she said, hoping that would end it. She led him through the living room and into the entrance hall.

Lucas had dreaded this meeting, not certain of how she was going to react to seeing him. The second she opened the door, she could have run screaming in terror and been justified in doing so.

He had been desperate the night he randomly chose her house to break into seeking food and shelter for a few hours. Desperate men did things they wouldn't ordinarily do. Like take a blameless Anglo woman hostage. It was still incomprehensible to him that she hadn't made him pay for that.

But now that he had accomplished his mission and thanked her, he was reluctant to leave. Odd. He had thought that once he had said what he had come to say, he would be more than ready to leave Aislinn Andrews for good and close that page of his life's history.

He hated to admit, even to himself, that he had thought about her while he was in prison. It had been months since that morning on the mountaintop, when she had given herself to him. He still found it hard to believe that it had really happened. Before his escape, his desire had been for a woman, period. Any and all.

But after his escape, his desire had had a face, a name, a tone of voice, a scent. And all of them belonged to Aislinn. Many nights, lying alone in his narrow prison bed, he had convinced himself that she wasn't real and that he had imagined the whole thing.

His body told him otherwise. Especially now, while his eyes were taking in the snug fit of her casual slacks over her bottom and thighs. She was shorter than he remembered, but maybe that was because she was barefoot. Her shirttail was out. It was an old shirt, a trifle too small for her. Oh, yes, while he had been sitting there sipping her soda, he had been thinking about sipping her breasts. He couldn't help but notice how amply they filled the front of the old shirt.

As she led him toward the front door, he was hypnotized by the swaying motion of her youthful ponytail. Was her hair as silky as he remembered? Had that rich blondness, such a flagrant trademark of her Anglo background, actually known his pillaging, Indian hands? And did her mouth, the one giving him a vapid, vacant smile now, remember the hard, searching strokes of his tongue inside it? He did.

"Good luck to you, Lucas. I hope all goes well for you now." She stuck out her hand.

"Thanks." He clasped her hand. Their eyes met. Held.

Then the sound.

It came from the back of the house. It was so out of context that at first he thought his ears were playing tricks on him. But then he heard it again. He glanced in that direction, his brows drawn into a puzzled frown.

"That sounds like a—"

Aislinn jerked her hand out of his. Surprised, his head snapped around. The instant he saw her face, he knew his ears hadn't been deceiving him. She looked as pale as a ghost and as guilty as sin. He went perfectly still. He stared at her with eyes razor sharp enough to flay her skin away, much less any deceit.

"What is that?"

"Nothing."

He moved her aside and stalked across her fashionable living room.

"Where are you going?" she cried, chasing after him.

"Guess."

"No!" She grabbed his shirt and held on with the tenacity of a bulldog. "You can't just come waltzing in here and—"

He spun around, knocking her hands away. "I did before."

"You can't."

"The hell I can't. Watch me."

He was intent on finding the source of that sound. Sobbing, Aislinn trailed after him, clutching at him ineffectually. He swatted her off like a pesky fly.

He glanced into her bedroom. It was exactly as he remembered it. Feminine, neatly arranged. He passed it. At the end of the hallway he came to a closed door. With no hesitation, certainly no apology, he turned the knob and pushed it open.

Then even he, the man with the heart and blood of an Apache warrior, was brought up short.

Three of the walls in the room were painted a soft yellow. The other was papered with a pastel Mother Goose print. A Boston rocker with thick cushions stood in one corner. A chest of drawers was topped by a quilted pad. It was lined with jars of cotton swabs and tubes of ointment. White shutters had been closed against the afternoon sun, but enough light seeped through the slats to silhouette the crib in front of the window.

Lucas closed his eyes, thinking that this must all be a bizarre dream from which he would awaken and have a much-needed laugh. But when he reopened his eyes, everything was unchanged. Especially that unmistakable sound.

He crept forward, illogically making as little noise as he could, until he reached the crib. It was rimmed with a padded border. A teddy bear smiled at him from the corner. The sheet was yellow to match the room. As was the downy blanket.

And beneath the blanket—squirming, squalling, flailing its tiny fists in rage—was a baby.

Chapter 7

The baby continued to cry, unimpressed by the havoc he had caused in the heart and mind of the tall dark man standing beside the crib. The face that was usually so remote was working with emotion.

Aislinn, standing slightly behind and to one side of Lucas, pressed her fingertips to her lips in an effort to stem her own emotions. They ranged from anxiety to abject terror.

Her first impulse was to tell him that she was babysitting, that the infant belonged to a friend or relative. But the uselessness of that was clear. The baby had been fathered by Lucas Greywolf. One had only to look at the child to dispel any doubts.

The beautifully rounded head, which hadn't been marred during the easy birth, was covered with midnight-black hair that hugged the soft scalp. The shape of the brow, the angle of chin, the slant of cheekbones, all were miniature replicas of Lucas Greywolf's features.

DISCOVER FREE BOOKS
& FREE GIFTS

From Silhouette

S	D	A	V	R	Y	B	X	N	M
G	I	F	T	N	C	A	S	P	Y
Z	D	L	N	B	U	L	T	R	S
R	T	N	H	N	E	F	T	A	T
D	H	I	A	O	V	K	D	M	E
N	W	E	K	H	U	O	W	S	R
O	C	T	M	U	T	E	D	D	Y
I	L	P	F	L	P	B	T	I	E
P	E	A	J	S	M	H	I	T	P
S	E	N	S	A	T	I	O	N	E

As a special introduction to Silhouette Sensation we will send you:

4 FREE SILHOUETTE SENSATIONS

plus a

FREE TEDDY

and

MYSTERY GIFT

when you return this card. But first - just for fun - see if you can find and circle five hidden words in the puzzle.

THE HIDDEN WORDS ARE:

SILHOUETTE • SENSATION
TEDDY • MYSTERY • GIFT

Now turn over to claim your
FREE
BOOKS & GIFTS

FREE BOOKS CERTIFICATE

YES! please send me FREE and without obligation, four specially selected **silhouette Sensation romances**, together with my FREE **teddy** and **mystery gift**. Please also reserve a Reader Service Subscription for me. If I decide to subscribe, I shall receive 4 superb Sensations every month for just £6.60, post and packing FREE. If I decide not to subscribe I shall write to you within 10 days. The FREE books and gifts will be mine to keep in any case. I understand that I am under no obligation whatsoever. I can cancel or suspend my subscription at any time simply by writing to you.

FREE TEDDY

MYSTERY GIFT

Mr/Mrs/Miss _____
(Please write in block capitals)

Address _____

_____ Postcode _____

Signature _____

I am over the age of 18.

3S1SS

Reader Service
FREEPOST
P.O. Box 236
Croydon
CR9 9EL

MAILING PREFERENCE SERVICE

The right is reserved to refuse an application and change the terms of this offer. Offer expires Dec 31st 1991. You may be mailed with other offers as a result of this application. If you would prefer not to share in this opportunity, please tick box ☐

Readers in Southern Africa write to:
Independent Book Services Pty. Postbag X3040
Randburg 2125. South Africa
*Overseas and Eire, send for details.

She watched in growing dread as Lucas stretched out a slender brown finger and touched the baby's cheek. Reverence and awe filled the light-gray eyes. His lips twitched slightly. Aislinn recognized the symptoms of keenly felt emotions. The same slight facial spasms seized her every time she held her baby. The kind of love that welled up inside her when she touched the child couldn't help but be registered on her face.

It terrified her that Lucas was experiencing the same kind of emotional tumult.

She jumped when he flicked the baby's blanket away with a swift motion of his hand. Her maternal instincts went into play when he tore open the tapes securing the disposable diaper. Lunging forward, she clutched his arm, but he negligently shook her hand off and pulled the diaper down.

"A son."

His rusty tone of voice sounded like a death knell to Aislinn. She was almost crazed with panic and wanted to cover her ears and shout denial. Frantically she prayed this wasn't really happening.

But it was. Helplessly she stood there and watched Lucas remove the one-snap sacque. Sliding his hands beneath the baby, he lifted him from the crib. All she could do was watch in mute despair as Lucas took the infant in his arms. The moment Lucas lay the baby against his chest, the child stopped crying.

The instant rapport between man and child gave Aislinn no peace. For once she would have preferred that her baby scream. He did nothing but make those sweet baby sounds against his father's shoulder.

Lucas carried the naked infant to the rocking chair. He folded his long legs low enough to sit in the rocker, awkwardly balancing himself while holding the baby. Under other circumstances, Aislinn might have thought that was a funny sight. As it was, her features were stark. All her worst nightmares were unfolding.

Had the situation not spelled such doom, Lucas's tender exploration of the baby would have touched Aislinn deeply. To see the dark, manly hands moving over the baby with such delicate curiosity was indeed poignant, and she would have had to be a pillar of salt not to be moved to tears by such instant adoration on the part of the father for the child.

Lucas gently turned the baby this way and that in loving inspection. He rolled him over and supported him in one large palm while he smoothed his other hand down the infant's back and over the tiny buttocks. He touched each toe, each transparent fingernail, and examined the baby's ears.

Finally he laid the child on his thighs and looked up at her. "What is his name?"

She wanted to tell him it was none of his business, but unfortunately it was. "Anthony Joseph." She saw an immediate reaction to the name in his gray eyes. "I had a grandfather named Joseph, too," she said defensively. "I call the baby Tony."

Lucas glanced down at the child who was beginning to wave his fists fretfully. "When was he born?"

She hesitated, giving thought to fudging on the dates and thereby negating Lucas's paternity. But his stare demanded the truth. "May seventh."

"You were never going to tell me, were you?"

"There was no reason to."

"He's my son."

"He has nothing to do with you."

He barked a short laugh. "From now on, he has everything to do with me."

Tony was crying in earnest now, the novelty of hearing a new, deeper voice having given way to hunger. Lucas lifted the baby to his shoulder, and immediately the wet little mouth went blindly searching. The most unexpected sound Aislinn had ever heard was Greywolf's soft chuckle. "That's one thing I can't do for you, Anthony

Joseph.'' Holding the baby in his arms, he stood up and extended Tony toward his mother. "He needs you."

She took the child and laid him back in his crib, hurriedly replacing the diaper Lucas had taken off. She was made clumsy by the baby's strenuous protests, his churning arms and legs, and by Lucas's watchfulness. When Tony was once again dressed and diapered, she lifted him to her shoulder and carried him to the rocker. Sitting there, she rocked him, patting his back and crooning softly. All ineffectually.

"He's hungry," Lucas said.

"I know that," she snapped, taking offense at his implication that she didn't know her own baby's needs.

"Well then? Feed him."

She looked up at Lucas, the baby acting as a fragile shield she held in front of her. "Will you excuse me?"

"You mean will I leave the room?"

"Yes."

"No."

They continued to stare each other down. Miraculously, Lucas was the first to relent. He turned his back and went to stand looking out the window after adjusting the shutters to allow him a view. Aislinn knew then that if this hard man were ever vulnerable about anything, it would be this son. An unbreakable bond had already been established between them, though Lucas hadn't even known the child existed until minutes ago. Would that he didn't know now. He could make her life hell.

"Why didn't you tell me?"

Aislinn, ignoring his question, unbuttoned her blouse and pulled down the cup of her nursing bra. Tony lustily latched onto her nipple and began to suck noisily. She draped a light flannel blanket over her shoulder to cover herself and the baby's head.

"I asked you a question." This time Lucas's tone was imperative.

"Because Tony is my baby."

"He's mine, too."

"You're not sure of that."

He swiveled his head around abruptly. Had modesty not made her flinch, the incisive gray eyes would have. "I'm sure." He was so positive there was no sense in arguing the point. So what if she beat him in a contest on semantics? The facts would remain the same. Tony was his.

"Tony was a biological . . . accident," she said by way of concession.

"Then why didn't you just get rid of him?"

A shudder ran through her body. "Why didn't you just get rid of it?" her mother had screamed at her when Aislinn informed her parents of her pregnancy. Purposefully she had waited to tell them until it was too late for an abortion, knowing that termination would have been their solution to "the dilemma."

Why *hadn't* she terminated the pregnancy? Before she went to the doctor, she had had a niggling suspicion in the back of her mind as to the cause of her afternoon malaise. Then there had been the morning bouts with nausea, the sudden bursts of appetite and the sour indigestion after satisfying it. All unusual.

She hadn't consciously entertained the idea that she might be pregnant. She hadn't allowed herself to. But when the doctor told her his laboratory-verified diagnosis, she hadn't been shocked or even surprised. In fact, her first reaction had been a stupendous rush of joy.

After that initial reaction, when reality had set in, she gave considerable thought to the negative ramifications of rearing a child as a single woman. She recognized the grave repercussions, but never did she consider having the pregnancy terminated.

From the moment she had learned of his existence, she loved the child fiercely. Her life suddenly had purpose and meaning. Now she had something to look forward to. There were goals to be met, horizons to move toward.

So now she could answer Lucas's question without hesitation or qualification. "I desperately wanted the baby." Reaching beneath the blanket, she laid her hand on Tony's soft head, lightly rubbing it while he avidly sucked at her breast. "I have loved him from the beginning."

"Didn't you think I was entitled to know about him?"

"I didn't think you'd care."

"Well, make no mistake; I do."

"What . . . what do you intend to do?" she asked fearfully, despising the tremulous quality of her voice.

"I intend to be his father."

Tony impatiently thumped her breast with his tiny fist. Only that could have distracted her from Lucas's hard stare. "I need to turn him," she said huskily.

Lucas looked down at her chest. Aislinn saw him swallow reflexively before he diverted his eyes.

She switched Tony from one breast to the other. Once he was resettled and nursing again, she said, "I ask nothing from you, Mr. Greywolf. I carried Tony for nine months. I went through the entire pregnancy and delivery without any assistance from you, from anyone. Financially I'm able to provide—"

He came around so suddenly, she fell silent out of fear that he might reach across the room and strike her.

"Do you think a checkbook can supply him with everything he needs?"

"I didn't mean that," she flared. "I love him."

"So do I!" He roared so loudly that Tony's mouth fell still for several seconds before he resumed nursing.

"Be quiet! You scared Tony."

Lucas lowered his volume but not his intensity. "If you think I'm going to abandon my son and let him grow up in your sterile, Anglo world, think again."

She clutched the baby tighter. "What do you mean?"

"I mean that when I return to the reservation tomorrow, he goes with me."

She paled drastically. Even her lips looked chalky. The only color in her face was the deep blue of her eyes, which looked abnormally large as she stared up at the man who was once again her enemy.

"You can't take him."

"I can. I will."

"No!"

"There will be no stopping me."

"I'll have you hunted down like the criminal you are," she threatened.

His lips quirked into a cynical smile. "If I didn't want to be found, I wouldn't be, Miss Andrews. But even if by some remote chance I *were*, I'd fight you to the Supreme Court if necessary to win my son away from you. I know how. I'm a lawyer, remember? I think he's finished."

His threats had frozen her with fear. By the time she assimilated his last sentence, he was already across the room and crouching down in front of her. Before she could stop him, Lucas removed the blanket from her shoulder.

Tony was lying in her arms, satiated. His plump cheek rested against her breast. His small mouth, pearlized with milk, lay close to her nipple. He was asleep, looking as full and contented as a despot after a three-day bacchanal.

Lucas caressed his sleeping baby's cheek. He touched the soft lips with the tip of his finger. His dark head moved closer. He kissed the top of Tony's head.

Aislinn sat petrified. Too stunned to move. Hardly able to breathe. Lucas slid his hands up over her stomach, wedging them between her and Tony, and lifted the child away from her. He stood and carried the baby to the crib. Tony burped and Lucas released another of those surprising chuckles.

Aislinn forced herself out of the trance that astonishment had imposed. Lucas's nearness had immobilized her. Feeling his breath on her skin had stupefied her. Now she hastily replaced the cups of her bra and buttoned her blouse. She swayed slightly when she stood up. "He's ready to go to sleep now," she said, shouldering Lucas aside as she joined him beside the crib. She turned Tony over onto his tummy.

"He sleeps on his stomach?"

"Yes."

The baby drew his knees up and poked his bottom into the air. He made a few sucking motions with his mouth, then lay still, fast asleep.

"He looks satisfied," Lucas said.

"For now," Aislinn said gently, drawing the light blanket over the baby.

"Well I'm not."

She looked up at Lucas and was startled to see the uncompromising expression on his face. "You wouldn't really try to take him away from me, would you?" she asked, willing herself not to beg.

She didn't think a father could ever win custody over a mother who was loving, caring and affluent, no matter what legal machinations he tried. But in the meantime, Tony would be a subject of litigation. He might even become a ward of the state and be placed in a foster home until the matter could be settled. That might take years. "Think of Tony."

"I am." He took her by the shoulders. "Do you think your society will accept him?" Not giving her time to answer, he said, "Never, Aislinn." His hands were hard on her shoulders. Hard and warm. She recalled other times he had touched her and dearly wished she didn't. "Believe me, I know. In an Anglo's opinion, being part Indian is tantamount to being all Indian. And he has so much white blood, he'll be an outcast in Indian society, too. He won't be accepted in either world."

"I'll see to it that he is."

The corner of his mouth tilted into a smile that was both scoffing and pitying. "You're naive and deluding yourself if you think that. I know what it's like to straddle the cultures, for christsake! I've had to live with the ambiguity every day of my life. I will protect my son from that."

"By doing what? What's your solution? Taking him to some remote part of the reservation where he'll never come into contact with other people?"

"If that's what it takes," he answered grimly.

She looked at him incredulously. "And you think that would be fair?"

"The circumstances of his birth weren't fair. Life isn't fair. I gave up on it ever being fair a long time ago."

"Yes, and you wear your bitterness where all the world can see it," she accused, angrily shrugging off his hands. "I won't let Tony grow up so steeped in hatred that he's made a prisoner of it as you are, Lucas Greywolf. And in the long run, who do you think he'd hate the most? *You!* He wouldn't thank you for separating him from the world."

Apparently he realized there was some merit to that because he gnawed the inside of his cheek in indecision. But he wasn't about to let her win the argument. "What did you plan to do, tell him that his Indian features were a fluke? Did you intend to keep my identity a complete secret from him?"

"I . . . I hadn't planned that far ahead."

"Well, you'd better be giving it some thought, lady. Because one of these days he'll ask about his father. I did."

For the beat of several seconds Aislinn let a tense silence reign, then she asked in a low voice. "And what were you told?"

He stared down at her for so long she thought he was going to refuse to tell her. But then he took up his stance at the window again, his broad shoulders almost spanning it. Unseeingly, he stared at the mountains on the horizon as he began to speak.

"The man who fathered me was an Anglo soldier stationed at Fort Huachuca. My mother was sixteen. She had graduated early from the reservation school and moved to Tucson where Joseph had friends who gave her room and board. She took a job waiting tables in a diner."

"Is that where she met your father?"

He nodded. "He flirted with her and asked her to go out with him after she got off work. She refused. But he kept coming back to the diner. She told me that he was very handsome, dashing, charming."

Turning his hands palms out, he slid them into the rear pockets of his snug jeans. If the father had looked anything like the son, if he had had that same long, lean physique, Aislinn could understand how easily Alice Greywolf's head might have been turned.

"Finally she consented to go out with him. To put it bluntly, Miss Andrews, he seduced her. I'm not sure how many dates it took. Mother was understandably not specific. Only weeks after she met him, he was shipped out to parts unknown. He didn't say goodbye. He just stopped coming by to see her. When she worked up her nerve to call the base to tell him that she was pregnant, she was informed that he was gone."

He turned around. His features were closed tighter than she had ever seen them. Intuitively she knew that meant he was hurting. It was an unbearable hurt that he kept tightly bottled up inside him.

"She never saw or heard from him again, nor did she try to contact him. She returned to the reservation in disgrace, pregnant with a white man's baby. She delivered me a month before her seventeenth birthday. She got a job making souvenir kachina dolls because she could work at home while taking care of me. Grandfather earned enough money selling horses to feed and house us in an old trailer. Mother and I lived with him until she met Gene Dexter. He offered her a job in town that vastly improved her standard of living. Thank God,'' he added softly.

He turned back to Aislinn. "So you see, I grew up knowing what a burden I was to my mother."

"She didn't think so, Lucas." Her throat was tight with emotion. "She loves you very much."

"I know that. She never became bitter because of what happened to her."

"You more than compensate."

"You can't know bitterness until you grow up a half-breed bastard," he said with an angry hiss. "So don't give me any lectures about it. And I'll see you in hell before I'll let my son be subjected to that kind of stigma. Do you think I'd do to him what my father did to me?"

"But your father didn't know. Maybe if he—"

"Don't even suggest anything so ridiculous," he interrupted sharply. "To him, Alice Greywolf, the beautiful Indian girl, was an easy roll in the hay. A novelty, no doubt. Even if he had known about the pregnancy, he probably would have deserted her. At best he would have driven her across the border for a cheap, speedy abortion." He shook his head. "No, the Anglo soldier would have wanted no part of his little Indian baby. But by God I want my son. He is going to know his father."

Reading his face, Aislinn knew that trying to deter him would be futile. He meant what he said. He would know his son and vice versa. And in so doing Lucas could make her life unbearable.

She had thought she would never see Lucas Greywolf again. She had imagined that he would view their morning on the mountaintop the way he supposed his father viewed his encounter with Alice. A roll in the hay. An *easy* roll in the hay.

Well, surprising as it was, he hadn't. Or if he had before, he had changed his mind about it when he saw Tony. Simply put, she had been found out. She had wanted to keep Tony's existence a secret from him forever. Such was not to be. The only choice she had now was to make the best of a bad situation.

"What do you suggest, Lucas? That we divide Tony's life between us? Don't you think that will only compound the confusion? It will be years before he's old enough to understand. Life here six months, life with you six months." It pained her to even verbalize the possibility that an arrangement like that might have to be made. "What kind of life would that be for a little boy?"

"I have no such arrangement in mind."

"Then what?"

"We'll get married. You'll both live with me."

It wasn't a suggestion. It wasn't even an alternative offered up for discussion. It was an edict.

When the words finally sank in, she splayed her hand over her chest and said on a soft laugh, "You can't be serious." But his unmoving features and unblinking eyes told her he was deadly serious. "Are you crazy? That's impossible!"

"It's essential. My child will not grow up branded a bastard."

"Don't say that word."

"It's ugly, isn't it? I want to guarantee that Tony will never hear it."

"But we can't get married."

"I didn't count on that either," he said, somewhat chagrined. "But we are, as soon as arrangements can be made. I'll be back tomorrow."

He leaned down and patted Tony on the behind, smiling down at him fondly and speaking something in his native tongue. Then, as though everything had been settled, he turned and left the nursery.

Aislinn ran after him, catching him by the sleeve as he reached for the knob on the front door. "I can't marry you."

"Are you already married?"

He fired the question at her and it stunned her for a moment. "No. Of course not."

"Then there's no reason why we can't marry."

"Except that I don't want to."

"Well, neither do I," he grated, bending down and putting his face close to hers for emphasis. "But we'll just have to put aside our own feelings for the sake of our son. If I can tolerate having an Anglo wife, you can damn sure tolerate having an Indian husband."

"Oh, for Pete's sake," she cried angrily. "This has nothing to do with my being Anglo and your being Indian. Don't you ever think of anything else?"

"Rarely."

"Well, make an exception this time. Considering the way we met, don't you think the idea of marriage is just a little ridiculous?"

"Meaning that a kidnapping is hardly a courtship."

"Exactly."

"What to you want from me? To go down on bended knees?"

She gave him a withering look. "I only meant to point out that we don't even know each other. We made a baby, but—" She broke off, alarmed by her own words. She didn't want to be reminded of that morning. She certainly didn't want to remind him of it.

She had been facing him squarely, her fists planted on her hips. Now, she quickly lowered her arms, suddenly aware of how her militant posture was stretching her blouse across her breasts. Nervously, she wet her lips with her tongue and looked someplace else besides Lucas's face.

"Yes, we made a baby," he said quietly. "That's really the point, isn't it? Tony had nothing to do with what happened between us, so he damn sure isn't going to go through his life paying for it. *We*," he said, waving his hand between his chest and hers, "we shared that lust. There's not a damn thing we can do about it now but share the responsibility for the life we created."

He placed a finger beneath her chin and yanked her head up, forcing her to look at him. "As surely as I planted my seed in you, Tony will know me." He released her and stepped back. "I'll be back tomorrow. Whether you consent to marry me or not, I'm taking my son with me when I leave."

"Under the threat of a knife?" she asked snidely.

"If necessary."

His eyes drove the words home. She believed him and was frightened into speechlessness. Nothing more was said before he left by the front door.

She was nervous. Chastising herself for acting like a ninny, she still jumped at every sound. She nearly came out of her skin when the doorbell rang. It turned out to be the postman hand-delivering a catalog that was too large for her mailbox. She felt foolish, but she couldn't curb her jitters.

She tried reassuring herself that her nervousness might all be for naught. Lucas Greywolf might never return. Seeing Tony might have made him think he wanted to take on the responsibilities of child-rearing. But upon thinking about last night, he might very well have changed his mind.

She didn't think so, however. Lucas—strange how her mind formed his name so easily—wasn't a man given to outbursts of emotion that were quickly spent. Nor was he likely to make promises he didn't intend to keep. Sometime today he would show up on her doorstep. When that happened, what would she do?

Exercise all the powers of persuasion at her disposal.

Throughout the long night, the problem had clattered around and around in her head like the ball in a roulette wheel. Lucas Greywolf was a fact of her life now, and she would have to cope with him.

She outlined what she thought would be a fair arrangement for Lucas to see Tony. Surely he would recognize the sound reasoning behind that. A baby needed his mother, especially for the first few years. Unless Lucas was totally unreasonable, he would admit that. And she knew that he didn't really want to get married, any more than she did.

She was enjoying the stability of her life now. In her fifth month of pregnancy, she had hired another photographer to take over her duties at the portrait studio. Then, since she had been busy converting the spare bedroom in her condo into a nursery, she hired a receptionist/bookkeeper. Both young women were doing well in their jobs, and the studio was prospering as it never had before.

She made periodic visits to check on things. Beyond that, her primary responsibility was to care for and love Tony. That was no chore at all. He was only a month old, yet he was such a vital part of her life that she couldn't imagine not having him.

Only one thing could have made her happier—that her parents would leave her alone. Resigned to the fact that their daughter had an illegitimate baby, they had turned their energies toward finding her a husband who would accept her and the child. Marriage to a respectable man would remove the blight on the family name.

Aislinn wasn't fooled by the tolerance of these prospective husbands, who were introduced to her under the most embarrassingly contrived circumstances. They overlooked Tony's illegitimacy and her indiscretion with amazing benevolence. However, she knew that each was keeping in mind her father's bank account and depending on his generosity. They expected recompense for their charitable attitude toward a wayward girl.

But stubborn as they were in wanting to dictate her future, her parents would be easier to dissuade than Lucas Greywolf. Of that Aislinn was certain.

When the doorbell rang for a second time shortly before noon, she knew who it was. For a moment, she clasped her hands together, squeezed her eyes closed, and drew a deep breath. The bell rang again and she didn't imagine the impatience behind that imperious ring. She moved toward the door with leaden footsteps.

Suddenly she wished she hadn't surrendered to vanity and dressed in "civilian" clothes. She had been wearing maternity clothes, giving her body time to slim down. Today, she had tried on last summer's skirt and found to her delight that it would go around her waist.

The full, calf-length skirt had always been one of her favorites. The soft blue fabric brushed against her legs when she walked. With it she had put on a white blouse with a white-on-white embroidered yoke. It buttoned down the front to facilitate nursing Tony. She had washed her hair in the shower and left it to dry in its natural waves. Now the sides were looped behind her ears, into which she had secured small gold rings.

Maybe applying makeup had been going too far. And fragrance. Why had she put on perfume today when she hadn't worn any for months? But it was too late to do anything about it now, because the doorbell was ringing for a third time.

She pulled open the door. She and Greywolf stared across the threshold at each other. Both wanted to feel antagonism. Instead each was experiencing a pleasurable jolt at the other's appearance.

Aislinn was never quite prepared for those light-gray eyes set in that dark, lean face. His shirt was different. Otherwise he was dressed the same as the day before, in jeans, which rode low on his narrow hips, and boots, which had seen better days. The silver cross lay against his chest in the open V of his shirt. The earring in his ear seemed to punctuate the pronounced intersection of his cheekbone and jaw.

Moving aside, she let him come in and closed the door behind him. Lucas looked down upon the crown of her head, then let his glance slide down her slender neck to her breasts. He could see the swelling mounds beneath her neckline.

His gut twisted with desire, remembering the shape of her breasts and the color of her nipples bedewed with milk. He shouldn't have looked at her yesterday. Then he wouldn't know what a lovely sight she was when nursing his baby, and he wouldn't be remembering it now. But he had had to look, or die.

Her breasts were noticeably fuller than they had been ten months ago. That only made the rest of her figure appear trimmer. Her feet looked incredibly childlike in the barefoot sandals.

He cleared his throat of congestion. "Where's Tony?"

"Asleep in his room."

With an economy of movement and an absence of sound, he turned and went toward the nursery. Aislinn marveled over how agilely and silently he could move.

By the time she had followed him into the nursery he was bending low over Tony's crib. The tenderness with which he gazed at his sleeping son coaxed an emotion from her that she didn't want to acknowledge. To deny it, she asked him, "Did you think I was lying? Did you have to see for yourself that he was still here? Did you think I had hidden him from you?"

With that same animallike grace, he turned around to face her. "You wouldn't dare."

For several beats, their eyes held. He glanced back at the child once more before crossing the room, taking her by the arm, and leading her back into the hallway.

"Get me something to drink," he said.

She started to snap something sarcastic like, "This isn't a tavern, you know." But she decided that sitting in the kitchen with the table between them was better than sharing the living-room sofa.

"All right. If you'll let go of me," she answered, working her arm out of his grasp. She didn't want to know the warm, strong pressure of his fingers, which seeped through the cloth of her sleeve. His touch evoked too many memories she had spent months eradicating from her mind. She wanted to yell at him to keep his hands off her, but she didn't want to provoke his temper unnecessarily. Now wasn't the time to gamble with his moods, not when she must appeal to his reason.

"None of Tony's things are packed," he observed, sitting down in the same chair as the day before.

"What would you like? Juice or a soft drink?"

"A soft drink." She took one out of the refrigerator and went through the same ritual as yesterday, finally handing the icy glass to him.

"None of Tony's things are packed," he repeated before taking a single sip of the drink.

She sat down across from him, willing her hands not to shake. "That's right."

"Then I take that to mean we're getting married."

"Then you take it wrong, Mr. Greywolf. I'm not marrying you or anybody."

He drank from the glass; then with careful thoroughness, scooted it away from him. "I will have my son."

Aislinn licked her lips. "I think Tony should know you. That's only fair to both of you. I won't keep you from seeing him. You may come here whenever you like. All I ask is that you give me several hours' notice to prevent any conflicts in schedules. I'll try to cooperate— Where are you going?" Lucas had suddenly left his chair and headed for the door.

"To get my son."

"Wait!" She bounded out of her chair and caught his arm. "Please. Let's be reasonable about this. You can't believe that I'll stand by and let you cart my son off with you."

"He's my son, too."

"He needs his mother."

"And a father."

"But not like he needs me. Not now, anyway. Yesterday you said yourself that you couldn't feed him."

His eyes dropped to her breasts. She held her ground. "There are other ways," he said tersely and tried to move away.

She gripped his arm harder. "Please. Maybe when he gets older."

"I told you my alternative. Apparently you've chosen not to accept it."

"You mean marriage?" She let go of his arm, realizing how close they were standing and how tenaciously her fingers were curled around his forearm. She turned her back and went to stand at the sink. As she tried to think of a graceful way to broach this subject, she nervously crossed her arms over her middle and ran her hands up and down her opposite biceps. "Marriage between us is out of the question."

"I fail to see why."

His obtuseness made her grind her teeth in frustration. He was forcing her to spell it out for him and she hated him for it. "I can't marry you because of all it entails."

"Leaving the city, this house?"

"That's part of it."

"What's the other part?"

"My studio."

"Your studio is being capably operated by two employees. Try again."

"All right then," she cried, spinning around to confront him. "Living with you. And . . . and . . ."

"Sleeping with me." He finished her sentence for her. The low, sandy sound of his voice was so intimate she could all but feel it brushing against her skin.

For answer, she turned her back to him again and bowed her head low. "Yes."

"Then we're not talking about marriage, are we? We're talking about sex. I used the term 'marriage' in a strictly legal context. Apparently you read more into my proposal."

"I—"

"No, no. Since you brought it up, let's explore all the possibilities."

He moved up behind her. She could sense he was there even before she felt his warm breath drifting over her neck as he bent his head down. It was a taunting movement, as though he had trapped her, but before devouring her, wanted to play with her.

"You can't stand the thought of having sex with me, is that it?" He slid his hand around her, pressing it flat against her midriff, drawing her closer. "You didn't seem to have any objections that morning on top of the mountain."

"Don't." Her breathy command carried little weight. It didn't stop him from nuzzling her hair with his nose until his mouth touched her ear.

"Did I miss something that morning? Or do white society girls say no differently from others?"

"Stop, stop this," she moaned. His fingertips lightly brushed her nipple, coaxing a drop of moisture from it.

"It sure as hell sounded like you were saying yes."

"It should never have happened."

"What's the matter, Miss Andrews? After all this time are you getting squeamish about screwing an Indian?"

She threw off his arms, spun around and smacked his hard cheek with the flat of her palm. The sound cracked through the room like a slashing whip. Both were as stunned by the sound as they were by her flare of violence and the crude words that had precipitated it.

She withdrew her hand quickly. "Don't ever talk to me like that," she said breathlessly, her breasts rapidly rising and falling with anger.

"All right," he growled, taking the few steps necessary to pin her against the countertop. "Then let's talk about why you're all dolled up today. Did you want to make sure I'd notice your blond beauty? Did you think you would intimidate the Indian boy with it? How dare I ask such a golden goddess to marry me? Is that what you wanted me to think?"

"No!"

"Then why do you smell so damn good? And why did you make yourself look good enough to eat?" he asked through clenched teeth. "And why do I want to?"

He couldn't resist the groan that rumbled from his throat, anymore than he could resist crushing her against him. He buried his face in the hollow of her throat and held her tight. He rubbed his chest against her breasts. His hips pantomimed lovemaking against hers.

The embrace lasted only a few seconds before he shoved himself away from her. His chest was heaving. A few buttons on his shirt had come loose. The color in his dark cheeks had deepened. To Aislinn's startled eyes he looked undisciplined and dangerous, and wildly sexy.

"You see, Miss Aislinn, I can control my lust. Don't flatter yourself into thinking that I want you any more than you want me. You're just excess baggage that has to come along with my son because I don't have mammary glands. But I'm willing to pay the price of living with you in order to make a home for Tony." He ran his hand through his hair and took several more restorative breaths. "Now I'm going to ask you one last time. Do you come along or not?"

Before she could collect herself enough to form an answer, the doorbell rang.

Chapter 8

"Who is that?"

"I don't know," Aislinn said.

"Were you expecting somebody?"

"No."

Always polite and adhering to the rules of etiquette, she asked him to excuse her. In light of what had just transpired, her courtesy was rather ludicrous. She left the kitchen and went to answer the front door bell, but she was distracted. Her mind had stayed in the other room with Greywolf. What was she going to do?

She swung the front door open and for several seconds didn't move. She just stood there wondering what else would happen to make this day one of the most disastrous of her life.

"Aren't you going to invite us in?" Eleanor Andrews asked her daughter.

"I...I'm sorry," Aislinn stuttered. She moved aside and her parents stepped into the living room.

"Is something wrong?" her father asked.

"No—I, uh, just wasn't expecting you." As usual, they intimidated her. Her parents could always make her feel like a child on the verge of being reprimanded. It wasn't something she liked to admit, but it happened every time she saw them. Today was no exception.

"We just left the club," Eleanor said, propping her tennis racquet against the wall, "and thought that as long as we had to come this way, we'd stop by."

Not very likely, Aislinn thought. If her parents had stopped by, there was a reason behind the impromptu visit. They didn't keep her in suspense long. "You remember Ted Utley," her father said for openers. "You met him at a symphony ball several years ago."

"He was married then," her mother supplied.

As Eleanor expounded upon Mr. Utley's unfortunate divorce and fortunate real-estate investments, Aislinn tried to view her parents objectively. They were both tanned and handsome and fit. They personified the American dream come true. They lived what most people would consider the good life. Yet Aislinn wondered if either of them had ever experienced any passion for living.

Oh, they smiled for the camera on Christmas mornings. Her mother cried daintily at funerals. Her father got emotionally involved when he discussed the national debt. But she had never once heard them either laughing lustily together or shouting in anger. She'd seen them kiss, formally, and pat each other affectionately, but she'd never intercepted a smoldering glance between them. They had produced her, yet she thought them to be the two most sterile people she had ever met.

"So we want you to come to dinner next Tuesday night," her mother was saying. "We'll eat on the patio, but wear something nice. And make arrangements with a sitter for...the...the child."

"The child's name is Tony," Aislinn said. "And I won't need to make arrangements with a sitter because I won't be coming to your dinner party."

"Why not?" her father asked, scowling. "Just because you've had an illegitimate baby doesn't mean you have to hide yourself away."

Aislinn laughed. "Why, thank you, Father, for your broadmindedness." Her sarcasm escaped them. "I don't want to go through an embarrassing evening where you and Mother try to match me up with some man who has a tolerant attitude toward fallen women."

"That's enough," he said sharply.

"We're only doing what we feel is best for you," Eleanor said. "You've made a mess of your life. We're trying to rectify your mistakes as best we can. I think the least you could do is—"

Eleanor ended her lecture with a soft indrawn breath. She even raised a fearful hand to her chest as though to ward off an attacker. Willard Andrews followed his wife's startled gaze and he, too, was visibly taken aback. Without even turning around, Aislinn knew what had ruffled her usually unflappable parents.

Indeed, when she turned and looked at Greywolf, she felt that tingling in her system that was a combination of fear and anticipation. Every time she saw Lucas, she experienced that initial reaction.

He stood straight and tall in the doorway between the living room and kitchen. His unwavering gray eyes were fixed on her parents. His mouth was set in a hard, thin line. His shirt was open almost to his waist, and his torso barely moved as he breathed. He was so still he could have been a statue had it not been for the latent energy he emanated.

"Mother, Father, this is Mr. Greywolf," Aislinn said, her voice cutting through the heavy silence.

No one said a word. Lucas gave the Andrews a curt nod of his head in acknowledgement of the introduction, but Aislinn thought that was because Alice Greywolf had probably grilled her son in proper manners and not because Lucas felt any deference or respect for her parents.

Lucas could have been an uncaged tiger for the fearful stare Eleanor gave him. Willard was almost as dumbfounded, but he finally asked, "*Lucas* Greywolf?"

"Yes," Lucas answered in a clipped tone.

"I read about your release from prison in this morning's paper."

"My God." Eleanor swayed and gripped the back of a chair for support. She had the white-faced look of a victim about to be massacred and scalped, who was calling on a deity for mercy.

Willard subjected his daughter to a hard look. Out of habit, Aislinn lowered her eyes. He said, "What I can't understand, Mr. Greywolf, is what you're doing in my daughter's house, apparently with her consent."

Aislinn kept her head lowered. She had thought her encounters with Lucas were bad, but nothing could be worse than this. From the corner of her eye, she saw Lucas leave the doorway and silently move into the room. He came directly toward her. Eleanor recoiled and uttered another gasp when he reached out and jerked Aislinn's chin up, forcing her to look at him.

"Well?"

He was giving her a choice, albeit not much of one. Either she was to tell them what he was doing in her house or he would. She lifted her chin off his index finger and turned her head slightly to meet her parents' incredulous stares. Taking a deep breath and feeling like she was about to step off a gangplank, she said, "Lucas is...is...Tony's father."

The following silence was so thick it could have been cut with a knife. Aislinn could hear the thudding of her own heart as she met the glazed expressions on the faces of her mother and father. Never at a loss for words in any social situation, they now stared at her as wide-eyed and gape-mouthed as dead fish on the beach.

"That's impossible," Eleanor wheezed at last.

"Lucas and I, uh, met when he escaped from prison ten months ago," Aislinn said.

"I don't believe it," Eleanor said.

"Yes you do," Lucas said scornfully, "or you wouldn't be so horrified. I'm sure it comes as an unpleasant shock to you to learn that your grandson is also the grandson of an Indian chief."

"Don't you dare speak to my wife in that tone of voice!" Willard ordered stridently and took a belligerent step forward. "I could have you arrested for—"

"Spare me your threats, Mr. Andrews. I've heard them all. And from men richer and more powerful than you. I'm not afraid of you."

"What is it you want?" Willard demanded. "Money?"

Greywolf's face went hard and cold with contempt. He pulled himself up straighter. "I want my son."

Eleanor turned to Aislinn. "Let him have him."

"What?" Aislinn fell back a step. "What did you say?"

"Give him the baby. That would be best for everyone."

Aghast, Aislinn stared first at her mother, then at her father, who, by his silence, had endorsed Eleanor's suggestion. "You expect me to give my child away?" It was a rhetorical question. She could tell by their expectant faces that her mother was sincere.

"For once in your life, listen to us, Aislinn," her father said. He reached out and clasped her hand. "You've always gone against our wishes, bucked the system, done what you knew we would disapprove of. But this time you've gone too far and made a ghastly mistake. I don't know how you could have..."

Unable to bring himself to say it, he merely cast a scathing glance at Lucas, a glance that said it all. He turned back to his daughter. "But it happened. You'll regret this mistake the rest of your life if you don't give the child up now. Apparently Mr. Greywolf sees the wisdom in it even if you don't. Give him the child to raise. If you like, I'll send money occasionally to—"

Aislinn wrested her hand from her father's and backed away from him as though he were diseased. At the moment, she thought he was—diseased in the heart. How could either of her parents even suggest that she give Tony away? Never to see him again. To dispose of him as though he were the incriminating debris of a wild party.

She looked at them and realized they were strangers. How little she really knew them. Even more, how little they knew her. "I love my son. I won't give him up for anything in the world."

"Aislinn, be reasonable," Eleanor said testily. "I can admire your attachment to the child, but—"

"I think you'd better leave."

Even if Greywolf's voice hadn't been so raspily commandeering, his stance was. He seemed to tower over the three of them when, as one, they turned at the soft dangerous sound.

Willard snorted scoffingly. "I sure as hell won't be ordered from my own daughter's house by an . . . by *you*. Besides, this discussion doesn't involve you."

"It involves him very much," Aislinn contradicted. "He's Tony's father. Whatever my decision is, it concerns him."

"He's a criminal!" her father exclaimed.

"He was unjustly accused. He took the blame for something others did." She noted that Lucas swung around toward her, revealing his surprise at the way she defended him.

"The courts didn't think so. According to the record, he's an ex-con. And, as if that isn't enough," Willard said, "he's an Indian."

"So is Tony," Aislinn said courageously. "That doesn't mean I love him any less."

"Well, don't expect us ever to accept him," Eleanor said coldly.

"Then I guess you'd better do as Lucas suggested and leave."

Willard came as close as Aislinn had ever seen him to losing his temper, but he held it in check and said tightly, "If you have anything, *anything*, to do with this man, you'll get nothing more from me."

"I never asked anything of you, Father." Tears were stinging her eyes, but she held her head up proudly. "I paid back your investment in the photography studio, which I didn't want in the first place. I don't owe you for anything, not even for a happy childhood. You said a moment ago that I had always bucked the system, but that isn't true. I always *wanted* to, but you always dissuaded me. I bowed to your wishes in every major decision of my life. Until now. If you and Mother can't accept the fact that Tony is your grandson, then I can't hold a place in your lives either."

They weathered her ultimatum with the same cool control they had every sad crisis and joyous occasion of their lives. Without a word, Willard took his wife's arm and steered her toward the door. Eleanor paused only long enough to pick up her tennis racquet before they left. They never looked back.

Aislinn's head dropped forward. The tears, which had been threatening for the past several heart-wrenching minutes, slowly slid from under her eyelids and rolled down her cheeks. Her parents wanted to dominate her life completely or have no part in it at all. She couldn't believe that they could be so resolute in their prejudice as to refuse to acknowledge their own grandson. She bitterly regretted their decision.

On the other hand, if they were that narrow-minded and unbending, she and Tony were better off without them. She wanted her son to be unashamed of the emotions he experienced. She wanted him to grow up having the freedom to express himself in a way she had never been allowed to. She wanted him to feel things intensely, as she had with...

Aislinn spun around and looked at the man standing so still and silent behind her. Her thoughts had inevitably brought her to those days she had spent as a captive of Lucas Greywolf. Then for the first time, life had been unpredictable. She clearly recalled the rushes of excitement, of joy and sadness. That brief period of time hadn't been romanticized in her mind, as she had later thought it had been. It hadn't all been wonderful. Far from it. But it had been *real*. She had never felt so alive as during those turbulent hours.

"What are you going to do?" Lucas asked her.

"Do you still want me to marry you?"

"For our son's sake, yes."

"Will you be a good, loving father to Tony?"

"I swear it."

It was the hardest thing she had ever had to ask another person, but she met his pale gray eyes steadily. "And to me? What kind of husband can I expect you to be?"

"You are the mother of my son. I'll treat you with the respect that deserves."

"You have frightened me on numerous occasions. I don't want to live in fear of you."

"I would never harm you. I swear it on the body of my grandfather, Joseph Greywolf."

What a bizarre proposal, Aislinn thought. Like most women, she had imagined candlelight and roses, wine and soft music, a full moon and professions of undying love. She smiled weakly and with self-derision. Oh, well, one couldn't have it all.

She had just closed the door on everything that was safe and familiar. There would be no going back. And besides, Lucas wasn't going to give up his son. He had made that perfectly clear.

It would be a loveless marriage, save for their common love for Tony. There was no love in her life now anyway, so it wouldn't be missed. Life with Lucas and Tony wouldn't be just an endless series of days, made monotonous by their sameness. It would at least hold some surprises.

Her eyes were steadfast as she looked up at him. Without further hesitation she said, "All right, Lucas Greywolf. I'll marry you."

She did, two days later at nine o'clock in the morning in a civil ceremony in the same courthouse where Lucas Greywolf had been found guilty of his alleged crimes almost four years before.

The bride held her baby on her shoulder as she recited the vows that legally bound her to a man who was little more than a stranger. She hadn't known what would be suitable to wear, but had finally decided on a peach-colored linen suit with a pleated skirt and unstructured jacket. Beneath the jacket was an ivory lawn shell so sheer that her lacy camisole showed through. The outfit was soft and feminine without being flagrantly bridal.

She held one side of her hair back with an ivory comb, an antique bequeathed her by her paternal grandmother. That was her "something old." She had chosen blue panties, not wanting to thumb her nose at tradition altogether.

Lucas had surprised her by wearing dark slacks and a sport coat over a pale-blue dress shirt and a sedate necktie. He looked incredibly handsome with his long, dark hair brushed away from his face and lying against his collar. Side by side, she knew they made a striking couple. Heads had turned to look at them when they entered the courthouse.

Before she even realized that the vows had been solemnized, the ceremony was over and they were leaving the building. Lucas had given her a light, perfunctory kiss when the judge had pronounced them man and wife. Now his hand rode loosely beneath her elbow as he guided her toward his parked pickup truck. It was at least a decade old. "We'll go load up the things you've packed, then get on our way."

He had told her the day before that he wanted to have the ceremony—though the few minutes they had spent in the judge's chambers hardly qualified as such—early, so they could reach their destination before nightfall. He wanted to waste no more time getting back to the reservation.

At her condo, while she changed Tony and herself into more comfortable traveling clothes, Lucas loaded the things she had set aside to take with them into the bed of the pickup. As she went through the rooms of the condo one last time, she couldn't conjure up an iota of regret for leaving it.

It had been a residence, not a home. No sentiment had been attached to anything. The only thing she hated to leave was the nursery she had prepared for Tony. Love had been poured into that room.

"Got everything?" Lucas asked her as she entered the living room from the back of the house after making sure all the lights had been turned out.

"I think so."

He had changed clothes, too. He was wearing the same shirt, but the sleeves had been rolled to his elbows. His slacks had been replaced with jeans, his dress shoes with boots, and there was a bandanna tied around his forehead. He hadn't worn the earring that morning, but he had it on now.

They locked the doors behind them, having agreed that for the time being they would leave her furniture there until they decided on the best way to dispose of it and the property. Knowing her husband might be sensitive about such things, she offered to leave her car in the garage. How much of a sacrifice that was soon became apparent.

"This damn thing isn't air conditioned," Lucas said of the truck. They were on the highway and the wind was wreaking havoc on Aislinn's hair. Tony rode in his carrier, which they had secured between them on the seat. He was protected by a light blanket. It was too hot to keep the windows rolled up. But it was a constant battle for Aislinn to keep her hair out of her face. She hadn't complained, but Lucas had noticed.

"It's not so bad," she lied.

"Open the glove compartment," he said. She did. Inside she found a variety of items. "Get that extra bandanna and tie it around your hair. That will keep it from blowing so much."

She removed the bandanna from the glove compartment and neatly folded it into a triangle, then into a narrow band. She twisted it before securing it around her head. Leaning forward, she checked her reflection in the rearview mirror. "Does this officially make me a squaw?"

She looked at him and smiled. At first he didn't know what to make of her question, but when he saw the teasing light in her blue eyes, he answered her smile with one of his own. It was slow in coming, almost as if his lips didn't remember how to form a smile. But at last it broke across his handsome face, relieving it of its foreboding austerity. He even gave a short laugh.

After that, the tension between them eased somewhat. Little by little, she drew him out. They exchanged stories about their childhoods, some funny, some painful. "In a way, I was as lonely as you," Aislinn said.

"After meeting your parents I can believe that."

"They don't have near the capacity to love that your mother does."

He only glanced at her and nodded.

As anxious as he was to get home, he consulted her frequently about stopping to rest, eat or drink. "We'll have to stop soon," she said shortly after noon. "Tony is waking up and he'll want to be fed."

He had been a perfect angel, sleeping in his carrier. But he woke up hungry and impatient for his lunch. By the time they reached the next town, his strenuous wails were echoing in the cab of the pickup.

"Where should I stop?" Lucas asked her.

"We can keep driving. I'll manage."

"No, you'd be more comfortable if we stop. Just say where."

"I don't know," she replied, gnawing her lip anxiously. She didn't want Tony's crying to aggravate Lucas. He might yet change his mind about wanting to be a parent. What if he quickly got tired of the everyday hassles?

"A rest room?" he suggested, his eyes scanning the buildings on the main street.

"I hate to take him into a public place when he's putting up such a fuss."

Lucas finally wheeled the truck into a municipal park. He found a private spot beneath a shade tree and parked. "How's this?"

"Fine." Aislinn hastily unbuttoned her blouse, adjusted her bra and positioned Tony against her breast. His cries ceased abruptly. "Whew," she said, laughing, "I don't know if we could have gone . . ."

Her sentence trailed off to nothingness because she had innocently lifted her gaze from her son's flushed face and looked up at his father. Lucas was staring down at his nursing son. The intensity on his face stopped whatever Aislinn was about to say. When he saw that she was watching him, his eyes flickered away to stare through the windshield.

"Are you hungry?" he asked.

"Sort of."

"How about a hamburger from a drive-through window?"

"That's fine. Anything."

"As soon as Tony is, uh, taken care of, we'll find a place."

"Okay."

"Did I hurt you?"

She raised her head and looked at him. He was still staring through the windshield. "When, Lucas?"

"You know when. That morning."

"No." Her denial was so soft even her own ears could barely detect it.

He tapped the steering wheel with his fist. He wagged one knee back and forth in a steady rhythm. His eyes darted over the landscape. In any other man these symptoms would have indicated nervousness. But that was unthinkable. Lucas Greywolf didn't get nervous. Did he?

"I had been in prison—"

"I know."

"And without a woman."

"I understand."

"I was rough."

"Not too—"

"And later I got to worrying about it. That maybe I had hurt you . . . your breasts . . . or your . . ."

"No, you didn't."

"You were so damn small—"

"It had been a while."

"And . . . and tight . . . and I—"

"It wasn't rape, Lucas."

His head snapped around. "You could have claimed that it was."

"But it wasn't."

The messages their eyes telegraphed to each other were laden with things better left unsaid. Aislinn bowed her head and closed her eyes as waves of heat, having nothing to do with the still, summer day, surged through her. Even now she could feel the driving thrusts of his body into hers.

And Lucas shut his ears to the delicious sound of his son nursing at her breast. He remembered his own lips tugging at her nipples, hard and peaked with arousal. His tongue had circled them, nudged them, stroked...

God, don't think about it or you'll get hard.

"When did you first know you were pregnant?" he asked gruffly after a long moment.

"About two months later."

"Were you sick?"

"A little. Tired more than anything. I didn't have any energy. And I had stopped having..."

"Oh. Yeah."

From the corner of his eye, he saw her gently lift Tony from one breast and transfer him to the other. She was modest. He knew what this enforced intimacy must be costing her. Yet, he wanted to reach across the seat, spread her blouse open and gaze at this marvel of nature. He wanted to look at her breasts. He yearned to touch them. To taste. Her femininity filled him—his nose, his throat, his loins. He was inundated with the scent and sight and sound of woman and he wanted to stay immersed in it for a long time.

"Was it an easy pregnancy?"

"As far as pregnancies go," she said with a smile.

"Did he kick a lot?"

"Like a soccer player."

"I prefer to think of him as a marathon runner."

Their eyes met across the narrow distance. The look they exchanged was mellow. What passed between them was the shared dream of parents for their child. "Yes. Like a marathoner," she agreed softly. "Like you."

His heart swelled with pride. Emotion welled so high inside his chest that for several seconds he could barely breathe. "Thank you." She looked at him inquiringly. "For carrying my son."

Then it was Aislinn's turn to become embarrassingly emotional. Thanks didn't come easily to a man with Greywolf's pride. To have made an issue of it would ruin the moment, so she merely nodded her head.

She gave Tony her attention until he was finished, then she passed the baby to Lucas. He held him while Aislinn readjusted her clothing. He even assisted as she changed Tony's diaper.

They said nothing more. Enough had been said.

"Gene's here," Lucas remarked as he pulled the pickup to a stop in front of a tiny, neat, white stucco house. Its fenced front yard was well manicured. A porch light burned in welcome. Zinnias bloomed in flower beds on either side of the front sidewalk.

It was well after dark. They had been driving on the reservation for hours, though this time they hadn't had to use back roads as they had when Lucas was a fugitive. Still, their trip had been long and tiring. Aislinn was exhausted. "Are we staying here tonight?" she asked hopefully.

"No, we'll stop and say hello. But I'm anxious to get to my own land."

His own land? She didn't know he had any land. Until then, she hadn't even thought to ask how he intended to support Tony and her since he couldn't practice law anymore. Somehow she wasn't worried about it. Greywolf had proven to be resourceful, intuitive, and capable. She had no doubts that he would make life as comfortable for his son as possible.

Lucas came around and helped her out of the truck. For the first time, she felt a twinge of apprehension. What if Alice Greywolf and Dr. Dexter reacted to the baby the same way her parents had? She was more an outsider here than Lucas was in her world. How would she be received?

Lucas seemed to have no such qualms. He jogged up the sidewalk and jumped onto the porch. He rapped on the front door twice before Gene Dexter pulled it open.

"Well, it's about time. Alice has been—"

When the doctor saw Aislinn coming up the sidewalk, his welcoming speech was cut short.

"Gene, is it Lucas?" Alice called from inside the house. "Lucas?" She stepped around Gene, her face wreathed in smiles. "Oh, you're here! We've been worried. Why didn't you come straight home? Did you decide to stay a few days in Phoenix?"

Lucas stepped aside. When Alice's eyes fell on Aislinn, they widened as prettily as a doe's. When she saw the baby nestled in Aislinn's arms, her mouth formed a small O. "I think you'd better come in out of the night air."

Aislinn knew then that she would come to love Alice Greywolf. No questions. No recriminations. No censure. Just gracious, unqualified acceptance.

Lucas held the screen door open for Aislinn and Tony. She stepped into a living room that was simply but tastefully furnished.

"Mother, Gene, you remember Aislinn."

"Of course," Gene said.

"Hello."

Alice smiled at her and asked shyly, "May I see the baby?"

Aislinn turned Tony so that he could be seen easily. Alice gasped softly. Tears filled her eyes as she reached out and touched the dark down on his head. "Lucas," she breathed.

"Anthony Joseph," Lucas proudly corrected her. "My son."

"Oh, yes, I know he's your son." Alice clamped her small, white teeth over her lower lip to keep from laughing and crying at the same time. "He looks just like you. Gene, did you see him? Isn't he wonderful? Anthony Joseph. After father." She looked at Aislinn with tear-sparkled eyes. "Thank you."

"I...we...call him Tony. Would you like to hold him?"

Alice hesitated for only a moment before opening her arms to receive the child. For years she had been taking care of newborns at the clinic, but she handled Tony so carefully he might have been made of porcelain. Her eyes never left him as she carried him to the sofa and sat down, crooning a Navaho lullaby.

"Guess that leaves me to take over as host," Gene said, finally thinking to shut the front door to preserve the air conditioning. "Aislinn, come in and have a seat," he said, sweeping his arm wide to indicate the living room.

"We got married today," Lucas said bluntly, almost as though he expected to be challenged.

"Well that's...that's great," Gene said dubiously.

Again the situation could have been awkward if Alice hadn't intervened. "Please sit down, all of you," she urged. "I'll get you something to eat and drink shortly. But I want just a few minutes with Tony."

"Don't go to any trouble, Mother. We can't stay long."

"You're leaving? But you just got here."

"I want to get out to the place before it gets any later."

Alice looked at her son with disbelief. "Out to the place? You mean to that *trailer*?"

"Yes."

"With Aislinn and Tony?"

"Of course."

"But you can't move them into that trailer. It's too small. It hasn't even been cleaned, and—"

"Alice," Gene said with gentle reproach.

She fell silent immediately. She glanced at Lucas and Aislinn uneasily. "It's none of my business, I realize, but I hoped you'd spend a few days here with me before moving out there."

Lucas looked down at Aislinn. She hadn't offered an opinion and he knew she wouldn't. God, she was courageous. When the occasion called for it, she was as steady as a rock. He had admired that in her from the beginning. But he could see the rings of fatigue beneath her eyes and the weary stoop of her shoulders. "All right. One night," he conceded, surprising himself.

"Oh, I'm so glad," Alice said. "Here, Aislinn, take the baby. I've been keeping some food warm on the outside chance that Lucas would show up tonight."

"I'll help you," Aislinn offered.

"You don't have to."

"But I want to."

Gene and Lucas followed them from the room. At the door, Lucas caught Gene's arm. "We're not putting you out of a bed tonight, are we?" he asked beneath his breath.

"Unfortunately no," Gene said ruefully.

"Still?"

The doctor shook his head sadly. "Still. Your mother is a rare woman, Lucas. I don't intend to give up on her until she is my wife."

Lucas slapped him on the back. "Good. She needs you."

As they entered the kitchen, he was thinking how rare a woman he was married to. That's why his eyes sought out Aislinn immediately.

She caught his glance and looked back at him shyly. This was a family scene, and yet it wasn't. Her new married status would take some getting used to. Yet she was inordinately pleased when Lucas sat down next to her.

"Lucas, why didn't you tell me about the baby?" Alice asked a half-hour later as she carried their supper dishes to the sink.

The significant pause broadened into a lengthy, uncomfortable silence. Aislinn finally broke it with her confession. "He didn't know about the baby. Not until he came to my house three days ago to thank me for not pressing any charges against him." She tried to meet the startled gazes of Lucas's mother and friend, but found that she didn't have the courage and lowered her eyes.

"I forced her to marry me," Lucas said with characteristic candor. "I threatened to take Tony away from her if she didn't."

Gene shifted uncomfortably in his chair. Alice raised her hand to her lips, hoping her shock wasn't too evident. At last she said, "I'm very glad to have you as my daughter-in-law, Aislinn."

"Thank you," Aislinn said, smiling at the older woman. She knew that Alice and the doctor must be burning with curiosity, so she appreciated their restraint from asking further questions.

"You must be tired after the long drive," Alice said kindly. "Why don't you let me get you settled for the night? You can sleep in my room."

"No." Before anyone could move, Lucas paralyzed them all with that single word. "Aislinn is my wife. She sleeps with me."

Chapter 9

The resulting silence was terrible. Gene stared into his coffee cup and fidgeted in his chair. Alice studied her hands, composed but embarrassed. Aislinn's eyes were riveted to the top of Tony's head while color rose high in her cheeks. Only Lucas seemed unaffected by his bold declaration.

"Do you need anything out of the truck?" he asked, scraping his chair away from the table and standing.

"The small suitcase and Tony's bag," Aislinn replied in a low voice.

"Mother, can you fashion Tony a crib out of a drawer or something?"

"Yes of course. Come on, Aislinn," Alice said, laying a hand on the girl's shoulder. "Let's get Tony settled for the night."

"I'll help Lucas." Gene seemed grateful for something to do. He followed Lucas from the kitchen.

The bedroom into which Alice led Aislinn was small, having room for only an old-fashioned vanity table with a padded stool, a chest of drawers, a nightstand, and a double bed.

"These drawers are empty," Alice said, taking one out of the chest of drawers. "I cleaned everything out after Father died."

"I didn't have time . . . before . . . to tell you how sorry I was," Aislinn said.

"Thank you. It was inevitable. He was old. He didn't want to linger for years in a hospital or nursing home. It happened just as he wanted it to. There, do you think that will work?"

While they were talking, she had lined the bottom of the drawer with a quilt, folding it several times in order to make it fit and to form soft bedding for the baby.

"That will be fine. For now. In another month or two he'll be kicking the sides out." Aislinn hugged Tony affectionately and kissed his temple.

"Oh, by then I'll have bought a crib. I'm counting on you to bring him to see me often."

"You don't mind about Lucas and me?" Her eyes shyly sought Alice's.

"Maybe I should be asking *you* that. Do *you* mind about Lucas and you?"

"At first, yes, very much. Now, I don't know," she said honestly. "We hardly know each other, but we both love Tony. The quality of his life is extremely important to us. On that basis, we might make the marriage work."

"Life out there on the ranch will be far different from what you're accustomed to."

"I was sick to death of the life I was accustomed to, even before I met Lucas."

"It won't be easy for you, Aislinn."

"Nothing worthwhile is."

The two women stared at each other, the younger with determination, the other with skepticism. "Let's make up the bed," Alice suggested quietly.

Once the clean sheets had been smoothed over the bed, Aislinn realized how narrow it was. How would she get through the night sleeping there with Lucas? He had come into the bedroom to deposit the bags she had requested from the truck, but had immediately gone out again. She could hear him conversing with Gene in the living room.

"I'd better leave so you can get some rest," Alice said. "Besides, if I don't say a special good-night to Gene, he might think I've deserted him in favor of Tony." She leaned down to kiss the baby who was lying contentedly in the makeshift crib. Before she left, she took Aislinn's hand. "I'm very glad to have you in the family."

"Even though I'm an Anglo?"

"Unlike my son, I don't harbor a grudge against a race for what a few have done."

Without thinking about it, Aislinn kissed her new mother-in-law on the cheek. "Good night, Alice. Thank you for your kindness to Tony and me."

When she was alone, Aislinn fed the baby, hoping he would sleep straight through till morning and not disturb Lucas. She rushed him along, hoping she could get done with the nursing before Lucas came in. She wanted to spare herself another scene like the one earlier in the pickup.

There was only one bathroom in the house. It was located in the hallway between the two bedrooms. Aislinn took her turn as soon as she put Tony to bed. When she came back into the bedroom, there was nothing left to do but get undressed.

Officially this was her wedding night, yet the nightgown she took from her suitcase wasn't exactly bridal. This was its second summer season, and though it was soft and the fabric sheer against the light, its modest, scooped, elasticized neckline wasn't sexually enticing. In fact it looked rather dowdy and plain.

She was sitting at the vanity table, smoothing lotion on her arms when Lucas came in and closed the door behind him. Aislinn fumbled with the bottle of lotion. She told herself that her clumsiness was due to the fact that her hands were slippery and not because she was facing a night alone in a bedroom with Lucas Greywolf.

Had she been looking at herself in the mirror rather than at her husband, she would have seen that her eyes were wide and apprehensive. They made her appear very young and innocent. In contrast, her hair fell around her shoulders seductively. Her lips were soft and dewy and naturally rosy. The nightgown looked maidenly. The total package, especially seen through the eyes of a bridegroom, was sexy.

The lamp on the nightstand was turned down low. The shadow that Lucas cast onto the walls and ceiling was long and ominous in the small, square room.

"Is Tony asleep yet?" he asked, his hands going to the buttons of his shirt.

"Yes. I don't think he minds sleeping in a bureau drawer at all."

In the mirror, Aislinn saw Lucas smile as he bent over the drawer, which she had placed on the floor near the side of the bed. Her heart fluttered at the way his face softened when he looked at his son. It would be very easy to fall in love with a man who could feel that kind of tenderness for a woman.

Mentally she jerked herself erect. Tender emotions like that would be foreign to most of the men she knew. For Greywolf, they would be impossible. As though to sweep the ridiculous musings from her mind, she picked up her hairbrush and began pulling it through her hair, though it already crackled with life.

Lucas sat down on the edge of the bed and tugged off his boots, dropping them to the floor. "Gene told me tonight that he's glad we got married."

It was so unlike him to initiate a seemingly innocuous conversation that her arms fell still and she looked at his reflection in the mirror. "Why?"

He chuckled. Another phenomenon. "He's been trying to get my mother to marry him for years. He made her promise she would when I got out of prison." He stood up and unbuckled his belt. "Our getting married was his ace in the hole. Now she really doesn't have any excuses left."

"He seems like such a dear, kind man. How can she help but want to marry a man like him?"

"A man so unlike *your* husband."

She was laying the hairbrush aside, but at his words, her eyes swung up to meet his in the mirror. "I didn't mean it that way."

"It doesn't matter what you meant. I'm the husband you've got."

She swallowed a knot of apprehension as he came toward her with a stalking, sauntering gait. He epitomized a confident male animal on the scent of a female. He had stripped down to his jeans. The fly was unbuttoned. Aislinn's eyes unerringly went to that narrow V that yawned open just below his navel. Her heart leaped with a mixture of desire and trepidation.

In the dim lighting, his skin took on a deep copper hue. His dark body hair was limned with golden light, especially that which spun around his navel. His cheeks were shaded by the drastic projection of his cheekbones, which were striped now with the long shadows of his eyelashes.

His gray eyes were trained on her like an eagle's on weakened prey. They seemed to penetrate the layers of her skin and see straight inside her. His look was hot. It seared her, but she shivered.

"Lucas?"

"You have beautiful hair."

He came to stand directly behind her, putting her shoulders on a level with his hips. Against the brown expanse of his hard stomach, her hair looked incredibly fair. It rippled like golden threads in his hands when he lifted bunches of it off her shoulders. Idly he let the heavy strands sift through his fingers.

Aislinn was entranced by the sensuous sight. And even though it was happening to her, she forced herself to become strictly an observer, to pretend that it was happening to someone else. That was the only way she could survive it.

Otherwise, when he spread a handful of her hair over his belly and rubbed it around and around like lather, her heart would have drummed its way out of her body.

If she let herself admit that she was actually participating in such a visually erotic act, she might turn around and kiss that taut stomach. She might treat her lips to a journey around the thin slit of his navel and down that strip of jet-black hair that fanned wide in the opening of his jeans. She might dampen that hair with soft, kittenish licks.

He let her hair fall back to her shoulders and closed his hands loosely around her neck. His fingers strummed it lightly. "Why does your white skin appeal to me so much?" he asked raspily. "I want to hate it."

He touched her earlobes, feathered them with the pads of his fingers, softly pinched them between his thumbs and index fingers. She made a whimpering sound. Against her will, her neck gave way and her head landed against the hard plane of his stomach behind her. Mindlessly, she rolled her head from one side to the other. She watched her hair swish across his dark skin and thought that, together, they were very beautiful.

His hands coasted over her shoulders and slipped beneath the lacy elastic top of her gown. Her eyes, which had been half-closed, opened and met his in the mirror.

"I want to see my hands on you," he said.

She watched, hypnotized, as his strong, tapering, widespread fingers slid down her chest. No protest broke across her lips when they moved lower, taking the gown down with them. Her breath rushed into her lungs when his palms slid down over her breasts. He pressed. He massaged. He rubbed.

Her body responded.

He cupped the undersides of her fully aroused breasts and lifted them, lightly whisking the crests with his thumbs. She moaned, grinding the back of her head into his belly, which was rising and falling with each of his rapid breaths.

Their eyes never wavered from the mirror. They were mesmerized by the contrast of his large hands, such testimonies to his masculinity, moving over the soft, velvety mounds of her breasts. He knew just how much pressure to apply to give her optimum sensation. His fingers played delicately with the dusky tips until they throbbed with a pleasurable pain.

Deep inside her, another ache was becoming unbearable. Her womanhood felt feverish and heavy as it flowered to readiness. Only one thing could ease that special kind of ache.

And that was impossible.

The realization struck Aislinn suddenly and she threw off his hands. Springing off the stool, she pulled her nightgown up over her breasts and, turning to face him, said "I can't."

The sound that emanated from his throat was that of an attacking mountain cat. He gripped the upper part of her arms and yanked her hard against him. "You're my wife."

"But not your possession," she flared. "Let me go."

"I'm entitled."

He tunneled his fingers through her hair, pressed them against her scalp and drew her face beneath his. Reflexively she reached up to ward him off. Her hands landed on either side of his torso, just under his arms. His skin was smooth and warm. The muscles were so hard they begged to be explored and admired. She wanted to sink her teeth into them. Her determination wavered.

But this wasn't right. They were married, yes. With that marriage license came certain privileges, yes. But shouldn't love be involved? And if not love, at least mutual respect? She knew that Lucas had only contempt for what she was and where she had come from. She refused to be merely a vessel for his lust.

And even if the wrongness of it weren't enough of a reason to discourage him, there was the other. Since it was the most expedient, that's the reason she would use.

A heartbeat before his mouth ravished hers, she said, "Think, Lucas! Tony is barely a month old." He paused. She saw his gray eyes blink with misapprehension, so she hurriedly clarified her point. "You asked me today if you had hurt me before, and I said you hadn't. That was the truth. But if you . . . if we . . . do this, you could hurt me. I haven't had time to completely heal."

He stared down into her face, his hot breath striking her in steady pants. When he had finally digested what she was telling him, he glanced down toward her middle.

Gradually his grip on her arms relaxed and he set her away from him. Nervously she wet her lips with her tongue. "For christsake don't do that," he growled. He ran his fingers through his hair, then covered his face with both hands. He pressed his fingers deep into his eye-sockets before slowly dragging his hands down his cheeks. "Get into bed."

She didn't argue. After quickly checking on Tony to make certain he was sleeping soundly, she slid between Alice Greywolf's sunshine-smelling sheets and pulled the top one over her. The air conditioning even required the light blanket.

She closed her eyes, but knew when Lucas peeled down his jeans and stepped out of them. Through the screen of her lashes, she saw his nakedness. Long limbs. Wide chest. A shadowy triangle between powerful thighs. And

an aroused virility. Then the room was pitched into
darkness when he switched out the lamp.

All she could think about as he lay down beside her
was that he was naked and that he was hard. Though they
didn't touch at any point, she could feel his body heat. It
scorched her skin. The rhythm of his breathing both
electrified and soothed. She held her body rigid until his
weight shifted and she knew that he had turned away
from her.

Only then did she relax enough to eventually fall
asleep.

Her eyes drifted open to meet the pinkish-gray, pre-
dawn light. Her breasts were full. Tony had slept through
the night without a feeding, but he would be waking up
soon. She hoped so. Her discomfort had awakened her
from a sound sleep.

She lifted her eyelids a fraction more and was alarmed
to see how close to her Lucas was lying. His chest was
scant inches from her nose. She could count each crinkly
hair. Secretly she thanked his father for giving Lucas
enough Anglo blood to have a beard and chest hair.

The bed covers were folded back to his waist. His
smooth, dark skin looked touchable beneath the rumpled white sheet. She longed to lay her hand in the valley
of his waist. But, of course, she didn't.

Lying perfectly still, she let her eyes wander up his
tanned throat to the proud chin. His lips were beautifully shaped, if a bit stern. His nose was long and
straight, not flat and wide like many Apaches'. Again she
blessed his father's seed.

She gasped softly when her eyes lifted to his and found
them steadily watching her. His hair looked very black
against the snowy pillowcase. "What are you doing
awake?" she whispered.

"Habit." Only an act of will kept her from flinching
when he raised one of his hands and picked a wavy strand

of hair from her cheek. Looking at it analytically, he rubbed it between his fingers. At length, he laid it with unwarranted care on her pillow. "However, it has not been my habit of recent years to wake up with a woman lying beside me. You smell good."

"Thank you."

Another man might have asked, "What perfume are you wearing?" or said, "I like your fragrance." But her husband was a man of few words. His compliments weren't lavish, but they expressed exactly what he wanted to say. "You smell good." She cherished the simple compliment.

He touched her. His fingers explored lightly, with the inhibited curiosity of a child allowed in the formal living room for the first time. Eyebrows. Nose. Mouth. He gazed at what he touched.

He glided his fingers back and forth across her throat and chest. "So soft," he said, as though marveling over the texture of her skin.

With one fluid movement of his arm he threw the covers off. She willed herself to lie still when he pulled her gown down. This was her husband. She couldn't withhold herself from him. And she discovered that she didn't want to.

He wouldn't hurt her. She knew that. If he were a truly violent man he could have hurt her so many times in the past. She remembered his gentleness when he tended the scratch on her arm. Besides, he had sworn he would never harm her, and she believed him. So she lay perfectly still while his eyes devoured her breasts and his finger traced a vein that rivered toward her nipple.

She saw his jaw bunch with tension. For a brief second, he looked directly into her eyes before he leaned forward and pressed his open mouth to her neck. Moaning low, he inched closer, until her breasts were touching his chest.

His lips sipped at her skin, nipping at it lightly with his teeth. She felt the brush of his tongue, soft and wet and warm. It took every ounce of willpower at her disposal not to dig her hands into his hair and hold his head against her. He was exercising such self-restraint that she dared not move. It would be cruel to instigate something that couldn't be satisfactorily finished.

His mouth moved lower, touching her damply, taking exquisitely gentle love-bites. He raised his head slightly and looked down at her laden breasts. "If I...? Would your milk come?" He looked at her. She nodded.

A spasm of regret flickered across his mouth. He leaned away from her and paused for a moment before easing the gown down farther. He looked at her. At everything.

His eyes fastened on her womanhood. He touched the golden cloud of hair. He started breathing heavily, rapidly. Indeed, since the covers had been thrown back, the strength of his desire was no secret.

Suddenly his hand clamped her wrist. Alarmed by the abrupt movement, she raised questioning eyes to his. "You're my wife," he grated. "I won't be denied."

Before she realized his intent, he dragged her hand down, below his waist, and opened it over himself. Pressing. Her lips parted in an effort to protest, but his were there to seal hers closed and the words were left unspoken. His tongue plunged deep, filling her mouth.

He rolled her to her back and straddled her thighs. Their hands were trapped between their bodies, locked in the cove of her femininity and grinding against his manhood. He used his hand to maneuver hers, keeping her fingers tightly closed around him. Her palm provided the friction.

What happened then was so personal, so heart- and soul- and gut-wrenching that they both quaked under the tumult of it.

It lasted forever.

Finally, he rested his head on her breasts. His breathing was labored. She could feel his fingers moving mindlessly through her hair, as though reaching for something greatly desired, but elusive and just beyond his grasp.

Then abruptly, he rolled off the bed and came to his feet. He picked up the articles of his clothing with jerky movements and pulled them on haphazardly and angrily. He shoved his feet into his boots and, without so much as a backward glance, flung open the door and walked out.

Aislinn was dismayed and heartsick. She lay there staring at the door through which he had passed, grieved that he couldn't even look at her after what had happened. To her it had been beautiful. When his mouth had softened, when his tongue had ceased to be aggressive, he needn't have forced her to caress him. Though she doubted he realized that.

The immensity of the act had left her weak and trembling. It had left him angry. Had he been ashamed? Embarrassed? Disgusted? With himself or with her?

Or had he been as shattered by the impact of it as she? And, like her, was he bewildered as to how to deal with his feelings about it?

Both of them had survived childhood by keeping their emotions hidden. She had been taught by her parents to do so. Because of the scorn he had suffered as a child, Lucas kept his emotions carefully guarded to protect himself from hurt. He didn't know how to demonstrate affection and tenderness. He was even less adept at accepting them.

Aislinn knew then. She loved Lucas Greywolf.

And if it took her from now until her dying day, she would make him accept her love.

It wasn't going to be easy. She realized that the moment she entered the kitchen a half-hour later. Lucas was sitting at the table talking with Alice, sipping coffee and eating a stack of pancakes. He ignored Aislinn completely.

It was ironic that her penchant to stare at him coincided with his avoidance of her at all costs. While Aislinn's heart was stormy with awakened love, his eyes were as turbulent as a thundercloud. Through breakfast, their departure from Alice, and their drive to Lucas's ranch, he remained practically mute.

He provided monosyllabic answers to the questions she posed. Each inroad she made toward conversation met with a dead end. While her eyes wanted to gobble up the sight of him, he wouldn't make direct eye contact with her. She was amiable; he was querulous.

Once, after they had driven miles with Tony sleeping in his carrier between them, Lucas whipped his head around and demanded, "What the hell are you staring at?"

"You."

"Well, don't."

"Because it makes you nervous?"

"Because I don't like it."

"There's nothing else to look at."

"Give the scenery a try."

"When did you get your ear pierced?"

"Years ago."

"Why?"

"I wanted to."

"On you I like it."

His eyes left the road for another brief moment. "On me?" he sneered. "Meaning that it's okay for a man to have a pierced ear if he happens to be an Indian."

Aislinn bit back a retort. Instead she responded with a softly spoken, "No, meaning that on you I find it very attractive." His stern expression faltered for a split second before he returned his concentration to the two-lane highway that was taking them into the higher elevations of the White Mountains. "I have pierced ears, too. Maybe we can swap earrings."

Her attempt at humor fell flat. If he heard her, he gave no evidence of it. She thought he was going to ignore her entirely. But after a minute or two he said, "I only wear this one earring."

"Does it have special significance?"

"My grandfather made it."

"Joseph Greywolf was a silversmith?"

"That was just one of his talents." There was a defensive edge to his voice as sharp as a double-edged sword. It couldn't have held more challenge if he had said *"En garde."* "Do you find it hard to believe that an Indian could have several skills?"

Again, she held back a rejoinder. Curbing her temper this time was more difficult, but she forced herself to control it. She understood that he was only being nasty because he was mortified over what had happened in bed that morning.

He had revealed a weakness to her, and he found that untenable. Underneath that implacable facade, Lucas Greywolf was an extremely sensitive man. He had the same needs and desires for love as any human being. Only he didn't want anyone to know it.

His hostility was a defense mechanism. He was punishing himself for being a bastard, for being a hardship on his teenaged mother, even for being Indian. He was so hard on himself he had served a prison sentence for a crime he didn't commit. Aislinn wouldn't be satisfied until she uncovered each injury in his soul and healed it with her love.

"You didn't tell me you had some land. I know, I know," she rushed to add, holding up both palms, "I didn't ask. Will I always have to ask to get information out of you?"

"I'll tell you what I think you need to know."

Her mouth fell open in dismay over such outrageous chauvinism. "You think a woman should be seen and not heard, is that it?" she cried. "Well, think again, Mr. Greywolf, because Mrs. Greywolf intends to be an equal partner in this marriage, and if you didn't want it like that, then maybe you shouldn't have been so hasty to force Ms. Andrews into marrying you."

He flexed his fingers around the steering wheel. "What do you want to know?" he asked tightly.

Somewhat mollified, she settled back against the seat of the pickup truck. "Did you inherit the land from your grandfather?"

"Yes."

"Were we there . . . before?"

"You mean at the hogan? Yes. It was just over that ridge," he said, hitching his chin in that direction.

"Was?"

"I had it burned."

That stunned her, and for several minutes she said nothing. Then she asked, "How large is your ranch?"

"We're not rich if that's what you're asking," he said with injured scorn.

"That wasn't what I asked at all. I asked how much land you own."

He told her and she was surprised and impressed. "That's what was left after the swindlers got to my grandfather. Uranium was found on his property, but grandfather never profited from it."

To save them a heated discussion on the exploitation of Indians, especially when she was already on his side of that argument, she asked, "What kind of ranch is it? Cattle?"

"Horses."

She pondered that for a moment. "I don't understand, Lucas. Why did your grandfather die in poverty if he had that much land and a herd of horses?"

Apparently she struck a cord. Lucas glanced at her uneasily. "Joseph was very proud. He thought things should be done according to tradition."

"In other words," she paraphrased, "he didn't advance to modern ranching techniques."

"Something like that," he mumbled.

It was endearing to her that Lucas defended his late grandfather, even though he apparently hadn't agreed with him on how the ranch should be run.

The rest of the trip was spent in silence. She knew they were getting close to their destination when he turned off the highway, drove through a gate and onto a dirt road.

"Will we be there soon?" she asked.

He nodded. "Don't expect much."

As it turned out, what they saw when they arrived surprised Lucas more than it did Aislinn. "What the hell?" he muttered as the pickup chugged up the last hill.

Aislinn's eyes darted around the clearing, trying to take in everything at once. Admonishing herself for behaving like a kid at her first circus, she slowed her eyes down and tried to digest everything she saw.

The compound was set between two low hills that formed a horseshoe. On one side of the open area there was a large corral. Two men on horseback were leading a small herd of horses through the gate. A barn, obviously old and weathered, was nestled against the mountainside.

On the other side of the semicircle, stood a house trailer. Its paint was chipped and faded, and it looked about ready to collapse upon itself.

Right in the center of this land harbor was a stucco house. Because of its color, it blended into the rock wall that rose almost perpendicular behind it. The house was well suited to its environment.

It was also a beehive of activity. Men were shouting to one another. The ring of a hammer echoed off the surrounding rock walls. From somewhere as yet undetermined, Aislinn could hear the high, shrill whirring of a buzz saw.

Lucas braked the pickup and got out. A man, dressed in cowboy garb, separated himself from the others who were working on the house. He waved and came jogging toward them. He was shorter and much stockier than Lucas and had the bowlegged, rolling walk of a man who spends a lot of time on horseback.

"Johnny, what the hell is going on?" Lucas said in lieu of a proper hello.

"We're getting your house finished for you."

"I was going to live in the trailer until I could get enough money together to finish the house."

"So now you won't have to," Johnny said, his black eyes twinkling jovially. "Hello, by the way. It's good to have you back." He shook Lucas's hand. But Lucas, still staring over his friend's shoulder up toward the house, barely noticed.

"I can't pay for any of this."

"You've already paid."

"What the hell does that mean? Does my mother know about this?"

"Yeah, but she was sworn to secrecy. We've been working on the house since we found out the date of your release, trying to get it finished before you got here. Thanks for giving us the few extra days."

Johnny was distracted as he spoke. Now he gazed openly at the blond woman who had gotten out of the pickup. She moved to stand at Lucas's side, holding a baby against her shoulder. The child's head was covered with a light blanket to protect it from the glaring sun. "Hi."

Lucas turned, noticing Aislinn for the first time. "Oh, Johnny Deerinwater, this is my, uh, wife."

"I'm Aislinn," she said, sticking out her hand.

In friendly fashion, Johnny Deerinwater shook her hand and swept off his straw cowboy hat. "Pleased to meet you. Alice told us Lucas had gotten married. The sonofa...gun was going to keep you a secret from his friends, I guess."

"Mother must have called you this morning."

"Yeah. She said you'd just left on your way here. As I said, we've been working on the house for several weeks, but we had to get our...uh, rears in gear when we heard this morning that you were bringing a wife and baby with you. Speaking of which, why don't we get them out of the sun?"

Johnny stepped aside, indicating to Aislinn that she should precede him up the path toward the house. She was conscious of the workmen's eyes as they followed her progress. When she ventured to smile at several of them, they returned her smiles with varying degrees of shyness and suspicion.

As Lucas and Johnny fell into step behind her, Johnny said, "Since Joseph died, we've all pitched in to keep the herd fed, but that's about all. The horses were scattered to kingdom come. We've been rounding them up for weeks. Not all of them are accounted for yet."

"I'll find them," Lucas said.

Aislinn stepped onto the low, wide front porch of the house and, because she didn't know what else to do, entered the front door. The smell of fresh paint and raw lumber was almost overpowering, but not unpleasant. She pivoted, taking in the white walls that added to the spacious feel of the house. There were windows on every available wall, naked beams in the ceilings, and quarry tile floors that gave the rooms unity. In the main room there was a hugh fireplace. She could imagine a glowing, cheery, crackling fire on a cold evening.

She gazed at Lucas in wonderment, but he seemed as surprised by the house as she. "When I left, there was nothing here but bare walls," he remarked. "Who's responsible for this, Johnny?"

"Well, Alice and I got to talking over a cup of coffee one day," he said, wiping his perspiring forehead with a bandanna. "We decided that we'd call in a few of your debts from people who owed you for legal services. Instead of collecting money, we collected favors. For instance, Walter Kincaid did the tile work. Pete Deleon did the plumbing." He went through a list of names, enumerating what each of Lucas's debtors had contributed to the house.

"Some of the fixtures and appliances are second-hand, Mrs. Greywolf," he said apologetically, "but they've been cleaned up good as new."

"Everything looks marvelous," Aislinn said, looking down at the beautiful, handwoven Navaho rug someone's grandmother had made for Lucas. "Thank you for everything, and please call me Aislinn."

He nodded, smiling. "The only furniture we could round up was a dinette set for the kitchen. This morning we got busy and found a, uh, bed." His dark cheeks flushed hotly with embarrassment.

"I have some furniture we can move up here," Aislinn said quickly, to relieve Johnny's bashfulness. Lucas gave her a sharp look, but said nothing. For that she was grateful. She didn't want to get in a row with him in front of his friends. Their marriage might not be conventional, but she didn't want that fact advertised.

"Linda, that's my wife, will be up later this afternoon to bring some groceries."

"I'll look forward to meeting her."

A truck rumbled to a halt outside. Johnny went to the door and looked out. "Here are the light fixtures we ordered."

"I can't pay for any of this," Lucas repeated stubbornly, his face set.

"You've got good credit." Johnny gave Aislinn a smile and left, bounding off the front porch, already calling orders.

"Maybe you'd better show me where the bedroom is," Aislinn ventured, "so I can lay Tony down."

"I'm not sure I know myself," Lucas said crossly. "This house was just a shell when I left it."

"Where were you living?" Aislinn asked, following him down the hallway. "In the trailer?"

"Yes. I'd been building this house for several years, taking it one step at a time whenever I could get some money together."

"I like it," she said, stepping into the room that was obviously the largest bedroom. It had a wide window that provided a view of the mountains.

"You don't have to say that."

"I mean it."

"Compared to that fancy condo you were living in, this is a slum."

"It is not! I'll decorate it and—"

"You can forget moving any of your furniture up here," he said, pointing his index finger at her.

She slapped it aside. "Why? Because you're too damn proud to use anything belonging to your wife? Didn't Indians barter with their prospective fathers-in-law for their wives?"

"Only in John Wayne movies."

"Consider this my dowry, which, whether you want to admit it or not, I know was a matter of pride to Indian women."

"I can provide for my family."

"I don't doubt that, Lucas. I never have."

"I'll buy furniture as soon as I sell some horses."

"But in the meantime, would you have your son sleeping on the floor?"

At the mention of Tony, Lucas glanced down at the baby. Aislinn had laid him on the wide bed the moment they entered the room. He was awake and looking around curiously, as though sensing he was in new surroundings.

Lucas bent over him and stroked his face with his index finger. Tony opened one of his waving fists and grabbed his father's finger, instinctively pulling it toward his mouth. Lucas laughed softly.

"You see, Lucas," Aislinn whispered, "whether you want to accept it or not, there are people who love you."

He gave her one of his most chilling stares before he swung around and stamped from the room.

Chapter 10

The next few weeks brought about miraculous changes in their lives. Lucas's friends, under Johnny Deerinwater's friendly supervision, finished the inside of the house. It wasn't fancy by any stretch of the imagination, but it was comfortable. Aislinn used her good taste and decorating skills, elbow grease and paint, until the stucco house looked like a magazine model home.

As soon as the telephone was installed, she called Scottsdale and made arrangements for her furniture to be moved to her new house. She itemized the pieces she wanted, including her washing machine and dryer, and double-checked the list with the moving company.

The van arrived several days later. As the furniture was being unloaded, Lucas rode up on horseback and deftly slid from the saddle. The first time Aislinn had seen him sitting astride a horse, he had taken her breath away he was so handsome. She liked him in his faded denim jeans, Western shirts, boots, hat and leather work-gloves. Often she paused from a household chore to watch him from a window as he went about his work outside.

Now, however, when he rode his horse right up to the porch before dismounting, she was made breathless by the angry expression on his face.

His spurs jingled as he crossed the porch, patently furious. "I told you not to send for this stuff," he said in a threateningly low voice.

"No you didn't." Despite his glower, she faced him squarely.

"We're not going to argue about this, Aislinn. Tell them to load it back up and return it to Scottsdale where it belongs, I don't need your charity."

"I'm not doing this for you. Or even for me."

"Well, Tony can't sit on a sofa yet," he said snidely, thinking she was going to use their baby as a lever to get her way.

"I'm doing it for Alice."

His face went comically blank. "My mother?"

"Yes, she's consented to hold her wedding reception here. Would you embarrass her by having her guests sit on the floor after all the sacrifices she's made for you?"

A vein ticked in his temple. She had him cornered. Worse, he knew she knew she had him cornered. And while he wanted to admire her cunning and congratulate her for being a worthy adversary, she was still his wife and he was so angry he could throttle her.

He glared at her for a count of ten, then turned on his spurred boot-heels, stamped off the porch and remounted his horse. He kicked up quite a cloud of dust as he rode out of the yard.

Aislinn worked all afternoon arranging the furniture, moving the pieces herself, no matter how heavy. Amazingly, the furniture looked custom-made for the house. She had always liked a Southwestern motif. When she had decorated her condo, that's what she had selected. But the furniture looked even better in this house, its desert tones accented by the native accessories that Lucas's friends had sent as housewarming gifts.

By late afternoon she was exhausted, but as consolation for their argument that morning, she cooked an especially good meal. Her kitchen lacked some of the amenities she was accustomed to, but made up for its deficiencies with space.

Tony was no help on this day when she particularly wanted to please her husband. The baby was cranky and cried fitfully, though she couldn't find any reason for it. While she was keeping dinner warm in the oven, she took a quick bath and made herself attractive as possible for Lucas's return.

She didn't chastise him for being hours late when he finally came in well after dark. "Would you like a beer, Lucas?"

"Sounds good," he said sullenly, taking off his boots at the back door. "I'm going to take a shower." Without a word of thanks, he took the opened can of beer from her hand and carried it with him to the back of the house. Had he turned around, even he might have laughed at the ogre's face she made at his back.

When he returned to the kitchen, she had dinner set on the table, which was covered now with one of her tablecloths and set with her dishes and cutlery.

He didn't say a word either about that or any of the other furnishings as he sat down and began to eat, virtually shoveling the food into his mouth. "What's that noise?" he asked after a moment.

"The washing machine."

"Washing machine?"

"Uh-huh. And the dryer," she said breezily. "Tony goes through so many clothes. It will be such a relief not to have to drive into town every few days to the laundromat. I was dreading those trips this winter, carrying Tony out in the cold."

Just as she had expected, Lucas glanced at Tony. She had set the baby's carrier on the table where he could hear their voices and be a part of the mealtime activity. Lucas seemed to weigh the advantages of having a washing machine and dryer under his roof and said nothing more.

One of the knots in Aislinn's chest eased considerably. "Having the nursery set up again is going to be wonderful," she ventured as she spooned another helping of potatoes onto Lucas's plate. "I won't have to worry about him rolling off the edge of something. Have you noticed how active he's getting?" She blotted her mouth with her napkin and coyly lowered her lashes over her eyes. "And he won't have to sleep between us anymore."

She saw Lucas hesitate as he raised his fork to his mouth. He chewed and swallowed that bite, then pushed his plate away. "I've got work to do." He left the table abruptly.

"But I made a pie for dessert."

"Maybe later."

Crestfallen, she watched his broad shoulders disappear through the doorway. She supposed she should be glad that they hadn't engaged in a battle royal over the furniture, but she was disappointed that he was so anxious to leave the table and her company, especially when she had just broached the subject of their sleeping arrangements.

Since they had moved into the house, Tony had, out of necessity, been sleeping in the bed with them. But Aislinn doubted that his tiny presence was the reason Lucas hadn't touched her since that morning at Alice's house. If they weren't in open dispute over something, he treated her with indifference. Rarely, if ever, did he look at her. When he did, it certainly wasn't with smoldering desire.

Not that she wanted him, she averred, as she readied Tony for bed. Still, the house was miles from their nearest neighbor. The nights were lonely. Lucas usually left right after a hurried breakfast. Often she wouldn't see him again until he came in for dinner. With only Tony for company all day, she looked forward to conversation with another adult. But Lucas remained taciturn.

She had grown up in a house where she had been discouraged from voicing an opinion or expressing herself. She didn't intend to live the rest of her life shrouded in silence. Stubbornly she decided to take the bull by the horns and not let Mr. Greywolf get away with his sulking.

She left Tony to sleep in his crib for the first time in weeks. A half-hour later, she carried a tray into the living room. Lucas was sitting on the sofa with papers spread out around him and spilling over onto the coffee table. He was making notes in a black notebook.

Aislinn went unnoticed until she switched on a lamp at his elbow. He raised his head and looked up at her. "Thanks."

"That should help you see better. How can you read without a light?"

"I didn't notice."

She thought he probably didn't want to use "her" lamp even though he was sitting on "her" sofa, but she refrained from commenting. "I brought your pie and fresh coffee," she said. She had set the tray on the end table.

"What kind?"

"Kind?"

"Of pie."

"Apple. Do you like apple?"

"I learned not to be too choosy in prison."

"Then why did you ask?" she snapped.

Ignoring her, he scarfed down the slice of pie in record time. She chided herself for not being more conscientious about his sweet tooth. Apparently it hadn't been satisfied in a long time. From now on she would see to it that every meal included dessert.

When he finished with his pie, he set the plate aside and bent back over his paperwork. "Is that ranching business?" she asked.

"No, a court record. My client..." he paused on the term, because he actually couldn't have clients any longer, "he, uh, wants to know if he should appeal the outcome of a lawsuit."

"Should he?"

"I think so."

She watched him make another brief notation in his tablet, then said, "Lucas, I want to talk to you."

He laid his tablet and pen aside and reached for his cooling coffee. "What about?"

She sat in the corner of the sofa and tucked her feet underneath her hips. "I had my camera equipment sent up with the furniture. I'm anxious to start using it again."

Fiddling with the fringe on a throw pillow, she drew a deep breath. "And I was wondering what you would think of my converting the old trailer into a darkroom."

His eyes swiveled toward her and she rushed on before he could say anything. "It wouldn't take much redoing. The sink is already there, in the kitchen area. I could do most of the work myself. Think how convenient it would be to take pictures of Tony and have them developed right away, as many prints as we wanted. And I could make enlargements and—"

"I'm not a fool, Aislinn." That was the first time he had addressed her by name in days and both were aware of it. Before they had time to reflect on it, however, he went on. "Making that trailer into a darkroom is hardly worth the effort just to have pictures of Tony readily available. What else did you have in mind?"

"I want to work, Lucas. Running the house doesn't keep me busy enough."

"You have a child."

"A very good one, whom I love and adore and enjoy taking care of and playing with. But he doesn't require my every waking moment. I need something to do."

"So you want to take pictures."

"Yes."

"Of what?"

This was the tricky part. The tallest hurdle. The one she had most dreaded. "Of the reservation and the people who live on it."

"No."

"Listen. Please. Before I saw it for myself, I had no idea of the—"

"Poverty," he said harshly.

"Yes and the—"

"Squalor."

"That, too, but the—"

"Prevalence of alcoholism. And despair. And the sense of utter hopelessness." He had surged to his feet and was now angrily pacing the area in front of the sofa.

"I guess that's it," she said softly. "The hopelessness. But maybe if I captured some of that on film, and my work got published—"

"It wouldn't help," he said curtly.

"It wouldn't hurt either." She sprang up, angry that he had squelched her idea without even hearing her out. "I want to do this Lucas."

"And dirty your Anglo hands?"

"You're an Anglo, too!"

"I didn't ask to be," he shouted.

"All the rest of us are monsters, is that it? Why is it you never ridicule Gene's work on the reservation?"

"Because he's not some grandstanding, bleeding-heart liberal doing us all a big favor."

"And you think I am?"

"Don't you think your charity would be a trifle hypocritical?"

"How?"

"Living like this," he said, waving his arms to include their house, made so much prettier and more comfortable by her contributions to it. "I have always despised Indians who profited off other Indians. Their skin is brown, but they forget that and live like Anglos. And now you've made me one of them."

"That's not true, Lucas. No one would ever mistake you for anything but what you are." He had turned his back on her. Now she caught his arm and spun him around. "You work damn hard at being Indian. Short of painting your face and going on the warpath, you do everything you can to let everyone know you're a big, bad Indian brave right through to the marrow of your bones, despite your Anglo blood. Or maybe because of it."

She paused for breath, but continued, warmed now to the subject. "You've taught me how mistaken I was. Until now, I thought Indian braves had hearts and souls and compassion as well as courage and daring." She poked him in the chest with her index finger. "Those you will never have, Lucas Greywolf. You have no compassion because to you that's a sign of weakness. Well I think bullheadedness is more of a weakness than tenderness. I doubt you even know what it is."

"I can feel tenderness," he said defensively.

"Oh really? Well I'm your *wife* and I've never seen any evidence of it."

She landed against him before she even realized that he had moved and drawn her forward. His arm curved around her waist while his other hand cupped the side of her face. He tilted it until her other cheek almost touched his shoulder.

Then he bent his head low and impressed a soft kiss on her lips. His mouth moved. Her lips parted. The intrusion of his tongue into her mouth was so gentle and sweet, so deliciously sexy, that she shivered. Where before his kisses had been characterized by violence, this one was exquisitely tender.

The kiss lengthened and became an outright act of love. He used his tongue to stroke the roof of her mouth. He explored and enticed until she was weakly clutching handfuls of his shirt in her hands.

When he finally lifted his mouth from hers, he buried his face in the fragrant hollow between her shoulder and neck. "I don't want you," he groaned. "I don't."

She rubbed against him. The lower part of his body unequivocally denied his words. "Yes, you do, Lucas. Yes, you do!"

She imbedded her fingers in his hair and lifted his head. She ran one finger over his sleek eyebrow, along the ridge of his cheekbone, and down his nose. She outlined his mouth. "You could never be a traitor to your people, Lucas."

The touch of her fingertip on his lips made him weak. The scent of her body filled his head and made him forget the stench of despair that permeated certain areas of the reservation. The sight of ill-dressed children was replaced by the desire he saw in her slumberous blue eyes. He could no longer taste the bitterness that kept him strong and resolute. All he could taste was Aislinn, the honey of her mouth.

She was the most dangerous of enemies because her ammunition was her allure. Her softness seduced him. What he felt deep in his gut at that moment terrified him. He used the weapon most readily at his disposal. It was also the most hurtful. His scorn.

"I'm already a traitor. I have an Anglo wife."

Aislinn recoiled as though he had struck her. She stepped away from him, her eyes glazed now with pain. To prevent him from seeing her tears, she turned and ran into the bedroom, slamming the door behind her.

When Lucas came in almost an hour later, she pretended to be asleep. They no longer had Tony serving as a buffer between them. But hostility was there, as sturdy as a brick wall, to keep them separated.

Antagonism continued to seethe between them. On the day Dr. Gene Dexter married Alice Greywolf, Aislinn did her best to put on a good front, pretending that her relationship with Lucas was nothing short of blissful. The wedding decorations weren't extravagant, but there was a distinct party atmosphere in the house. All the guests had a good time. Aislinn had been trained to give good parties. She was a gay, gracious hostess and seemingly enjoyed herself.

The bride wasn't fooled.

"I can't believe you're finally my wife."

Gene and Alice had driven to Santa Fe for their honeymoon. Now, as he held her tenderly, stroking her straight black hair, he couldn't quite believe that his dreams had finally become a reality.

"The church looked beautiful, didn't it?" she asked him.

"*You* looked beautiful. But then you always do."

"Aislinn went to too much trouble over the reception. I wasn't expecting anything so lavish."

"She's a lovely girl," Gene murmured absently as he kissed Alice's velvety cheek.

"Tony seemed fretful."

"Aislinn told me he'd been crying more than usual. I recommended that she bring him in for a checkup when we get back."

"They're unhappy, Gene."

His arms fell to his sides and he sighed heavily. "I didn't know that we had brought Lucas and Aislinn along on our honeymoon."

"Oh, Gene," Alice said, wrapping her arms around his waist and hugging him tight. She laid her cheek against his chest. He had removed his suit coat as soon as the hotel bellman left the room, but they were both still fully clothed. "Forgive me. I'm sorry. I know I shouldn't be worrying about them, but I can't just shut my mind off. Aislinn looks like she's walking a tightrope and Lucas looks—"

"Like a keg of dynamite about to explode," Gene finished for her. "He's more truculent than ever. I've never seen him so brooding and angry." He laughed softly into her hair. "Personally, I think it's a good sign."

"How?" she lifted her head to ask.

He ran a finger along her jaw. "If she didn't disturb him so much, he wouldn't be so touchy and defensive. I think the lady is getting to him in a way no one else ever has. That scares hell out of the fearless Lucas Greywolf."

"Do you think Aislinn loves him?"

"Yes. Undoubtedly. I've done some checking on her father. Willard Andrews is on about every board of governors and chairs about every committee in Scottsdale. A woman of her means, whose father holds that kind of position in the community, could have fought one lone Indian and won hands down. I don't care what he threatened her with, she didn't have to marry your son. Yes, I think she loves him."

"And what about Lucas. Does he love her?"

Gene's brow furrowed as he thought back on the reception brunch held in honor of Alice and him. Every time he had looked at Lucas, Lucas had been looking at Aislinn. And not just casually looking, but watching her with total concentration, oblivious to what was going on around him.

Now that he thought about it, Gene remembered Aislinn carrying a heavy bowl of punch to the buffet table she had set up in the living room. He had seen Lucas rush forward, as though to relieve her of it. But Lucas had stopped short of reaching her, suddenly changing his mind.

And while they had been saying their goodbyes, Gene would bet Lucas's mind hadn't been on his mother and her new husband. The young man had seemed captivated by his wife. His whole body had looked stiff, as though he was physically restraining himself from touching her as she waved goodbye, laughing and calling out good wishes, her blond hair blowing against Lucas's shoulder.

"In my professional opinion, he's got a touch of lovesickness," Gene said now, in answer to Alice's question. "He might not know he loves her yet. Or if he does, he doesn't want to admit it, especially to himself."

"I want them to be happy."

"I want *us* to be happy. Do you know what would make me deliriously happy right now?" He tipped her head back with his knuckle beneath her chin and kissed her, tenderly at first, then with mounting passion. His arms slid around her waist and drew her up against him. "Alice, Alice," he moaned when he finally lifted his lips from hers. "I've waited so long for this. I can't remember when I didn't want you, when I didn't ache for Alice Greywolf."

"Alice Dexter," she whispered shyly.

He took that as her way of saying that she shared his love and desire. He reached for the back buttons of her simple, apricot linen dress. Ruffles and lace would have swallowed a woman as petite as Alice. For adornment she wore only a pair of gold earrings, the gold chain he had given her last Christmas, and the slender gold wedding band that now encircled her finger.

When all the buttons were undone, he eased the dress forward. "I'm not young anymore, Gene," she said tremulously. "I'm a grandmother."

He only smiled and pulled the dress off her shoulders. His gasp and the shudder that ran through him testified to his delight in her body. She was small, trim, perfect. Her ecru lingerie was alluring without being overtly sexy.

It suited the woman who was wearing it. She was modest but had a latent sensuality waiting to be kindled.

He adored his bride.

Holding her gently and kissing away her nervous shyness, he removed the rest of her clothing. Lifting her in his arms, he carried her to the bed and laid her down. She kept her eyes closed while he undressed.

Then he came to her, gathered her in his arms, and held her body close to his while sheer ecstasy, as sweet and thick as honey, rivered through him. She was trembling.

"Alice," he whispered, "don't be afraid. For as long as you want, I'm content to just hold you. I know you're frightened and I know why. But I swear to you and to God that I would never do anything to hurt you."

"I know that, Gene. I do. It's just that it's been so long and—"

"I know. You don't have to say any more. Nothing will happen until you want it to." He held her protectively, commanding his body to hold itself in check. He knew he must practise infinite patience with this woman who was worthy of being cherished.

Eventually she relaxed and he felt encouraged enough to stroke her caressingly. Her skin was satiny smooth, yet vibrant. She had the body of a woman twenty years younger. He worshipped the breasts that were still high and round and firm. When he touched her there, she moaned, but after one quick glance at her face, he knew it was out of pleasure and not out of fear. The lips that kissed the dusky crests were as soft as a spring rain.

He wooed her that way, alternately arousing and soothing, until he knew she was ready. And then the loving was achingly sweet, exquisitely tender, and in the end, wildly passionate.

Later, holding her against him, he sighed into her hair. "If I had had to wait another twenty years for you, Alice Greywolf Dexter, you would have been worth it."

"And you, Gene," she said, kissing his chest. "And you, my love."

Lucas closed the barn door and latched it. This might be his mother's wedding day, but on a ranch the work never ended. As soon as all the guests had departed, he had changed clothes and put in a full day's work. He was tired, having had to get up early that morning and drive into town for the wedding.

Tomorrow a buyer was coming to look at some of his horses. He'd spent all day grooming them. If they brought a good price, which he planned on demanding, maybe he would have enough money to hire a ranch hand.

Perhaps his being disbarred had worked out for the best after all. He doubted that he could run a ranch and a law office at the same time. He loved the land and the herd because they had belonged to his grandfather. He liked working outdoors. He didn't even mind the long hours.

But he missed practicing law. He had always enjoyed a good fight. When he had matured to the point of knowing that brawling never solved anything, the courtroom provided him an arena. He had been an excellent courtroom gladiator. He missed the legal skirmishes and the satisfaction of having done his best whether he won the case or not.

He peeled off his shirt and went to the outdoor faucet on the foundation of the house. He sluiced water over his head, his neck, shoulders, arms and chest, rinsing off the top layer of dust and sweat.

Every time he thought about the kindness of friends like Johnny Deerinwater, he got a lump in his throat. Without them he wouldn't have the house. It would have taken him years to finish it in his spare time, not to mention the money it would have cost. He and Aislinn—

Damn! He hated it when his mind automatically paired them together. Aislinn and I. Aislinn and me. We. Us. He didn't ever like thinking of them as a unit, yet his brain stubbornly continued to.

Fuming over the mental slip, he rounded the corner of the house. If he had walked into a wall, he couldn't have come to a more abrupt standstill. He was standing only a few yards from their open bedroom window. Aislinn walked past it. He could hear her humming and see her shadow gliding across the walls as she moved about the room.

That rectangular patch of light looked inviting in the darkness that surrounded the house. It beckoned him as a lighthouse does a sailor. It represented all things warm and cozy and comfortable. Home. He was hypnotized by that open window. He couldn't force himself to move away from it, even though he supposed that this was an invasion of Aislinn's privacy. *Would you stop thinking like a damn fool? The woman is your wife.*

Still, he felt just a little ashamed of his window-peeping. Especially when she stepped into full view again. Especially when she began to undress.

He stood stock-still in the deep shadows, not moving so much as an eyelash.

Lucas watched her unbutton the cuff on the sleeve of her sheer blouse. Much as he hadn't wanted to notice, he had to admit that she had looked beautiful that day. The blouse she had worn was cut like a man's shirt, except that the sleeves were much fuller and the cuffs much wider. The tips of the collar reached far down on her chest.

The blouse had small pearl buttons. As she bent over the ones on her cuff, her hair fell forward in a golden cascade. He wanted nothing more then than to bury his face in the stuff, to feel its cool silken movement against his skin. He already knew what it felt like against his belly. What about his thighs? His—

Sonofabitch! Don't even think about that.

When she pulled her blouse off, which she did with a provocative lack of haste, he had an unrestricted view of the lingerie that had teased him all day. Held up by spaghetti-thin straps, it was lacy and feminine and cupped her full breasts as if it adored them. They swelled over the top of it, creamy and enticing in the lamplight. God, he wanted to taste her there. The camisole wasn't sheer enough to see through, since it had obviously been designed to show beneath the blouse. But even from this distance, Lucas imagined he could see the dark centers of her breasts through it. He imagined his mouth there, too.

The skirt she had worn was the color of the eastern sky just before daybreak. It was made of a rustling fabric that had driven him into a fine madness all day as it moved against her body. He held his breath as she reached behind her to unbutton it. It seemed to take forever. Then the skirt slithered past her hips, over her thighs, and down her legs, which were encased in pale stockings.

He cursed beneath his breath and ran his damp palms up and down his thighs. The camisole was a one-piece affair. Lacy suspenders held up her stockings, which he had supposed were panty hose. Between the top of the stockings and the teddy, her thighs looked as soft and warm as velvet. He imagined himself— Damn! What was he doing out here lusting after his own wife like some pervert? If he wanted her so badly, and his body was insisting that ''badly'' didn't even come close to describing how much he wanted her, why didn't he just go in there and take her? She belonged to him, didn't she? They were legally bound and he was entitled to conjugal rights, wasn't he?

So move, damn you. Go in there and take what is yours for the taking.

But he didn't, because he knew it would be too risky. If he could take her dispassionately, then he would use her body to rid his of this raging fever. It would be over and done with and he wouldn't even think about it until the next time he got in this condition.

No, it wouldn't be like that at all. She had bewitched him, that's what she had done. Somehow she had wormed her way into his mind and heart, and what he was thinking and feeling somehow interfered with what his body wanted. His sex couldn't participate without his head getting involved.

He kept remembering that morning on the mountaintop. She had climbed up there to offer him comfort when she sure as hell had had every reason to be fleeing from him. He remembered what her face had looked like as his body moved inside hers.

And at the most inopportune times, when he wanted to feel his bitterest toward her, he thought about her bearing his child and how lovingly she treated Tony. Then, too, there were the generous things she did for him, like keeping the coffee in his cup warm even when he hadn't asked for refills. And the way she was sometimes waiting on the porch for him when he came riding in after working long hours. She always smiled, as though she was glad to see him.

What puzzled him was why she treated him with such consideration and kindness. He couldn't figure out what her motive was. She had every reason to hate him. If she would just demonstrate resentment instead of understanding, then life would be a helluva lot easier. They might even have some rowdy sex every once in a while to let off steam and clear the air. As it was, his blood simmered.

Looking at her through the window now, he felt his blood heating to a full boil. She was no longer standing in full view, but he could tell by watching her shadow on the wall that she was removing her stockings. She lifted one foot to the edge of the bed, unhooked the garter and rolled the stocking over her knee and calf and ankle, peeling it off her foot with studied leisure. She performed the ritual on the other leg.

He stared transfixed when she shrugged the straps of the teddy off her shoulders and shimmied until it slipped down. She stepped out of it gracefully, and when she straightened, her shadow was in profile. Everything was perfectly, painfully silhouetted.

Lucas mouthed a series of scalding obscenities.

Why wouldn't she give him a fight? Huh? Did she feel sorry for him? Was that it? Or did she feel obligated to be an exemplary wife? Well, by God, he didn't need her largess.

He moved then, spinning around on his heels and stalking toward the rear of the house. He slammed through the back door, barely remembering to lock it behind him, before he stamped through the house, viciously turning off lights as he went. By the time he barged through the bedroom door, he was good and mad.

"Just what the hell do you think you're doing?" he roared.

Aislinn looked up at him with innocent, blue-eyed, wide-eyed dismay, which made her look even more guiltless than she already did. She was sitting in the rocking chair. A madonna. Blond hair rippling over her shoulders. One side of her nightgown was open. Tony nursed contentedly at her breast.

"I'm nursing Tony," she answered simply.

Lucas, standing braced in the doorway by his arms, was spoiling for a fight. Shirtless, the recently washed skin on his chest gleamed in the lamplight. The dark hairs were damp and curly. The cross dangling from his neck caught the light and shone almost as brightly as his eyes.

The joke was on him. Feeling like a fool, he dragged his eyes away from his wife and glanced toward the bed. The teddy and stockings lay spread out there like me-

mentos of an indolent afternoon of loving. They enflamed him all over again.

"Next time, you might think twice before parading around half naked in front of an open window with the light on."

"I don't know what you mean, Lucas."

Pointing toward the window with a finger shaking with rage, he blustered, "The window, dammit, the window. Don't undress in front of the window."

"Oh," she said, following the direction of his finger. "I didn't think about it."

"Yeah, well, think about it from now on, okay?"

"But there wasn't anyone out there to see me."

"I was!" he shouted. "I could see you all the way from the barn."

"You could?"

"Hell yes, I could."

"But you're my husband."

There was just a trace of mockery in her voice, but it was so slight that he was afraid to challenge her on it. He was ready for hand-to-hand combat, but he couldn't handle a contest of wits. He had never felt more witless in his life. Nor so out of control. In an entirely different way, she looked just as tempting now as she had a few moments before, doing her guileless striptease in front of the window. Blood pounded in his head and in his sex.

"I'm going to take a shower," he said quickly and left the room before he disgraced himself further.

When he left the bathroom, Aislinn was in the other bedroom, bending over Tony's crib. "Let me hold him a minute," Lucas said. He had calmed down considerably. He was still wet. Drops of water clung to his teak-colored skin. He was naked save for a towel that cut a swath across his loins and looked much like the breech-cloths his ancestors had worn. He looked primitive and dangerous except for the lambency in his eyes when he lifted his son and held him close to his face. He murmured Navaho love pledges he remembered from his childhood and kissed Tony's cheek before laying him in the crib. The child fell asleep instantly.

"He looks so peaceful now," Aislinn said with a tired sigh. "I wish he'd sleep till morning. I'm exhausted."

"Why is he waking up so much lately?"

"I don't know. Gene's going to give him a checkup when they get back. Oh, I almost forgot about this," she said as they entered their bedroom. She picked up an envelope that was lying on the dresser and handed it to him. "This came in the mail for you today."

He studied the envelope for several moments before tearing it open. Aislinn feigned disinterest, though she was consumed by curiosity. The return address was the warden's office of the prison camp where Lucas had been incarcerated.

After he read it, Lucas refolded the letter and stuffed it back in the envelope. His face gave away nothing and Aislinn couldn't stand not knowing. "Is it something important?"

He shrugged negligently. "Warden Dixon thinks I should be exonerated. He thinks he knows the men responsible for the violence that broke out at that demonstration. They've been convicted and sentenced for similar crimes. If he can get them to sign affidavits as to my innocence, he thinks he can get a judge to have me vindicated."

"Lucas, that's wonderful!" she cried. "That would mean you could be reinstated to the bar."

He whipped the towel from around his waist and got into bed. "I've learned not to trust anybody's promises. Especially an Anglo's."

She got into bed beside him. His harsh words hadn't fooled her. She had seen his face a second before he switched off the light. He might pretend to be nonchalant over this unexpected ray of hope. But he wasn't.

Chapter 11

She had learned where the worst chuckholes were and how to avoid them. Recently Johnny and Linda Deerinwater had gone to Scottsdale and offered to drive her car back when they returned. She and Lucas's pickup had never had a meeting of the minds, so driving her car again was a pleasure.

Today she barely noticed the pitching and rolling as she drove her car up the uneven road toward home. She was happy on several accounts, and when Lucas came riding up on a roan gelding to meet her and Tony, that was an extra bonus. She braked the car and lifted Tony out of his safety seat, just as Lucas swung his long leg over the saddle and dismounted.

"You were gone longer than I expected," he said.

Could that mean he was worried about her, she wondered. Or was he concerned only for Tony? She wanted to think she was included. "Gene's clinic was overflowing. There's a virus going around. He and Alice had their hands full."

"How are they?"

She grinned, her blue eyes glinting mischievously. "Positively glowing. I've always thought your mother was beautiful, but wait until you see her now. She's radiant. And Gene wears a perpetually sappy grin."

Lucas smiled and chucked Tony under the chin. He was holding the reins of his horse in his free hand. "What did Gene say about Tony?"

"He has a slight cold. Actually Gene called it an upper respiratory something-or-other. He gave him a liquid decongestant that should take care of it in a few days."

"Is that why he's been crying so much?"

"Not solely. There's something else."

"What?" he asked, his brow beetling.

"Tony is hungry."

"Hungry?"

"Yes," Aislinn said, blushing under the tan she had acquired. "He's not getting enough milk. Gene suggested that I switch him to formula and start him on fruit and cereal."

Lucas shifted from one booted foot to another. "So you won't be, uh, breast-feeding him anymore?" Aislinn kept her eyes trained on the buttons of his shirt as she shook her head. "How do you feel about that?" he asked.

"I'll miss it. But of course I want to do what's best for Tony."

"Of course."

"I stopped at the grocery store and bought bottles and cans of formula and baby food."

"One little baby can eat all that?" he asked incredulously.

She followed the direction of his gaze into the back seat of her car and laughed when she noticed the cartons stashed there. "Only part of it. Most of those boxes contain the chemicals I had ordered. They were waiting for me at the post office.''

"Will your darkroom be operable now?"

"Yes. All I needed were the chemicals." She had taken his silence on the subject of the darkroom as consent and had proceeded to convert the kitchen area of the derelict trailer.

Much to her surprise she had come out of the house one morning to find Lucas painting the trailer. Before she even posed the question, he said querulously, "This paint was left over from the house. No sense in letting it go to waste." Besides giving it the paint job, he had done some repairs that made the portable building more habitable.

"I won't be able to process color film," she told him now, "but I can do black and white. I thought I'd start with the snapshots I took at the wedding reception. If they're good, I'll give enlarged prints to Gene and Alice. I invited them to come to dinner soon."

"Good."

"And I took some pictures in town today. You know that housing area where the conditions are so bad?"

He nodded grimly. "All too well."

"There were some little girls playing beneath a clothesline. I think I got some good stuff, but it will take me a while to get back into practice."

"What did you do with Tony?"

"He was on my back in the sling carrier." She smiled up at her husband. "Just like a good little papoose."

His mouth twitched with the need to smile. He held it back as long as he could, but it overpowered his stubbornness and the remote face broke into a wide grin that dazzled his wife. His teeth were straight and white, a brilliant contrast to his dark face.

"I don't want the grandson of a chief to turn into a mama's boy. Give him to me."

He lifted the baby out of Aislinn's arms and turned toward the horse, which was still standing by docilely. "Lucas, what are you doing? Lucas, you're not—"

"It's past time that Anthony Joseph Greywolf had a horseback-riding lesson."

"Don't you dare!" Aislinn cried.

Heedless of her protests, Lucas cradled the child in his right arm. Using his left hand to grasp the pommel, he pulled himself into the saddle. With one smooth motion he and Tony were sitting on the horse. Tony was waving his hands happily.

"Lucas, give me that baby before you break both your necks," Aislinn said sternly. Unconsciously, she laid both hands on Lucas's hard thigh to forestall him.

He grinned down at her teasingly. "Shall we race to the house?"

"Lucas!"

He wheeled the gelding around and nudged it with his knees. The horse cantered off. Aislinn propped her hands on her hips and glared after him with exasperation. Most of it was faked. Actually her heart had never been so full of love.

For several days after she had weaned Tony, she was uncomfortable and he was cranky. But he learned to like the pre-mixed formula. He was a creative eater, splattering her, Lucas, and anything within yards of him with mushy cereal and strained fruit, but he gobbled up the food greedily and soon Aislinn could tell he was gaining weight.

Lucas received another letter from Warden Dixon. He had been in consultation with a judge and was making progress toward having Lucas vindicated. Aislinn took heart; Lucas kept his feelings on the subject to himself.

Due to his hard work, the ranch was prospering. From the hills surrounding the ranch, he had rounded up an impressive herd of horses that wore the Greywolf brand, but that had strayed since old Joseph's death. Several of the mares were pregnant. Those that weren't were artificially inseminated, a practice his grandfather had resisted.

The Greywolfs were fortunate to have a stream that flowed out of the mountains across one corner of their land. Water was the most valued commodity. Joseph had never sold water rights as a matter of principle, but Lucas was of the mind that what was good for one was good for all. There were several small ranchers, Indian and Anglo alike, who were now paying for the use of Greywolf water.

Nor did Lucas allow himself to become attached to the horses to the point of not being able to sell them, as his grandfather had. Customers who bought Greywolf horses got their money's worth. Lucas was a fair but shrewd dealer.

Aislinn spent a few hours every day in the trailer in her darkroom. She always took Tony with her, placing him in a playpen she had bought in a secondhand store. After she painted the slats and furnished it with a new pad, it looked as good as new.

One afternoon she was working in the darkroom, experimenting with different techniques, when she heard the distant rumble of thunder. At first she paid no attention to it. Her ears were trained to pick up any sound Tony made, but to tune out other distractions.

The thunder became louder, and she realized that a storm was fast approaching. Wending her way through the dark curtains surrounding the nucleus of her darkroom, she stepped into what had previously been the living area of the trailer.

Tony lay asleep in the playpen. Aislinn was alarmed by how late it had gotten, but when she consulted her watch, she saw that it was only the middle of the afternoon, not nearly as late as the darkness indicated.

She went to the door of the trailer and looked out the small diamond-shaped window. Dark clouds were brewing over the mountains. Her first thought was for Lucas. He had left on horseback early that morning, saying he was going to ride up into the higher elevations to see if he could locate any more strays. Not liking the looks of the weather, she hoped he would return soon.

The wind was picking up. Dust was swirling in the wide yard between the trailer and the house. She decided to wait for Lucas before she tried carrying Tony and all his paraphernalia back to the house. Besides, the storm would probably blow over in a few minutes.

After checking on the baby again, she went back into the darkroom and became engrossed in her work. It took a jolt, literally, to rouse her. The trailer swayed as a gust of wind socked it like a mighty fist. Aislinn heard Tony whimper. Hurriedly, she left the darkroom. The trailer was lit by a ghostly, greenish light.

Tony began to cry. Aislinn rushed toward the door and opened it. The wind tore it from her hand, and it went crashing against the exterior wall of the trailer. Raindrops pricked her exposed skin like needles as she stepped out onto the concrete steps and reached for the door. Hailstones pelleted her. Within seconds the ground was white, covered with them.

"Oh, God," she cried, straining with all her might to pull the door closed against the wind. Inky black clouds boiled overhead. The sky was completely blocked out by the low clouds, which looked as opaque as a velvet curtain. Jagged forks of lightning struck the ground, dancing and popping, before disappearing again into the clouds. Thunder roared so loudly that she could hardly hear Tony's piteous cries over the racket.

She finally got the door closed and latched, though it had required all her strength. Crouched over with fatigue, she practically crawled to the playpen and lifted Tony out. She didn't realize her clothes were wet until she held him against her. Her hair was plastered to her skull and dripping onto the child.

"Shh, shh, Tony, everything will be all right," she crooned, wishing she believed it herself.

Where is Lucas?

She squeezed her eyes shut as she envisioned him wandering lost in the storm, with the wind and rain and hail beating against him unmercifully.

Each time a fresh gust of wind buffeted the trailer, she feared it would overturn and she and Tony would be crushed. She could hear debris being hurled against the exterior and expected something to come crashing through one of the windows at any moment.

Tony was wailing, and she clutched him tightly against her breasts. That did nothing to comfort him because he could sense his mother's fear. Aislinn paced the length of the room, cringing each time she heard the lightning crack, knowing that it could very well strike the trailer.

"Lucas, Lucas," she chanted. Had his horse been spooked and thrown him? Was he lying unconscious somewhere? Had he fallen into a crevice and broken his leg?

The grisly possibilities were endless, yet she seemed to think of every conceivable one. She pressed her cheek to the top of Tony's head and bathed it with her tears.

She felt small and insignificant. God's wrath was awesome, and He was showing it off. What did He care if one woman and her child perished in a storm of His making?

The waiting was the worst part. But what else could she do? Getting across the clearing to the house would be hazardous even if she were alone. Carrying Tony and protecting him in her arms would make the trip impossible. The ground was already a sea of mud, unable to absorb the pelting rain quickly enough. Her vision would be hampered by the consuming darkness between blinding flashes of lightning. She could easily lose her way.

Why hadn't she left the trailer at the first signs of the impending storm? She would be frightened inside the house, but it would certainly provide more protection than the trailer.

Self-recriminations were useless now. She had made an unwise decision, and she would have to pay for it, possibly with her own life and that of her child.

Lucas. Lucas. Lucas.

She sat down in a rickety chair that had been left behind when Alice and Lucas moved from the trailer. Holding Tony against her, she rocked him, mindlessly humming, waiting for Fate to do with them what it would.

When she first heard the pounding noise, she thought it was another piece of debris banging against the trailer. But when she heard her name being shouted in accompaniment to the noise, she uttered a glad cry and went stumbling across the trailer.

"Lucas!"

"Open the door!" he shouted.

Holding Tony in one arm, she clumsily unlocked the door with her other hand. When the door opened, Lucas almost fell inside, propelled by the wind. Aislinn collapsed against him, sobbing uncontrollably. Only his surefootedness kept the three of them from toppling to the floor.

She repeated his name as she clung to him. His shirt was soddenly molded to his body. His boots were caked with mud. His hat, secured to his head by a leather cord beneath his chin, dripped rainwater. He had never looked better to her.

They hugged each other tightly for a long moment, unmindful of the rain that fell in sheets through the open door. Between them, Tony squirmed and squalled. Lucas pressed Aislinn's face into his neck and rubbed his hands up and down her back until her wracking sobs subsided.

"Are you hurt anywhere?" he asked at last.

"No. I'm f... fine. Just scared."

"And Tony?"

"He's okay. He's frightened because he could tell I was." She bit her lower lip hard to keep it from trembling. "I thought something had happened to you."

"Something did. I got caught in the storm," he said wryly. "I could see it coming, but I couldn't get back in time. The horse threw a shoe and I had to walk him back. He was reluctant and scared."

She touched his face. It was wet. She didn't notice. "I thought you were lost. Or lying hurt somewhere. I didn't know what would happen to us without you."

"Well, it scared hell out of me when I got to the house and you and Tony weren't there." He pushed a strand of her wet hair away from her mouth and touched her lips. "But we're all safe. Now our only problem is getting across the clearing to the house. I don't trust this trailer to stay in one piece much longer. We'll be safer outside than we are in here. Can you make it?"

She nodded without even having to consider the danger. Lucas was there. She felt safe again.

"Do you have something to wrap Tony in?" he asked.

She had stockpiled some extra baby blankets in the trailer. While Lucas stared out the door, planning the path of least resistance, she wrapped Tony in several of them until he looked like a living mummy. She ignored his crying, knowing that once he was fed and dry and calm, he would be all right.

Lucas took an extra blanket, draped it over Aislinn's head and tied it beneath her chin. "That won't give you much protection, but it's better than nothing. Now," he said, catching her shoulders in his hands and looking directly into her eyes, "your only job is to hang on to Tony. I'll do the rest." She nodded. "Okay, let's go."

She never remembered the details of that journey, which usually took less than sixty seconds. In her mind, it would forever be a blur of wind and rain and lightning and fear. No sooner had they left the steps of the trailer than her shoes got stuck in the mud. When she fished for them with her toes, Lucas shouted above the storm, "Leave them," and she went the remainder of the way barefoot. She slipped and slid in the oozing mud, but Lucas's strong arms kept her from falling. She held on to Tony so tightly that she was afraid she would break his ribs. She kept her head bowed and, for the most part, her eyes closed.

At last her shin rapped against something and she realized it was the porch of the house. With Lucas's assistance, she staggered up the steps and beneath the shelter of the overhang. He opened the front door and pushed her inside. He propped her against the wall and, while she regained her breath, pulled off his hat and boots and threw them out onto the porch.

He untied the blanket he had wrapped around her head and sent it the way of the boots and hat. "Don't move," he said sternly. "I'll get a blanket." Barefoot, he headed toward the bedrooms, his clothes dripping water onto the tile floors. While he was gone, Aislinn unwound the blankets covering Tony.

"My brave boy," she said, lifting him for her to kiss. "You and Daddy are so brave."

Lucas came back and threw a blanket around her shoulders, bundling her into it. "My teeth are chattering," she said needlessly.

"I noticed. Hurry, let's get Tony dried off. Then we'll work on you." Together they went into the nursery. The electricity wasn't working, but Lucas carried in two candles from their bedroom, which until now had served only as decoration. By candlelight, Aislinn swiftly undressed the baby and dried him off. While she was doing that, Lucas went to fetch a bottle from the kitchen. He waited for it to warm and came back with it just as Aislinn was snapping Tony into his sleeper.

"Let me feed him while you get into a tub of hot water. I've already turned the taps on. Take one of the candles." To keep the dry baby from getting wet and chilled again, Lucas was peeling off his clothes as he talked. When he was stripped to the skin, he took the towel Aislinn had used on Tony and whisked it over himself. Then he lifted Tony from the crib and carried him to the rocking chair.

Any other time, the sight of the huge, naked Indian man, sitting in the rocking chair with the gingham cushion, feeding a baby a bottle, would have been a hilarious sight. But Aislinn was still too benumbed by fright to notice the hilarity of it.

"Don't forget his medicine," she said, nodding toward the prescription Gene had ordered for the baby's congestion.

"I won't."

Knowing that Tony was in capable hands, she left the nursery to take her bath. It was almost a half-hour later when she came out of the bathroom carrying the candle. She had immersed herself in the tub until the hot water covered her shoulders. Its warmth had seeped into her comfortingly, relieving her chill and dulling the serrated edges of her nerves. Before she got out, she washed her hair. Brushing it back and leaving it to dry naturally, she wrapped herself in a long terry-cloth robe.

She checked the nursery first and found Tony sleeping soundly in his crib. She laid her hand on his head, tears forming in her eyes. He was so very precious to her. She couldn't imagine life without him now. What an empty, barren existence hers had been before she had been blessed with him.

She asked God to forgive her for her momentary lack of faith when she had been in the trailer. He had favored her by giving her Tony. He had brought them through a terrible ordeal safely. She would never doubt His grace and goodness again.

She left the sleeping child and tiptoed through the darkened rooms, which were illuminated only by occasional flashes of blue-white lightning and the faint, wavering glow of the candle she carried.

Lucas was in the kitchen, standing at the stove, stirring something in a saucepan. When she entered, he turned. She hadn't made a sound, and yet he had known she was there. "I knew this old gas stove was good for something. Just the other day I was wishing I could buy you a better one to cook on."

"I like that one." He had pulled on a pair of dry jeans. He was still bare-chested and barefoot. His hair was beginning to dry. She hoped he would never want to cut it short. She loved the way it shimmered each time he moved his head. "What are you cooking?"

"Cocoa. Sit down."

She set her candle on the table and pulled out a chair. "I didn't know you could cook."

He poured the steaming drink into a waiting mug and turned off the burner. "Better taste it before you make any snap judgments," he said, handing her the mug.

She sipped it cautiously because it was extremely hot. It was rich and sweet and delicious. It warmly trickled its way into her stomach and spread a welcome heat all through her. "It's delicious, Lucas. Thank you."

"Would you like something to eat?"

"No." Then she lifted her head quickly and looked up at him. "Would you? I'll fix—" She made a movement to get out of her chair, but he laid his hands on her shoulders.

"No. I'm not hungry. Drink your chocolate."

He removed his hands and soundlessly crossed the floor toward the window. "The storm is moving away." Rain was still falling, but the wind had died down considerably. The thunder sounded like low drumrolls coming from far away and the lightning was less sinister.

Aislinn raised the mug of chocolate to her lips and swallowed several sips. She tried to drink all of it, but the knot in her throat kept getting in the way. She couldn't take her eyes off Lucas. His profile was sharply outlined against the gray window. She thought he was a beautiful man.

The trauma of the day caught up with her. Emotions assailed her. She began to tremble, so drastically that the chocolate sloshed out of the mug onto her hand, burning it. She set the mug on the table. She was unable to stifle the whimper that escaped her trembling lips.

"Aislinn?"

She didn't answer because she knew her voice would only be a croak if she tried to speak. Cramming her fingers hard against her lips, she tried to contain the emotion that seemed determined to erupt.

"Aislinn?" Lucas repeated.

The concern in his voice was her undoing. Tears burst through the dam of her pride and false courage. Her shoulders shook. She buried her face in her hands.

"What's the matter? Is something wrong? Are you hurt?" Lucas knelt in front of her chair. He ran his hands up and down her arms, across her quaking shoulders, as though searching for injuries.

She lowered her hands from her face, but tears continued to stream down her cheeks. "No, no. I'm not hurt. I...I don't know why I'm doing this," she stammered. "Delayed reaction I guess. I was so scared." She dissolved into another bout of tears.

He reached up, touched her hair. "Don't," he whispered. "Don't. It's all over."

One side of his face was obscured by darkness, but the candle lit the other side. Aislinn extended both hands toward him. Reaching. Beseeching. She touched his face with feather-light fingertips. "I was afraid I'd never see you again. I didn't know how I would survive if anything happened to you."

"Aislinn—"

"More than fear for my safety, or even Tony's, I was frightened for yours." She ran her hands over his head and down his bare biceps before touching his face again.

"I was safe."

"But I didn't know that," she said with desperation.

He pressed three of his fingers against her lips to still their trembling. "I was frantic to get back to you, too."

"You were?"

"I was worried." His fingers moved over the delicate features of her face, exploring it even as she was exploring his.

"Lucas?"

"What?"

He leaned forward and kissed her, briefly, softly. She made a tremulous, catchy sound in her throat and rested her hands on his shoulders. Reflexively her fingers clenched and unclenched. "I don't ever want to be alone and without you again."

"No."

"Don't ever leave me."

"I won't."

"I depend on you to protect Tony and me."

"I always will."

"Am I a fool? A coward?"

"You're very brave. I'm proud of you."

"You are?"

"Very."

"I love you, Lucas. I love you."

The declaration acted as a lever on a floodgate. Words came pouring out of her mouth, professions of love that had been fermenting inside her for weeks. Now they came frothing out of her like the bubbles in a bottle of uncorked champagne, undisciplined and uncontainable and beyond capture or control. And in between the rushing words, their lips met in brief little exchanges of breath.

But soon that wasn't nearly enough. His arms swept around her swiftly. He angled his head to one side, claiming her mouth in a searing kiss. His lips were hungry; hers were the feast. With a low groan, he pressed his tongue inside her mouth. He rubbed it against hers. The kiss was purely carnal.

His hands slid from her back to her front. He untied the belt of her robe and thrust his hands inside. She was warm and soft and womanly. Her breasts filled his hands and he massaged them.

He trailed kisses down her neck. She watched with wonder and love as he touched the tip of one breast with his tongue, flicking it softly. A small cry of joy escaped her. His mouth gave her even more reason to rejoice. Moving from side to side, it performed acts of love on her flesh.

From over his shoulders, Aislinn could see the smooth expanse of his back. The muscles beneath the sleek skin rippled with each movement he made. She smoothed her hands over his naked skin as though spreading on lotion.

Still kneeling in front of her, his hair brushed her belly. He touched it with his mouth. He kissed her navel. When he pressed his face into her lap, she threw her head back in a spasm of delight. She sobbed his name as he drew her hips forward.

Slowly, he parted her thighs and kissed her.

Aislinn was drawn into a maelstrom of passion. It welled up over her and she seemed to drown in it. She was barely conscious when he lifted her in his arms and carried her through the house.

Only when he gently deposited her on the bed did she become aware of her surroundings again. She heard the whispering sound of cloth as he unfastened his jeans. Her eyes opened in time to see him stepping out of them. As though for her benefit, lightning lit up the sky and provided her with enough light to see him, naked and splendid.

He didn't lie down as she expected, but knelt between her thighs. He lowered his head. "Lucas," she said in feeble protest.

"I owe you this, Aislinn. The first time, that morning so long ago, was for me. This is for you."

His mouth brought her to a crescendo of feeling, unlike anything she had ever experienced. Her head thrashed on the pillow as she tried unsuccessfully to draw breath, but wave after wave of ecstasy prevented that. He was relentless in his determination to give her ultimate satisfaction, but he withheld the finale until she thought she would die of pleasure almost unendurable.

When at last he released her from that glorious prison of rapture, her body was dewy with perspiration and her lips were bruised by her own teeth.

His lips were incredibly considerate of that as he brushed kisses over hers. He licked them gently, then bathed her entire face with his tongue. Once again, sensations began to ribbon their way through her body. Lucas lowered himself over her carefully.

His sex was hot and hard. She felt it against the inside of her thigh. She wanted him and conveyed that want by raising her hips and moving them against him.

"I won't hurt you?" he asked gruffly.

"No."

He was as hard as steel, but velvety smooth. His penetration was so complete that she winced. "I am hurting you," he said, alarmed. But when he tried to withdraw, she closed her thighs against his.

"I want to have all of you."

Burying his face in the curve of her shoulder, he groaned with immense pleasure, both at her words and at the way her body smoothly, tightly, and creamily gloved his. He wanted it to last forever, and he sustained it for as long as he could.

But his body was starved and wouldn't be delayed indefinitely. Once he began to move, the climax came quickly. It rushed upon them, as tempestuous as the storm had been.

When it was over, he rested atop her until their breathing subsided, then he rolled them to their sides, so they still faced each other.

Every time the lightning flickered through the windows, he enjoyed the reflection of her back and derriere in the mirror across the room. It made a provocative picture, her hair in wanton disarray, her skin so pale compared to his hands that moved over the curves of her body.

He touched her with astonishing familiarity, yet she murmured not a single word of protest. He was bold. He satisfied every curiosity he had entertained. The liberties she afforded him made him breathless and lightheaded. She didn't shrink from even the most intimate caresses, indeed she purred beneath his touch.

He remembered praying for death that first time, because he had thought then that nothing else in his life would ever be so good as being inside Aislinn. He felt equally good now, but selfishly he didn't want to die.

What a fool he had been to deny himself the privilege of making love with her. She had been healed from childbirth for weeks. Gene had even surreptitiously given him the go-ahead.

Yet he had stubbornly denied his desire for her, because he was terrified of the emotions that accompanied it. He didn't just want the woman's body; he wanted the woman. It was the first time in his life that he had felt a real need for another human being.

Now, mellow and languid in the sweet aftermath, he eased away from her, raised her chin with his finger and kissed her mouth. He thought it would be a benediction, a good-night, but her tongue initiated a deeper kiss and played with his lower lip.

"The day of your mother's wedding..." she whispered against his lips.

"Yes?"

"I knew you were outside when I undressed by the window." He leaned his head back and looked down at her. "I wanted you to see me," she confessed. "I wanted to seduce you."

His face remained remote, but after a lengthy silence, during which she was held captive by his compelling eyes, he said, "I was seduced."

Rolling quickly to his back, he pulled her atop him and rasped, "Ride me."

Taking him inside her, she fulfilled his fantasy. Eagerly, she carried him beyond his most vivid imaginings. It was a supreme effort, but Lucas kept his eyes open to enjoy the blond beauty of her skin and hair. He caressed her breasts, giving special care to their responsive peaks. And when she arched her back with the pleasure of that caress, he stroked her in places that caused her thighs to quiver against his.

At last, with a shudder, she collapsed on his chest. He wrapped himself around her and gave her all of himself that was in his power to give. Her body celebrated his gift.

Then, weak and spent, they lay there, his body nestled in hers, for a long time. And finally, when he moved her to his side and tucked her back against his chest, they fell into a sleep more peaceful than either had ever known.

Chapter 12

I'm glad you chose my house to break into that night."

Greywolf tilted his head to look down at her. "So am I."

She lightly plucked at his chest hairs. They had made love frequently through the night, dozing in between. Their passions had been quick to kindle each time one touched the other. Now, their desire momentarily replete, they lay indolently among the tangled sheets. Last night's storm had long since passed. Morning light tinted the bedroom with a rosy glow.

"I was scared to death of you," she said.

"I was scared to death of you, too."

Laughing in surprise, she propped herself up on her elbows so she could look down on his face. "Of me? You were afraid of me? Why? Did you think I could overpower you?"

"Not in the sense you mean, but at that point in time, if anything could have overpowered me, it would have been a beautiful woman. You totally disarmed me. Why do you think I picked up that knife?"

"Did you think I was beautiful?" She glanced at him through a screen of demure lashes.

"Fishing?"

"Yes, husband. I'll never get tired of the compliments you continually shower on me." Her sarcasm was softened with a smile.

He had the grace to smile back. "I do think you're beautiful. But do you want to know what I thought when I first saw you?"

"Yes. What did you think?"

"Damn it all."

"What?"

"That's what I thought. *Damn it all*. Why did you have to be gorgeous and have the body and face of an angel? I wanted to curse you to perdition for looking the way you did. If you had been a man I would have clipped you on the chin and fled. Or if Miss Aislinn Andrews had been ugly, I would have tied her up, eaten her bread and sausage, drunk her milk, possibly stolen her car, and then hightailed it out of there."

"You did all that . . . but you spent the night, too."

He slanted a look down at her. "Even when I knew that multiplied my chances of getting caught."

"Why, Lucas?" Her fingers strummed his hard, flat stomach.

"Because I wanted to sleep with you."

She sucked in a short little breath. "Oh."

"But all the time I was wanting you, I hated myself for wanting you."

"Scruples?"

He laughed robustly. Aislinn loved the deep, rich sound still new to her ears. "Hardly. I've never had many scruples when it came to women."

"That's odd."

"Why?"

"After what happened to Alice."

He frowned. "I made sure I never got a woman pregnant." She gazed up at him inquiringly, and he gave her a rueful smile. "Except once."

They kissed.

"That time I wasn't thinking about anything but this." He touched her lower body, letting his fingers luxuriate in the soft, tawny hair. "I never took advantage of any woman. Until you. You were the exception to every rule I'd ever imposed on myself."

"It seems that way. I'm very glad. But why did you hate yourself for wanting me?"

"I didn't want to feel such desperate desire for any woman, much less an Anglo."

She looked pleased. "That's what you were feeling, a 'desperate desire'?"

"Yes," he admitted in a hoarse voice.

"The whole time we were together?"

He nodded seriously.

"And all that about my being your insurance policy?"

"Was my flimsy rationalization. Crazy as it was, I wanted to keep you with me. I felt guilty about disrupting your life and dragging you into that mess, but..." He gave a helpless shrug. "I couldn't bring myself to let you go even though all along I was so afraid you'd get hurt." He laid his hand on her throat and rubbed the soft skin. "I guess you got hurt anyway, didn't you?"

"I don't think so."

"Is that true, Aislinn?"

"That's true."

"God, I don't know why you haven't murdered me in my sleep."

She smiled down at him. "Because I was counting on that desperate desire still being there."

"It is. More desperate than ever." He wound her hair around his hand and, holding her head still for his fervent kiss, rolled her to her back.

After a lengthy kiss that left her breathless, she said, "We could have been doing this for weeks if you weren't so damned stubborn. You never give an inch, do you?"

He grinned lecherously. "Right now I know of several inches I could give you."

She pulled his hair by way of punishment for his ribaldry, but then she giggled. "I can't believe you actually made a joke."

"I can be extremely funny."

"With everyone but me. With me you're hardheaded and unbending. You can't be humorous because you're too busy being defensive about what happened that morning at Alice's house." He tensed up and started to move away, but she locked her arms across the small of his back. "You stay right where you are, Lucas Greywolf."

"I shamed myself."

"You needed me." The very softness with which she said it arrested his defensive reaction. "Needing someone is nothing to be ashamed of. Why is it so difficult for you to admit that you need another person occasionally, Lucas? None of us is entirely self-sufficient." Her finger touched his lips lovingly. "I liked being needed by you that morning. I wasn't offended by what you did. I was only sorry you didn't let me participate more."

She raised her head off the pillow and kissed him. At first he was resistant, but as her mouth continued to move over his, he began to thaw. When her head reclined on the pillow again, he followed it down and showed her just how much he needed her.

Later her hands glided down his sweat-dampened back, past his waist to his buttocks. "Do you hear something?"

"Yes," he mumbled into her neck. "My heart. It's still pounding."

She smiled against his shoulder, biting it softly, loving even the slightest trace of vulnerability he demonstrated. "Mine is pounding, too. But I was referring to something else."

"Like Tony?"

"Precisely Tony. Better let me up to check on him."

He moved away from her and lay sprawled on his back, watching with hot, possessive eyes as Aislinn pulled on the wrapper she'd been wearing the evening before and padded out of their bedroom.

Lucas didn't recall a time in his life when he'd been happy. He'd lived through happy occasions like birthdays and Christmases. He'd loved the times he and Joseph had hunted in the hills. He exulted in winning races at track meets. But happiness was something that other people had, people with normal families and backgrounds, people with undiluted blood, people who didn't live under stigmas, people who weren't labeled.

This morning Lucas Greywolf came as close to being happy as he ever had been. He even allowed himself to smile broadly just for the hell of it. He stretched like a sinuous mountain cat who had nothing more to worry about than what to eat for breakfast. Being happy wasn't nearly as frightening as he had thought it would be.

Aislinn, too, floated into Tony's bedroom on a cloud of joy. All the horrors of yesterday had been banished by Lucas's loving. Radiant sunlight was pouring through the windows. Her future looked sunny because she loved Lucas and had finally gotten him to accept her love.

He hadn't said he loved her, but one couldn't have everything at once. He desired her. He loved having her in his life and in his bed. Maybe love would grow out of that eventually. In the meantime, she would be satisfied with what she had. Life was good.

"Good morning, Tony," she called gaily as she entered the nursery. He was crying, whimpering actually. "Are you hungry? Hmm? Want a dry diaper? Wouldn't that feel better?"

The moment she bent over the crib, she realized that something was terribly wrong. With that inexplicable maternal instinct, she instantly realized that something wasn't right. The rattling sound of his breathing alerted her immediately. When she touched him, she screamed, "Lucas!"

He was pulling on a pair of jeans. He recognized Aislinn's cry as one of distress. He knew better than anyone that she didn't panic easily. Within heartbeats he was clearing the door of the nursery.

"What is it?"

"Tony. He's burning up with fever. And listen to his breathing."

His breath was making a hideous whistling sound as it rushed in and out of the tiny lungs. His respiration was quick and shallow. His face was mottled. And instead of making a lusty cry, which both his parents would have welcomed, he seemed barely to have the strength to mew pitiably.

"What do you want me to do?"

"Get Gene on the phone." Already Aislinn was stripping the infant and reaching for the rectal thermometer, which her baby books had advised she keep close at hand. Lucas didn't argue, deferring to her expertise in this situation. He raced through the house into the kitchen and quickly punched out the telephone number.

"Hello," Gene sleepily answered the second ring.

"Gene, Lucas. Tony's sick."

"A cold. I gave—"

"More than that. He can hardly breathe."

By now Gene had recognized the no-nonsense tone of Lucas's voice. "Does he have a temperature?"

"Just a minute." Lucas cupped his hand over the receiver and called out the question to Aislinn.

She appeared in the doorway of the kitchen, holding Tony against her chest. Her eyes were filled with fear. "One hundred and four," she whispered. "Lucas." It was a plea.

He reported the baby's temperature to Gene, who cursed. Lucas could hear Alice's voice in the background, asking of her husband who was calling and what was wrong.

"Dammit, Gene, what do we do?" Lucas demanded.

"You calm down for starters," Gene said reasonably. "Then you bathe Tony with cool water, try to get his temperature down. Bring him in as soon as you can get here."

"To the clinic?"

"Yes."

"We'll be there in half an hour or less."

Lucas hung up the phone without another word and repeated Gene's instructions to Aislinn. He finished dressing while she cupped cool water over Tony in the bathroom sink. Then they switched places. He took the baby and she slung on clothes, not caring what they were.

She diapered Tony, wrapped him in a light receiving blanket and left by way of the front door, where Lucas already had her car idling.

The clearing in front of the house was a quagmire from the torrential rain the night before. The spongy ground sucked at the tires as Lucas plowed the car toward the road. It wasn't much better. He skidded into the ditch several times, the back tires fishtailing in the mire.

Lucas's hands were clenched around the steering wheel and his back was hunched. The hard expression on his face reminded Aislinn of another time he had driven her car with the same kind of concentration. At the time that had seemed like a life-or-death situation. How tame it seemed compared to this. Now she knew the real meaning of fear: when one's child is in life-threatening danger.

The drive into town seemed to take forever. Tony's little body generated so much heat that he branded himself into his mother's breasts. He was fretful. Every time he dropped off to sleep, he would come awake choking, struggling with his effort to breath.

Gene and Alice came rushing out of the clinic the moment they saw the car race into the parking lot. "How is he?" Gene asked, opening Aislinn's door.

"Oh, Gene, help him," she pleaded. "He's burning up. I think his fever has gone back up."

They all hurried toward the doors of the clinic, scrambling over each other in their haste. Aislinn carried Tony into an examining room. The clinic wasn't open for business yet, so there were no other patients vying for the doctor's attention.

Alice and Gene methodically went about examining the baby, kindly elbowing his hovering mother aside. Aislinn looked toward Lucas for reassurance, but he was staring down at the baby. He had said little on the trip into town. She wanted to offer him comfort, but knew that anything she said would sound like just what it was, an empty platitude. And how could she comfort him when she was so terrified herself?

Gene listened to Tony's chest through a stethoscope. When he lowered the earplugs he said, "He's got fluid in his lungs. That upper-respiratory infection has gotten much worse."

"But he was getting better," Aislinn protested. "I've been giving him his medicine faithfully."

"No one's blaming you, Aislinn," Gene said kindly, laying a hand on her shoulder. "These things happen."

"He...he got wet last night. And chilled." She told them about the storm. "When Lucas took us back to the house, I kept Tony covered up as well as I could. Is that why this happened?"

There was a trace of hysteria in her high, thin voice. Both Alice and Gene hastened to assure her that the infection could have spread in any event. "He wasn't on any antibiotics," Gene said. "And it certainly wasn't negligence on your part."

"Make him well."

Lucas, who had remained silent until then, spoke from the side of the examination table where he continued to stare down at his son as though Tony were the center star of the universe and the light was about to burn out.

"I don't think I can, Lucas."

"What!" Aislinn gasped. She clasped her hands together and raised them to her white lips.

"I can't do much here," Gene said. "My suggestion would be to take him to one of the hospitals in Phoenix. Get him to a natal intensive-care unit where specialists can treat him. I'm not properly equipped."

"But that's hours from here," Aislinn said frantically.

"A guy I went to med school with heads up a helicopter ambulance service. I'll go call him. Alice, give the baby a shot to bring down the fever."

Unable to shake off the paralysis of fear, Aislinn watched Alice prepare a syringe and give Tony an injection. When that was done, she rediapered him and handed him to his anxiety-ridden mother. Aislinn leaned against the examination table and rocked back and forth, comforting the baby as best she could.

Gene returned and informed them, "He's dispatching a chopper immediately. It'll set down in that pasture on the north side of the highway just outside town. The pilot he's sending was here last year to pick up a snakebite victim, so he knows the way. Aislinn, Lucas, there will be a pediatric nurse in the helicopter and specialists standing by when you reach the hospital."

"Is he that critical?" Aislinn asked, her voice wavering.

Gene took her hands in his. "I wouldn't alarm you unnecessarily. Yes, he's that critical."

A few hours later, the specialist at the Phoenix hospital confirmed Gene's diagnosis. Those intervening hours had been a nightmare for Aislinn. Lucas and she had met the helicopter and were hustled aboard. From that moment on, she realized she would forever have a greater appreciation for people in medicine. The nurse on board the chopper began administering to Tony immediately; by radio, she was in constant contact with the doctors at the hospital, so that by the time they set down on the roof, Tony was already getting the best of medical treatment.

As soon as he was carried into areas of the hospital restricted to them, Aislinn turned to Lucas, seeking the strength of his embrace. But even though he folded his arms around her, it was a mechanical gesture. His heart wasn't in it. She could feel the spiritual distance between them, yawning as wide as a gulf. Since they had left their home that morning, she had felt him slipping further and further away from her.

His face was closed, as though he had removed himself from the tragedy. But Aislinn knew he was suffering terribly. How he could enforce such rigid control over his emotions, she didn't know. She felt that at any moment she would begin banging her head against the wall, stamping her feet, tearing out her hair.

They waited, sharing a silence that was intolerable to Aislinn. Where was the loving comfort Lucas had given to Joseph and Alice when the old man had lain dying? Why was there none for her now? But Joseph had been an old man. Lucas had had years to prepare himself for the day his grandfather would die.

She was relieved when the specialist approached them. "Mr. and Mrs. Greywolf?" he asked politely. They nodded. "Your little boy is very sick," he began. He delivered a spate of medical terms that meant nothing to Aislinn, but he finished with, "Pneumonia."

"Then it's not so bad, is it?" Aislinn cried in relief. "I've known many people who have had pneumonia. They recovered without any difficulty."

The doctor glanced worriedly at Lucas before looking back into Aislinn's expectant face. "The recovery rate for pneumonia is high, but we're talking about a three-month-old pair of lungs. I'm afraid that reduces your child's ability to throw it off quite so easily."

"Then it *is* serious?"

"His current condition is extremely serious."

"Will he die?" She could barely control her wobbling lips long enough to ask the hateful question.

"I don't know," the doctor replied honestly. "I'm gonna fight like hell to keep him." He squeezed her shoulder in reassurance. "Excuse me, now. I should get back."

"May I see him?" she asked, clutching at the sleeve of his lab coat.

"I don't advise it. He's got tubes going in and out. To see him now would only frighten you more."

"She wants to see him." Lucas's sibilant whisper was more threatening than a shout. He and the doctor stared each other down for several seconds before the doctor relented.

"For one minute, Mrs. Greywolf. No more."

When she returned to the corridor, she was crying copiously. Lucas placed his arms around her and patted her gently on the back. But as before, she felt the invisible barriers between them, and there was little solace to be found in his aloof bearing and cool, gray eyes.

They spent the entire day and night in the hospital waiting room. Aislinn refused to leave even long enough to eat, though the nursing staff kindly urged her to. No one approached Lucas. Aislinn thought it was because they were afraid of him. What went on in the brain behind that implacable face remained a mystery to everyone but him.

Shortly after dawn on the second day, the doctor reported that Tony's condition was still serious. "But when he first arrived, I wouldn't have laid odds on him making it this long," he said, with a hint of optimism. "I think he's a fighter."

Aislinn took heart. She grasped at any straws of hope.

Gene and Alice arrived soon after that. They had posted notices that the clinic would be closed and had made the long drive, unable to stay away any longer. Their sudden appearance had such an impact on Aislinn that she dissolved into tears of gratitude.

The Dexters expressed alarm at how drawn and pale she looked and begged her to check into a hotel and rest. She steadfastly refused. But they did talk her into eating the hot meal the hospital cafeteria sent up on trays for Lucas and her.

They were sitting in the waiting room, finishing their breakfast, when Lucas glanced up. He angrily tossed his napkin down and stood up, banging the table with his shin. "Who invited *them*?" he asked rudely, apparently not caring if the approaching couple overheard him.

"I did." Aislinn's voice was as unsteady as her knees as she stood up to confront her husband, who was obviously furious, and her parents, whom she hadn't seen or spoken to since her marriage. "Mother, Father," she said, stepping forward, "thank you for coming."

The Andrews seemed at a loss as to what to say or what to do. Eleanor fidgeted with the ivory handle of her purse, and Willard looked everywhere but at his daughter and son-in-law.

"We thought it was the least we could do," Eleanor said to break a silence that had grown uncomfortably long. "We're very sorry about the baby's illness."

"Do you need anything, Aislinn? Money?" Willard offered.

Lucas said something thoroughly obscene and went around them, shouldering them aside as he passed. "No thank you, Father," Aislinn said softly.

She was ashamed that her parents' solution to any problem was money, but she forgave them. Their being there was a comfort to her and, in light of their bigotry, more of a concession than she had had any right to expect from them.

She was relieved of having to deal with the awkward situation when Alice stepped forward. "I'm Alice Dexter, Tony's other grandmother. Please forgive my son's bad behavior. He's extremely upset."

She spoke softly. What impressed Aislinn, as it had from the night she met Alice in the hogan, was the absence of censure or prejudice in her tone. She looked directly at Eleanor, whose dress cost more than what Alice would spend on clothes in several years. She was neither hostile toward nor intimidated by the other woman. She extended her hand. "Please come meet my husband, Dr. Gene Dexter."

Aislinn left the four of them to get acquainted and went to find Lucas. He was standing at the end of the hall in front of a window. He was broodily staring out at a cloudless day very much the way Aislinn imagined he must have stared out the barred windows of the prison. For a man who enjoyed being outdoors as much as he did, it must have been hell.

"Lucas?" She saw his shoulders tense; otherwise he didn't respond. "Are you angry with me for notifying my parents?"

"We don't need them."

"Maybe you don't; I do."

He spun around. Only an act of will kept her from recoiling from the rage burning in his eyes. Taking her hand, he dragged her into a room that the nurses had made available to them, but which neither had used so

far. When the heavy door silently swung closed, he faced
Aislinn furiously.

"I guess you miss their damned money after all, don't
you? What's the matter? Didn't you think I could provide sufficient medical care for my son? Did you call
Daddy, begging forgiveness for marrying beneath you
and asking him to please drop by with his checkbook?"

"I don't deserve that, Lucas!" She slapped him hard,
hard enough for his head to follow the path her flying
palm had taken. When his face came back around, his
teeth were bared, and he raised his hand in retaliation.
However, he stopped the downward arc of his hand before it could make contact with her cheek.

She threw herself against him and gripped handfuls of
his shirt. "Go ahead. Hit me. Maybe then, just maybe,
I'll know you're alive and not made of stone. I'll gladly
invite you to strike me if that's what it takes for you to
show some emotion, some feeling."

She shook him, grinding her white knuckles into the
hard wall of his chest. "Damn you, Lucas! Talk to me!
Yell. Scream. Show me your pain. I know it's there. I
know you love Tony even if you love no one else. He
might die and I know you're hurting because of it. Use
me as your punching bag, as your sounding board. Let
me share your grief."

She was crying, but the tears ran heedlessly down her
cheeks. She licked them from the corners of her mouth.
"You're so proud, aren't you? Nothing can touch you."
She shook her head in denial of her own words. "I know
differently. I heard you keening when Joseph died. I
witnessed your pain. And that heartache can't begin to
compare to what you're feeling now for your son. Your
own stupid prejudice keeps you separate from the rest of
the world, not the other way around. Are you so heart-
less that you can't even cry at your son's deathbed?

"You say you don't need anybody. But you do, Lucas. You just won't admit it. I needed my parents' sup-

port during this time, so I swallowed my pride and called them, having no guarantee that they wouldn't hang up on me. I need all the support I can muster today. I don't want to go through this crisis alone. Even if it meant losing face, I would have begged them to be here with me. You ridicule them, but you have more in common with them than you think. You're as cold and unyielding as they are. Only they relented. They're here for me now and you're not."

She gripped his shirt harder, almost tearing the fabric. "Whether you love me or not, you're my husband. I need you. Don't you dare withhold your support from me. You married me because you felt honor bound to do so. But is there any honor in deserting your wife when she needs you the most? Does it make you less a man to weep with me?"

She slapped him again. And again. Tears rained from her eyes and rolled down her face and dripped off her chin. "Cry, damn you! Cry!"

With a suddenness that snatched the breath from her body, he flung his arms around her and bent his head low. He buried his face in the crook of her shoulder. At first Aislinn didn't realize that her fondest wish had been granted. But then she felt his broad shoulders shaking and heard the wracking sounds of his weeping.

She encircled his waist with her arms and held him close while his tears bathed her neck and dampened her blouse. He cried on and on, and when she couldn't support his weight any longer, they sank to the floor, their arms still around each other. She pressed his head between her breasts, curved herself over it protectively and held him dearly, rocking back and forth as she often did with Tony. Her own tears were unstemmed and fell into his hair.

Lord, she loved him. She hurt with love.

"I want our baby to live," he sobbed. "You can't know what it was like for me to learn that I had a son. I want him to live. I want him to know me. When I was a kid, I wanted a father so badly, Aislinn. I want to be the kind of father to Tony that I used to dream about having." He burrowed his head deeper into her flesh. "Would God be so cruel as to take my son from me?"

"If he is taken from us, Lucas, I won't be able to bear your pain. I love you too much."

After a time, his tears ceased, but he kept his head nestled in her cleavage. He kissed her through the damp cloth of her blouse and murmured endearments, sometimes in English, sometimes in a language still foreign to her.

"I didn't want to love you."

"I know," she replied softly, combing her fingers through his hair.

"But I do."

"I know that, too."

He raised his head and looked at her through tear-washed eyes. "Do you?" For an answer, she lifted a tear off his glossy black eyelashes, looked at it, then at him, and gave him a bittersweet smile.

They shared one poignant second before there was a gentle knock at the door. Their expressions turned bleak. Lucas stood up and extended his hand down to her. Trustingly, she laid her hand in his, and he pulled her to her feet, placing a strong, supportive arm around her. They faced the door as though facing an executioner. "Come in," Lucas said. They expected the doctor.

But it wasn't the doctor who came through the door. It was Warden Dixon. Aislinn didn't recognize the man, but Lucas did. She could tell by the tensing of his muscled body.

"Hello, Mr. Greywolf. I know this is an awkward time for you." He was embarrassed, for it was apparent that they had both been crying. "I'm Warden Dixon," he said to Aislinn when it became obvious that Lucas wasn't going to make introductions.

"What are you doing here?" Lucas asked, curtailing the pleasantries.

"As I said, I know this is a terrible time for you. I apologize, Mrs. Greywolf, for the untimely intrusion. If I wasn't delivering good news I wouldn't trouble you at a time like this."

"How did you know I was here?"

"Mr. Andrews's secretary. I telephoned him this morning when I failed to contact you after trying all day yesterday."

"You've been diligent, Mr. Dixon," Aislinn said. "Have you come to see us about something important?"

"Your husband's exoneration." He looked at Lucas. "A judge has reviewed the transcripts of your trial. He has also considered the affidavits submitted to him freely by two men who have confessed to their crimes. The documents absolved you from any and all guilt. In fact, they stated that the only reason you were in the fracas at all was to break up the fighting. You were trying to prevent the violence, not perpetrate it. You are to be officially vindicated and immediately reinstated to the bar."

Aislinn slumped against her husband's arm with profound joy. Lucas, however, was barely able to support her. The news had made him weak-kneed.

Before either of them could voice their thanks to the warden, Gene came running into the room. "Lucas, Aislinn, come quickly. The doctor is looking for you."

Epilogue

Smile!"

"Aislinn, my face is about to crack from smiling."

"I don't doubt it. It's so unusual an expression for you." She laughed at her husband's dark scowl. "Look this way, Tony. Look at Mommy."

She clicked off two pictures while Tony had his head turned in the right direction. He even proudly displayed his new front teeth in a slobbery grin.

"Now stop working with those cameras," Lucas said, moving toward his wife. "This is supposed to be a party."

"I'm having a wonderful time," she said happily, standing on her tiptoes to kiss his cheek. Her eyes were sparkling. "I'd rather be taking pictures of you and Tony than anything in the world."

Lucas looked at her with open skepticism. "Bet I can name something you'd rather be doing."

"Lucas!"

Now it was his turn to laugh . . . at his wife's exasperation. "However, I'll admit Tony and I do make good subjects, don't we?'' he said, proudly looking at his son, who resembled him so remarkably.

Tony's eyes were already turning the same gray color as his father's, and they had a rim of blue around them which he had inherited from his mother. His hair was jet black, but not as straight as Lucas's. His cheekbones were just as prominent, but he had enough baby fat to round out the cheeks beneath them. He was a picture of good health.

''You are my favorite subjects anytime.'' Aislinn hugged them both, nuzzling her husband's strong throat, while her son tugged on fistfuls of her hair.

''Hey, will the three of you break it up?'' Gene said, handing Aislinn a glass of punch. ''You're supposed to mingle.''

''Give Tony to me,'' Alice said, joining them. She had a cookie in her hand and that was bribery enough. Tony put up no fuss when Lucas passed him to his grandmother, though he was usually reluctant to leave his father's arms. ''Willard and Eleanor want to see him.''

''Now, stop making goo-goo eyes at each other and go shake some hands,'' Gene told Lucas and Aislinn, pushing them toward the crowd of people milling around the office.

The reception was to celebrate the official opening of Lucas's law office. The publicity surrounding his vindication, coupled with the publication of Aislinn's photographs in a national magazine, had brought renewed public awareness of the plight of many of the Indians who lived on the reservations.

Lucas wasn't deluded by this rush of interest. In his lifetime he wouldn't see an end to all the oppression, whether it was intentional or not. But every step he took in that direction was gratifying.

He was extremely conscientious about appearances. He never wanted it to seem that he had profited from his conviction and the subsequent reversal. He never forgot who his clients were. Even today, he had worn a white shirt, tie and sports jacket, but he had on jeans and boots with them. He hadn't worn a headband, but the silver earring was in his ear. And behind his desk, hanging on the wall, was a framed portrait of Joseph Greywolf dressed in the full regalia of a chief. Many of the attending dignitaries commented on the photograph, which had been taken when Joseph was in his prime.

"How much longer before we can go home?" Lucas asked Aislinn after an hour of smiles and handshakes.

"The invitations Alice sent out said from two till six. Why?"

"Because I want to get you home and in bed."

"Shh! Somebody might hear you."

In full view of their guests, he lowered his head and kissed her on the mouth.

"Behave, Lucas. This reception is in your honor." She tried to sound scolding, but couldn't mask her pleasure in his spontaneous display of affection.

He toyed with a strand of her hair. "I could just haul you out of here, you know."

"Kidnap me?"

"Uh-huh."

"You did that already."

"It was the smartest thing I ever did."

"It was the best thing that could have happened to me."

Unaware of the conversations buzzing around them, they stared searchingly into each other's eyes, finding the love they knew they would. Johnny Deerinwater finally broke them apart by coming up and thumping Lucas on the back while he heartily shook hands.

They played host and hostess for the time required and eventually the crowd began to dwindle. "We haven't spent any time with Mother and Father," Aislinn said, taking Lucas's arm and guiding him toward the couple who were sitting across the room talking to Gene. Lucas made a complaining sound. "They've come a long way, Lucas, and I'm not referring to the distance they drove today."

"I know," he conceded. "I'll be kind. After all, he's building that new wing to Gene's clinic."

As soon as Willard and Eleanor departed for Phoenix, Alice asked if she and Gene could keep Tony overnight. "We don't get to see him often enough. And you have to drive back tomorrow to clean up the office for Monday's business anyway. Please?"

They consented and left for home, just the two of them. It was a beautiful evening. The sky was star-studded and a full moon hung low over the mountains.

"You know, I think I've become part Indian myself," Aislinn said musingly. "I love all this," she said, nodding toward the horizon.

"You gave up a lot, Aislinn," Lucas said quietly, keeping his eyes on the narrow road that led to the ranch.

She took his hand from the steering wheel and held it, pressing it hard until he looked at her. "In that other life, I didn't have you. I didn't have Tony. I would never trade back."

Indeed, she had severed all her connections in Scottsdale. The condo had been sold. She used her equity in it to buy playground equipment for several of the schools on the reservation. She had sold the photography studio as well, and after using part of the profits to expand her darkroom and camera equipment, bought Lucas a magnificent stud for his herd. The day the animal was delivered, he had struggled with his pride to accept the gift.

Aislinn had laid her hands on his chest and gazed up at him imploringly. "You've given me so much, Lucas. Let me give you this."

He had accepted the horse because it was a gift of love from her. Too, the stud would strengthen his herd. Its offspring would be valuable. The more profitable the ranch, the more young men Lucas could hire as hands

who might otherwise go jobless. One of the first buildings to go up on his property had been a bunkhouse to
house the six cowboys he had already hired. They ably
ran the ranch so he could devote more time to his law
practice.

Now, Aislinn looked at Lucas's stern profile etched
against the moonlit sky and her heart swelled with love.
She could barely contain the happiness that had been hers
since Tony had survived the bout with pneumonia.

"I hope the pictures I took today turn out well. Especially the ones of Tony." Her husband seemed to sense
that she wasn't finished, so he said nothing. "I still get
the shivers when I think how close we came to losing
him."

He withdrew his hand from hers and rubbed the backs
of his fingers against her cheek. "We promised that we
would never forget it, but we also promised that we
wouldn't dwell on it either."

"I know," she said, softly kissing his knuckles as they
stroked her lips. "I was just thinking about that day. You
telling me that you loved me, then Warden Dixon showing up with his news, and almost immediately after that
the doctor informing us that Tony would pull through."
She smiled at him. "Whew! So much good stuff at one
time nearly did me in."

"You're certainly in a reflective mood tonight."

"My way of celebrating how happy I am."

He pulled the car to a halt in front of the house and slid
his gray eyes toward her. "Well, I've got another form of
celebration in mind."

"And what would that be, Mr. Greywolf?"

They didn't even waste time turning on lights, but let
the moonlight, shining in through the windows, guide
them through the house into the bedroom.

Lucas whipped off his jacket and slung it onto a chair.
He unbuttoned his shirt. That's as far as he got before his
passions ruled him. He reached for Aislinn and pulled her

into his arms. She dropped the jacket of her suit onto the floor, barely having had time to take it off.

His mouth retained the same hot fierceness it had had the first time he kissed her. His bitterness might have mellowed, his prejudices might have been tamped down, he might have come to accept and appreciate the Anglo half of himself, but Aislinn hoped that the savage nature of his lovemaking would never be tamed.

He touched the front of her blouse, groping for buttons. He released them one by one as she plowed all ten of her fingers through his hair, holding his mouth hard against hers. He tugged the blouse from the waistband of her skirt, unfastened the clasp of her bra and pushed the lacy cups aside, then covered her breasts with his hands.

His callused fingertips and palms were excitingly abrasive against her smooth flesh. They worked their magic, and when she was primed for his mouth, he took her between his lips and made her very wet.

They both groaned with pleasure when he lifted his mouth once again to hers and drew her breasts against his chest. He held her tight against him, wrapping his arms as far around her as he could reach, bending his head down low over hers.

"I don't ever want to remember when you weren't a part of my body," he said huskily, squeezing her closer. "I don't want to remember when I didn't love you."

The romantic speech was so unlike him that she treasured it all the more. He had learned that admitting to profound emotions didn't compromise his heritage or manhood. Still, he rarely voiced aloud his deepest feelings. When he did, as now, Aislinn cherished every precious word.

With their mouths fused in an ardent kiss, he slipped his hands beneath her skirt and moved them up her thighs. He played with the tops of her stockings and the suspenders of her garter belt, which he had expressed an extreme liking for and which she favored him by wearing often.

He cupped her derriere and positioned her against him, maximizing the sensations for both of them. Moments later, she stepped out of her panties. His hand slid between her thighs. And up. And inside. And he let her die a little before bringing her back down with soothing kisses and whispered endearments.

"Lucas," she murmured weakly, wilting against him like a flower that has experienced full bloom.

"God, you're beautiful." He wound his fingers through her hair, pulling hard. "My wife. My woman," he murmured possessively, and held her even tighter.

After sharing a violently passionate kiss, she backed away from him. To his eyes, she was a vision of sexy disarray, with her mouth dewy from their kiss, her hair tangled about her head and shoulders, her blouse and bra open but not off, her skirt rumpled.

He stood still, slightly surprised, when, keeping her eyes riveted to his, she peeled his shirt off his shoulders. After letting it trail from her fingertips to the floor, she pushed her hand beneath his ornate, turquoise-studded belt. "Remember when you carried the knife here?" she asked. "It was extremely phallic."

"It was?"

"It was."

She worked her hand into the waistband of his jeans, the backs of her fingers pleasantly gouging his hair-dusted belly. Then her eyes still focused on his, she backed toward the bed, towing him with her, until the backs of her knees touched the edge of it and she sat down.

He looked sinister and dangerous with the moonlight shining on his dark beauty. It made his hair appear blacker, his eyes lighter, his body lithe and sleek and menacing. The cross hanging from his neck only made his throat and chest appear stronger by contrast. The silver earring winked at her.

With an airy touch, her hands drifted over his chest, his nipples. Her fingers combed down the ridges of his lean ribs until they reached the shadowy dell of his navel. He raised his hands to his belt buckle.

"No," she said.

When his hands obediently moved back to his sides, she made a ballet of unfastening the belt buckle. Fingers had never been so nimble, yet so agonizingly controlled and unhurried. The metal clinked musically in the darkness. His rushing breath was the only other sound breaking the total stillness.

One by one she popped free the heavy metal buttons on his jeans until all were undone and the fly was open. The smell of his soap and his skin and his sex greeted her warmly, muskily. She wanted to swallow his smell.

"You are so beautiful," she whispered. "So tall and strong and...hard."

Tipping her head forward, she pressed her open mouth to his navel. She slid her hands inside his jeans and eased them down. Slowly. Seductively. Softly.

He gave a hoarse cry when her tongue touched him.

Again and again and again....

Much later, as they lay entwined, naked now, basking in each other's body heat, she kissed his neck and whispered into his pierced ear, "I love you, Lucas Greywolf."

"I know."

And because he did, she was content.

Silhouette Sensation

COMING NEXT MONTH

IN SAFEKEEPING
Naomi Horton

Linn Stevens was determined to protect five-year-old Nathan who'd been entrusted to her care, but perhaps she was being too careful. She'd attracted the interest of rugged espionage author Trey Hollister whose bold sensuality was impossible to resist!

For days Trey had been secretly watching over the woman and child. He knew she was running from something or someone and that she needed his help. Would she let down her guard with him?

A CHANGE OF SEASONS
Carin Rafferty

Sam Dillon was determined to give his grandfather something special and he'd decided that it would have to be a set of stunning photographs of the majestic Rocky Mountains. When Sam saw Liana's work he knew the photographer he wanted too.

Liana didn't want to work for Sam; she didn't want to use her camera again or start to feel once more, but Sam wasn't giving her any choice. When Sam was determined even an armoured tank couldn't stop him; what chance did Liana have?

Silhouette Sensation

COMING NEXT MONTH

TENDER OFFER
Paula Detmer Riggs

Casey O'Neill never would have gone looking for her ex-husband, Alex Torres, if she'd seen any other way out of her dilemma. Alex had turned his back on her more than five years ago and Casey still had no real idea of why he had lost interest in her.

But now her company, her whole town, was under threat. Alex Torres had been known as a formidable, ruthless corporate raider and Casey knew that if she could get him to help she would keep control of her firm. But what would persuade him to become involved?

DUAL IMAGE
Nora Roberts

From the pain of a bitter marriage Booth De Witt had written his greatest script, a bitingly brilliant story. Ariel Kirkwood wanted to play the scheming wife, but her portrayal was eerily perfect and Booth mistrusted anyone who could appear to be so coldly seductive.

It was inevitable that they become lovers but, beyond that, could they have a future together?

NOW YOU CAN ENJOY
4 SILHOUETTE SENSATIONS, A CUDDLY
TEDDY AND A MYSTERY GIFT FREE

❤ ❤ ❤ ❤ ❤ ❤ ❤ ❤ ❤ ❤ ❤ ❤ ❤ ❤ ❤ ❤

Now you can enjoy 4 Silhouette Sensations, a
cuddly teddy and a mystery gift absolutely FREE
and without obligation. Then if you choose,
you can look forward to receiving your new
Sensations delivered to your door each month
at just £1.65 each (post & packing free) plus a
FREE newsletter packed with author news,
competitions offering great prizes, special offers
and lots more. Send no money now. Simply fill
in the coupon below at once and post it to:-
Silhouette Reader Service, FREEPOST,
PO Box 236, Croydon, Surrey CR9 9EL.

– – – – – – – `NO STAMP REQUIRED` – – – – – – →

Please send me, free and without obligation, four specially selected Silhouette
Sensations, together with my FREE cuddly teddy and mystery gift - and reserve
a Reader Service Subscription for me. If I decide to subscribe I shall receive 4
new Silhouette Sensation titles every month for £6.60 post and packing free. If
I decide not to subscribe, I shall write to you within 10 days. The free books
and gifts are mine to keep in any case. I understand that I may cancel or
suspend my subscription at any time simply by writing to you. I am over 18
years of age.   Please write in BLOCK CAPITALS

Mrs/Miss/Ms/Mr _____   EP09S

Address _____

_____

_____ Postcode _____
                                   (Please don't forget to include your postcode)

Signature _____

The right is reserved to refuse an application and change the terms of this offer. Offer
expires December 31st 1991. Readers in Southern Africa please write to P.O. Box 2125,
Randburg, South Africa. Other Overseas and Eire, send for details. You may be mailed
with other offers from Mills & Boon and other reputable companies as a result of this
application. If you would prefer not to share in this opportunity, please tick box. ☐